Excellent Sons

A Love Story in Three Acts

Larry Benjamin

Beaten Track
www.beatentrackpublishing.com

Excellent Sons: A Love Story in Three Acts

First published 2021 by Beaten Track Publishing
Copyright © 2021 Larry Benjamin

Print ISBN: 978 1 78645 421 8
eBook ISBN: 978 1 78645 422 5

Beaten Track Publishing,
Burscough, Lancashire.
www.beatentrackpublishing.com

Dedication

For my brother Vernon, who embodies the concept of an
"excellent son," which was the inspiration for this book.
And for Space, whose story is told in part within these pages.
And as always for my husband, Stanley H. Willauer, Jr.

Acknowledgements

Where do I begin? I have said before it takes a village to write a book. I owe a huge debt of gratitude to my parents, Kathleen and Ray (aka Space) Benjamin, for raising my brothers and me. We could not have asked for better, more supportive parents.

I cannot express how grateful I am to my family at Beaten Track Publishing, especially my friend, publisher, and editor extraordinaire, Deb McGowan. Thank you for believing in me from the start.

Thank you to the immensely talented John Kicksee of Kix By Design for another splendid book cover.

And I'd like to acknowledge my husband Stanley who put up with my distraction and inattention during the year-plus it took me to write this book. I appreciate you.

And finally, in no particular order, my deepest gratitude to: Grace O. Kraybill, Tim Green, Courtney Walton, and every random stranger who in some way contributed to what appears within these pages.

Excellent Sons

Act 1:
Thunder & Lightning

They call us Thunder and Lightning because where there is one, there is sure to be the other. I am Thunder, scowling dark and stormy; he is Lightning, all smiles and glittering light.

Chapter 1

TRISTAN

Now I lay me down to sleep,
I pray the Lord my Soul to keep,
If I should die before I 'wake,
I pray the Lord my Soul to take.

THAT'S THE PRAYER my mother put me to bed with each night. Can you imagine? Yet that prayer before bed was representative of my upbringing, which was a combination of unbridled love and domestic terrorism, much like the honorific "excellent son," most often attached to me as a child, was both praise and bludgeon. I grew up buffeted by my mother's erratic affection, her scalding disappointment, the positive and negative, the yin and yang of her personality.

. . . .

I was my mother's most constant companion. We went grocery shopping and shoe shopping and to the movies; she sought my opinion on matters way beyond the scope of my experience and interest—would *this hairstyle* on *that actress* look becoming on *her*? Should she buy the brown suede pumps or the black patent leather ones? Sometimes I worried that she'd forgotten she had a husband. If this oddity bothered my father, he didn't show it. He bore the slight like he did all other things—with stoic indifference.

3

Once a month, before we ran our errands, we would pay a visit to my mother's favorite store. The eponymous Albrecht's, a small, fashionable boutique, sat complacently along a bustling avenue of commerce and fashion in the shadows of the great EL. We never met the mysterious Albrecht himself, though he always sent my mother a handwritten thank-you note after her many, frequent purchases.

Her main and favorite saleswoman was Miss Dorothy, who usually attended her alongside Miss Minnie. They would both fawn over my mother and examine and discuss in endless detail every aspect of her dress as if she were a member of the royal court and they her devoted ladies-in-waiting. Mostly, I was consigned to eating peanut brittle in a lime-green suede swivel chair until my mother emerged from the dressing room, at which point I would be called upon to offer an opinion.

Once a year or so, my father would accompany us to Albrecht's so he could replenish his seemingly inexhaustible supply of made-to-measure, monogramed Oxford button-downs. Miss Dorothy and Miss Minnie would make a fuss over him. He would charmingly call them Salt and Pepper because he said they were always together. Miss Dorothy, who was black, was Salt, and Miss Minnie, who was white, was Pepper.

Miss Dorothy would be invited to Easter dinner and our occasional cookouts. Once, she even went on vacation with us to Puerto Rico. One afternoon, I drifted into the deep end of the hotel pool and panicked. Miss Dorothy, who couldn't swim, made her way over to my flailing body by holding on to the pool's tile edge and drifting towards me. When she was close enough, she grabbed me with one hand and dragged us along the side of the pool until my father, who'd been in the hotel bar when he heard our screams, could reach in and pull me out.

"Thank you, Salt," he said when I'd landed, spluttering and crying, on the pool's deck.

Every Saturday, my mother would grant me a reprieve from her company when she had a group of her church friends over for lunch in the afternoon after we'd done the week's grocery shopping and run errands. Free, I would wander down to the creek behind our house or draw in my room. Inevitably, I would be called back into her presence to play the piano as a background to their gossipy chatter. I would sit unobtrusively at the piano, quietly playing for their enjoyment. During rare breaks in their conversation, my mother or one of her friends would make a special request, and I would play as their conversation drifted over me.

"He is such a good boy."

"So talented!"

"He's an excellent son. Only having the one," said Miss Lilith, who had a multitude of dirty, noisy children, "you are so lucky. He's devoted to you."

"Oh, I'm sure that devotion will end one day. Some pretty girl will come along and turn his head, and he'll forget all about his poor Omma," my mother said cavalierly, looking over at me.

"He won't," Mrs. C said emphatically, glancing in my direction. She was a mild, disheveled widow who lived with a multitude of ancient dogs and a seemingly immortal cat named Pablo. I often walked the multitude of dogs and fed the immortal cat when she was away.

"He won't marry. Some boys don't," Mrs. C continued, shrugging, "and I can look at him and tell he's one of them." She patted my mother's hand. "You'll always have him. He'll be a treasure in your old age."

An awkward silence ensued, and I played louder as I tried to understand Mrs. C's words and the odd interruption in their chatter it had prompted.

Once I was old enough to understand I'd never have a wife, I accepted the idea that wifeless, I would be consigned to being an excellent son my entire life, living in my parents' house and dancing attendance on my mother. At least, I consoled myself, that conscription would guarantee me eventual entry into Glory. I was instantly depressed.

Chapter 2

TRISTAN

I'D DEVOTED MUCH of my young life to being an excellent son because my mother told me that is what all good boys did. If they did, they would make their mothers proud, and after they died, they would go straight to heaven. From that moment on, I pursued perfection with an almost religious fervor.

I played golf until I was nine, when I switched to tennis. If you've ever seen Rafael Nadal in tennis whites, you might understand my sudden infatuation with the sport. I played the piano and the organ, went to church without complaining, got straight As in school. The problem was, the more I achieved, the higher my mother raised the bar until meeting her expectations became tantamount to climbing a stairway to heaven. Yet failure was not an option; my fall from grace was inconceivable even as I stumbled and took the first steps backward.

Failing to meet her gold standard, which was nothing less than perfection, was sure to result in some punishment, but I was a difficult child to punish. I didn't watch television, so she couldn't rescind a privilege I didn't exercise; I didn't like sweets, so denying me dessert was pointless; and I was already so skinny that sending me to bed without supper was sure to result in me showing up at school looking like a Biafran refugee, and that in itself was sure to prompt a visitation from Child Protective Services. I had no friends to hang out with and seldom left the house except to go to school and church, so I couldn't be grounded.

I was, however, oddly obsessed with kissing my mother goodnight. Noting this, when I displeased her, my mother would send me to bed without granting me a kiss. This inevitably prompted me to cry and wail and swear I would do better. One day, when I brought home a B+ on a Social Studies paper and my mother's outrage and demands for an explanation prompted only a shrugged shoulder from me, she waited until bedtime and denied me a kiss. I looked at her bitterly but did not cry. I went instead quietly to bed and slept the whole night through. When I awoke in the morning, I discovered calamity had not befallen me. I had not died, and neither had my mother. The playing field between us leveled just a bit that morning. After that, I would occasionally catch my mother watching me with a look of bewilderment and hurt.

By seventeen, I was exhausted from being an excellent son, from the relentless pursuit of perfection, from the next race never being the last, from being ridden hard and put away wet. I was chafing under the bridle of others' expectations; my skin split from the near-constant crack of my mother's whip and threatened to expose the dark secret beneath—a secret whose discovery would reveal me lame and ultimately useless, no longer an excellent son. The belief that my mother would shoot me mid-race rather than face a very public defeat at the finish line haunted my every waking hour. My depression deepened.

. . . .

My depression lifted the fall I turned seventeen and met Max. He was tall and slim, vaguely Asian in aspect, dressed completely in loose-fitting black clothes. From the top of his head sprang a short, lively ponytail like the last gasp of water from a hose after the spigot supplying it had been turned off. He looked like the type of boy who might sneak cigarettes in the boys' restroom between classes or who would pilfer Scotch from his parents' liquor cabinet while they were out on a Saturday night. Or who had a secret tattoo in a hidden place on his body.

As it would turn out, none of those things were true, but I thought they might be, and that added to his allure: he was like a half-opened door at the end of a long, dark corridor. I don't remember how I worked up the courage to speak to him. As I remember it, one moment, he was a stranger, an intriguing shadow, and the next, he was my friend, my most constant companion.

Chapter 3

MAX

I LAY ON MY bed staring at the picture of my mother. It was my favorite picture of her. In it, she was just sixteen—my age—surrounded by her sisters, all three of whom were much older than she. She was a change-of-life baby, born after they and their mother left Jamaica and settled in Toronto, my aunts explained in whispers as if sex late in life was a shame. She was lighter-skinned, and except for her two fat pigtails, she was sharper, more angular than her sisters, with high, sloping cheekbones, light-colored eyes, and bony arms and legs.

The picture was taken the year she met my father, and I wondered, looking at her picture, if she had been as lonely as I was now. Did she know she would meet the love of her life in just a few short weeks? Would I, at sixteen, meet mine?

My mother died young—when I was just three. I don't really remember her, though I have the vaguest recollections of playing hide-and-seek with a laughing shadow, quick as the wind, a light, giggly thing, bright as a sprite. There were, of course, other pictures of her: Mama with my father and me; Mama standing at the back of a church in a cocktail-length white dress and a veil cascading over her shoulders; Mama looking unsure, holding the squirming, unhappy bundle that was me at my christening. But the photo of her and her sisters which rests beside my bed remained my favorite.

After she died, it was just me and my father and The Aunts—my mother's three older sisters. Though they were individuals and I loved one of them, Tashelle, more than the others, they stood in my imagination as a dark monolithic being in sensible shoes and a felt hat.

"You going to school today?" my father shouted from the kitchen. It was then I realized I'd been daydreaming. Every morning before the sun rose, I'd get up to run, even though I had track practice after school. I loved running, alone, through our neighborhood in the quiet pre-dawn light as the papers were being delivered and mothers were stirring to begin making breakfast. Then I'd go home and shower and get ready for school. Sometimes, like today, I'd lie on my bed and dream.

Now, as I got up, I wondered: would today be the day?

"Love is heartache," I once overheard Aunt Tashelle tell her sisters.

Good morning, heartache…sit down.

Chapter 4

MAX

"Excuse me. May I sit here?"

I looked over at the sound of his voice. He was short, slight, and Asian like me. I hurriedly gathered my backpack and placed it on the floor between my legs. "Sure, please."

"Thanks." He sat, rather daintily, I thought, and as far away from me as he could get in the narrow seat. He seemed to fold in on himself as if determined to take up as little space as possible.

"I—I'm sorry about taking up two seats. That was inconsiderate, but I was tired of holding my backpack in my lap and no one ever sits next to me, anyway."

"I'm not surprised. Your scowl is quite intimidating. I myself thought twice about asking you if I could sit here."

"Oh!" I was surprised by his forthrightness; looking at the other empty seats in the car, I wanted to ask him why he'd decided to sit next to me but didn't.

"Well, this is my stop—"

"You go to my school, don't you?"

He nodded. I *thought* he looked familiar.

"The next stop is closer."

"I know, but I like getting off here. The walk is only a few minutes longer, but there's more people to see."

"Why would you want to see more people?"

He shrugged. "I like to make up stories about people I see—you know? Where they're going, what they did last night, who their lover is and whether or not they have a future. And if they both feel the same way." He laughed. The train pulled into the station, and then he was gone.

As the train pulled out of the station, I wondered why I was irritated at his abrupt departure.

Chapter 5

TRISTAN

I SAW HIM THE next morning and the morning after that. He made room on the seat for me each time, without my asking. Eventually, we exchanged names and spoke about classes we were taking. His name was Maximillian Wong, but everyone called him Max. We were both Juniors. I learned he was on the track team, and he learned I played the organ at church on Sundays and the piano in recitals for the middle and grade school with which we shared a campus.

We fell into a routine, and I wondered if he looked forward to seeing me each morning as much as I looked forward to seeing him. One morning, lost in conversation, I missed my stop.

MAX

TRISTAN. HIS NAME was Tristan James. We were both Juniors. He was musical. That was, he played the piano and organ. He said I'm a jock cuz I'm on the track team.

This morning Tristan missed his stop, so he got off with me for the first time. When we came out from underground, he said, "OK, I'll let you go on your way now."

"We can walk together—if you'd like," I said.

He smiled. "Sure. I just thought you might want to be alone—"

Everyone always describes me as a "loner." Just because I'm alone all the time doesn't mean I want to be.

"No, it's fine. I could use the company."

"OK," he said, falling in step beside me. For someone so much shorter than I, he kept up. He talked a blue streak. As we walked, he shared random facts and lame jokes; he commented on things we passed and made up entire life histories for anyone going by who caught his fancy. His nonsense soothed me like healing hands. His voice blew like a cool breeze over my burning flesh. His words, caressing fingers, touched and teased me.

We fell into a routine after that. Since I caught the train first, I'd save him a seat and text him what car and row I was in. Once, when a woman, overburdened with purse, briefcase, various assorted, recyclable bags, and an umbrella, attempted to sit next to me, I said, "Sorry, this seat is taken."

"Really?" she snapped. "It looks quite empty to me."

Tristan appeared, and stepping around her, quickly sat beside me. "Look again," he said.

She stared down at him in astonishment. Her lips formed an upside down "U"—a cartoon character's dismay. Then she stomped off, adjusting her many bags on her shoulders; her clogs sounded like a mad horse's hooves.

"Is she wearing...*clogs*?"

"Poor little Dutch Girl." Tristan murmured, making me dissolve into uncharacteristic giggles.

Chapter 6

TRISTAN

MAX HANDED ME a motorcycle helmet. Once I put it on, he fastened the strap under my chin. He climbed on the motorcycle and, turning to me, said, "Hop on."

"Where's *your* helmet?"

"You're wearing it."

"But what about you?"

"I'll be fine. My head is a lot harder than yours. Now get on."

I climbed on behind him.

"Put your legs there," he said pointing to the stirrups. "Just hold on. You don't have to do anything. I'll take care of everything else."

"OK. Um…what should I hold on to?"

He turned to me smirking slightly. "Me. Put your hands around my waist."

I did. He started up the bike and we were off. The wind in my face was stronger than I'd expected, so I leaned in closer to him and tightened my hands around his waist. He was thicker around the middle than I'd expected, his shoulders broader. From where my face pressed against his back, I could smell his skin. It was a scent so clean it was almost antiseptic.

MAX

I took Tristan for a first ride on my motorcycle. Until him, no one had ever ridden with me. I hadn't wanted a passenger until…him. As I walked my bike down the drive, him seated behind me, I saw my dad standing in the open door of our house watching us.

I loved riding my bike because it made me feel free, dangerous, as if I were soaring above the clouds, weightless. With Tristan seated behind me, his arms tight around my waist, I felt anchored, earthbound, safe. I found I no longer wanted to soar free.

Returning home, lost in my reverie, in the feel of his hands tight around my waist, the warmth of his breath on my neck, I parked my bike, hopped off, and removed my helmet. My dad walked out of the house and handed me a helmet exactly like the one I had just taken off. I took the proffered helmet and looked at him, puzzled.

"I saw you give your helmet to your friend earlier."

"I—"

"I know you wanted to protect him. It was an honorable thing to do. But I need you to be protected too."

Chapter 7

MAX

I REMEMBER AT THIRTEEN standing in the bathroom and looking out the window, catching sight of Martin cutting his grandmother's grass. Catching sight of my expression in the mirror over the sink, I felt like I was staring at a stranger I would soon know. The words formed for the first time: *I like guys.*

Brushing my teeth, I watched myself in the same mirror. My expression was undeniably one of happiness. I was happy to be going to school, to be meeting up with Tristan on the train. New words again formed for the first time: *I like Tristan.*

TRISTAN

HEY, MEET ME by the bike stand out front, Max texted.

I was surprised because this morning, he was quieter than usual, almost surly. I thought he might be mad at me, but when I asked, he said he wasn't. As we sat in unaccustomed silence, I glanced over at him; he appeared to be studying me, perplexed, like I was a French textbook or the map to a hidden Incan city.

Now, as I leaned against the bike stand, he walked up to me.

"Hey."

"Hey."

"I have some time before practice, so I thought I'd walk you to the train station if that's OK."

"Yeah, cool."

Without asking, he took my backpack from me and slung it over his shoulder.

Realizing Max was staring at me in a most curious manner, I stopped talking abruptly, self-conscious that I was, as my mother often pointed out, probably talking too much. I asked him, "What? Am I talking too much? I'm talking too much, aren't I?"

"You are so handsome," he said.

Sure I'd misheard him, I was about to ask him to repeat what he'd said, when he suddenly leaned forward and pressed his lips against mine. I can't say he kissed me; the touching of lips was too hesitant, too afraid of its own power to be called a kiss.

He drew away almost immediately. "I'm sorry," he said, his eyes wide, looking everywhere but at me.

"I'm sorry," he said again. "I shouldn't have done that." Then he started beating the sides of his head with his fists. "Stupid, stupid, *stupid*! I hate myself!"

"Max!" I tried to grab his flailing fists. "Max, stop it!"

He stopped. He looked about wildly for a few seconds then said, "I have to go. I'm late for practice." Before I could say anything, he turned and sprinted off. I stared after him, dumbfounded. My lips burned.

MAX

TRISTAN. SWEET TRISTAN was musical. I don't mean literally, though he was that, too. That musicality of his slipped under a door I'd always kept closed and locked, and it turned the key, unlocking it. The door sprang open, and l saw what I'd always been afraid to see, but now, unlike before, I couldn't turn away, could only stare in mesmerized wonder.

And now I'd gone and kissed him and probably lost the only friend I'd ever had. As soon as I kissed him, I felt I'd made a mistake. *What if Tristan doesn't like me the same way?* I wondered after it was too late. I grew frightened and literally ran away.

Chapter 8

TRISTAN

W<small>E WERE SITTING</small> on the grass outside the cafeteria. Judy was trying to engage me in conversation, but I was lost in thought, worried about Max, so I was only half listening. She'd been my closest friend since forever, but since I'd met Max, she complained I was spending so much time with him she felt eclipsed or neglected or some such. She stopped talking and looked past me, over my shoulder. Her expression grew so sour I knew without turning around that Max was standing behind me.

"Sorry. I didn't mean to interrupt," Max said.

I sprang to my feet, dusting off the seat of my pants. My open book fell out of my lap as I stood.

"Max."

"Hey," he said and walked away.

"Max, wait." I grabbed my backpack and hurriedly retrieved my book and stuffed it inside. He kept walking. I ran after him.

"Tristan, where are you going? We were—" Judy called after me.

Catching up to Max, I said, "Hey."

"Hey," he said, not looking at me as I fell in step beside him.

"Hey," I repeated, determined not to say more. Then, failing, added, "I thought you were sick. I mean, you were on the sick list."

"Yeah, I told my dad I was sick."

"Are you?"

"No."

"Look, can we stop for a minute?"

"What?"

"What's with the attitude? *You* came looking for *me*, remember?"

"I just wanted to apologize."

"For what? Running off and leaving me? Kissing me? Not answering any of my texts?"

"All three, I guess." He stared at the ground, digging the toe of his sneaker into a patch of weeds. "But mostly for kissing you. I should have asked for your consent. I should have—"

"Oh, for God's sake, Max!"

"What?"

"Come here," I said, grabbing his shirt front and pulling him into an alcove.

"What?"

"You know that kiss you just apologized for? Well, I've wanted you to kiss me almost from the moment I first saw you." I leaned forward and kissed him. A proper kiss. At least, it mimicked the kisses I'd seen in movies. His eyes widened, and I felt his lips move against mine as he smiled. He opened his mouth, and our tongues met. He pressed me against the wall as his hands traveled up and down my body.

MAX

THE BELL ANNOUNCING the end of sixth period rang. "I have to go," Tristan said. "Meet me after school?"

"I have practice—that's why I came in. Well, that and to see you," I added shyly.

"Can I meet you after practice?"

I nodded, not trusting myself to speak. Even as he walked away, I could still feel his lips against mine, his hot hands on my fevered flesh and the taste of him: bubblegum and Chapstick. All last night I'd been consumed by fear: *What if he doesn't like me like that?*

I noticed people in the hall were looking at me funny and I realized it was probably because I was smiling. I laughed out loud, and a few students walking towards me actually moved closer to the walls, eying me warily as they passed. They probably thought I'd gone mad, and perhaps I had.

Yesterday, I'd kissed Tristan and I'd thought the world ended. Today, *he* kissed *me*, and the world began again.

Chapter 9

TRISTAN

Come sit with me," Judy whispered. "I have to tell you something."

"So, tell me."

"Not here."

She lured me to a bench outside the cafeteria. It was hot and uncomfortable, but I could tell she had something on her mind. Giving her time to collect her thoughts, I spoke of other things: the antics of our classmates, the terrible lunch we'd abandoned. Once, or twice, she stopped frowning and laughed. "So, what did you want to tell me?" I asked finally.

She sighed heavily, looking past me. I followed her gaze.

"Max!" I stood, but he kept walking. When I caught up to him, I tugged his arm. He tried to shake me off. I could feel Judy's eyes on us. I let go of his arm and stood still as if his rejection had nailed my feet to the ground. He stopped suddenly and turned around. He looked at me sullenly, his eyes burning. In his loose-fitting black clothes, he looked like a postmodern Samurai: regal, distant, wounded.

"Max, what is it?"

He shrugged. "Nothing. Sorry I interrupted you and your girlfriend."

"She's not my girlfriend!"

"Well, it looks like she is."

"Well, she isn't! You *know* that."

He sucked his teeth, a frustrated, dismissive sound that nearly broke my heart. "Max, why are you acting like this?"

MAX

Looking for Tristan during his lunch period, I found him and Judy sitting together on a bench in the courtyard between the cafeteria and the main building. She was sitting too close to him and laughing coquettishly at his nonsense. The casual onlooker would have assumed they were a couple. That pissed me off for some reason. And so I just muttered a curt, "Hey," and kept walking. Tristan ran after me, which I hadn't realized until he grabbed my arm. "Leave me alone," I barked, trying to shake him off, trying to forget we had kissed.

He stopped and let go of my arm. "Max why are you acting like this?" he asked.

The hurt and confusion in his voice tore at my heart. "I don't know," I answered honestly. "I suppose I'm jealous."

"You have nothing to be jealous of."

"Don't I?" How could I explain to Tristan how afraid I was of losing him? I thought I'd be alone my whole life. And then he came along. Did he think I didn't know how lucky I was? He could do so much better than me. I'm surly and difficult and jealous and kind of ugly. I told him this in kind of a rush. He stared at me.

"You're not ugly. I think you're handsome."

I smiled. "You don't have to lie to me."

"I'm not lying," he protested, then seeming to study my face for a moment, he added, "OK. Maybe you're not what other people would call handsome—I can't tell. I just think you're the most attractive guy I've ever seen."

"Really?"

"Really. Before I met you, I'd see guys all over I'd think were handsome, maybe even hot, and then they'd pass by, and sometimes I'd come across them again, maybe just a few minutes later, and I'd be surprised because in their absence I'd forgotten all about them. But from the moment I first saw you, your face and body stayed with me—you haunted my dreams. I couldn't get you out of my mind."

Speaking around the lump in my throat, I mumbled, "Judy likes you. I know she does."

"I don't care," he said. "*I* like *you*."

And just like that, my anger dissipated.

Chapter 10

TRISTAN

M AX INVITED ME to his house on Saturday. Besides Judy's, I had never been to another classmate's house before. His house was one of a cluster of similar tract houses, all clad in aluminum siding in need of a power washing, all listing on the same side, as if gravity was stronger on the north. The houses were lined up neatly along both sides of a narrow street littered with cars in varying stages of decrepitude and the occasional van or pickup truck.

He opened the door, grinned ecstatically, then stepped aside and waved me in. I walked into vivid color: robin's-egg blue and egg-yolk yellow and fire-engine red. I'd never imagined rooms painted such lively colors. Adding to the visual cacophony was an auditory assault—the sounds of car alarms and horns and barking dogs, straining at the end of chains, and the regional rail trains rumbling past on their squeaky tracks and a dozen mother tongues—some guttural, some lyrical and romantic, all beguiling—tumbling over each other like a dozen different choruses sung all at once. And beneath it all the sound of drums beating, alongside the beating of my own excited heart. I imagined this is what chaos would sound like, or maybe the halls of hell.

In the living room, huddled around the biggest flatscreen TV I had ever seen, was oversized black leather furniture, all of which looked like it would recline at the touch of a cleverly hidden lever. There were piles of discarded newspapers and sports magazines strewn on the floor; the dining room table was stacked with unopened mail; in the kitchen, there were dishes in the sink and cups a quarter full of coffee and Coca-Cola on the countertops.

I fell in love with the disorder. And in the midst of it, Max stood cool and orderly, watching me survey his surroundings.

MAX

"Is it just you and your dad?" Tristan asked me.

"Yeah. My mom died."

"Oh! I'm so sorry."

"It's OK. I was only three when she died, so I don't really remember her. We have pictures of her all over the house, of course, but I look at them, and because I don't remember her, it's like looking at one of those anonymous models' pictures you get when you buy a picture frame. The Aunts tell me that after she died, I walked around for months asking where she was and looked for her behind curtains and under beds. The only thing I remember about her is playing hide-and-seek. It was our favorite game."

"I can't imagine not having a mother."

"Oh, I didn't say I didn't have a mother. I have *The Aunts*—my mother's older sisters. They're this trio of chick-less mother hens who do nothing but obsess over and criticize my dad and me."

TRISTAN

"Speaking of the devil," Max said as the front door creaked open and three elderly women stepped into the house.

They were soberly dressed in white blouses and dark skirts of some nubby, itchy-looking fabric. They each wore their salt-

and-pepper hair in two long plaits. Two of them were plump and looked like they brooked neither nonsense nor joy. Max introduced them as Kaleisha and Tianara. The third was smaller and wore a jaunty red bandana about her neck at the open collar of her white blouse. This seemed to indicate that she was the fun one, the reckless one, the one who would indulge Max's boyish enthusiasms and excesses. Max introduced her as Tashelle. She beamed at Max.

"I'm a Christmas baby," she informed me apropos of nothing and added confidentially, "Max is my favorite nephew."

Max rolled his eyes. "I am your *only* nephew."

"Oh, hush," she said.

Kaleisha and Tianara were singular and fierce; their soft voices belied a pride and self-assuredness that bordered on arrogance. Because of their clear disapproval of me, I thought of them as Christian missionaries confronting the dancing heathen that was me, ignorant of my affront to their lord and his disciples. By contrast, Tashelle, both her forearms covered from wrist to elbow with jangly silver bracelets, seemed to contain multitudes, like an army of mad elves.

"Max's father tells us you two boys are spending a lot of time together, so we wanted to meet you," Kaleisha said, sitting in one of the big black leather recliners.

I nodded but said nothing. On the sofa beside me, Max leaned forward.

"So, you are Korean?" Kaleisha asked me.

"Yes—well, half. My mother was born there. My dad served in Korea, but he's an American."

"Ah, a *war bride*," Tianara stage-whispered to her sisters, both of whom frowned.

I guess because Mom was Korean and Dad served in the Korean War, everyone assumed they met there, that she was a war bride. In truth, they met here, and in fact, Mom hadn't even been born until decades *after* Dad had left Korea. I explained this now.

"So, your father is...an older gentleman." Half question, half accusation.

"Yes. He's thirty years older than my mother. People often assume he's my grandfather."

Tianara shook her head as she tutted, "Tut! Tut!" She reminded me of The Church Saints, a group of spotless women who had appointed themselves the moral yardsticks against which all others would be measured and found lacking. "That must be so embarrassing for you."

"Not really. I mean, I suppose it might be if I cared what other people think, but I don't."

Kaleisha and Tianara looked at each other while Tashelle let out a delighted bark of laughter. I decided I liked her.

"Pizza is probably ready," Max said to no one in particular. "I'll go get it." He stood. "The Aunts" ignored him. He shot me an apologetic look and, mumbling, "I'll be right back," went to the kitchen.

As soon as he disappeared into the hall, Tianara pounced. "I must say, we're surprised you have so much time to spend with Max."

"What do you mean?" I asked.

"Well, you're...what? Seventeen?"

I nodded.

"You're a very good-looking boy. I would think you'd be so busy with girls you wouldn't have time for old Max here."

"My mother doesn't allow dating. She says I need to concentrate on my schoolwork," I stated flatly. When you're gay, you learn early on to deflect and misdirect, if not outright lie. Tianara stared at me hard, a prosecuting attorney trying to decide if the witness was lying.

"Can we stop this inquisition now, please?" Max asked, returning with two plates containing pizza that was slightly burned at the edges.

"Leave the boys be, nuh?" Tashelle said. "Max is entitled to have his...*friendships*."

The missionary aunts tutted to themselves again and stared furiously at Tashelle but fell silent. To us, Tashelle said, "Pay these two old biddies no mind." She adjusted the red bandana around her neck.

"Who you calling old?"

"You! I calling you old."

"We are not old," the other aunt said.

"Please! You were born in the year two, and she was born before the flood! The two of you are so old you fart dust."

The missionaries wrinkled their noses and said, "Don't be so vulgar in front of the children."

They began to bicker.

Max nudged me. "Come on."

"Should we leave them?"

"Yeah, they'll be fine. They'll get bored fighting with each other without an audience."

I followed him to his room. The blinds were drawn. The trim and doors were painted a glossy black. Every other surface—walls, ceiling, floor—was painted a different flat color: blue, yellow, white, red.

"What do you think?" Max asked.

"I like it. It's like stepping into a three-dimensional Mondrian," I said.

He looked at me in surprise. "That's exactly right. No one ever gets that. Mondrian is my favorite artist."

Chapter 11

TRISTAN

WHO IS THIS boy Judy says you're spending time with?" my mother asked.

"Max? He's my friend."

"Where did you meet him?"

"On the train. We go to the same school. I don't spend that much time with him. Judy is always exaggerating things."

"Well, if he's your friend, I should meet him."

"Meet him?"

"Yes. Invite him over to dinner next Saturday."

Reacting to my decided lack of enthusiasm, she volunteered, "I'll make an authentic Korean meal."

The subject evidently closed, my mother extended her hands and asked, "What do you think of my new nail color?"

Her nails were painted a matte reddish brown. "It's ghastly," I said.

"What do you mean?" she asked, folding her hands and inspecting her nails.

"It looks like dried blood."

"Well, I think it's a lovely color." She sounded unsure.

"What's it called? 'Crime Scene'?"

Now she was really offended. "I still think it's lovely," she repeated.

I shrugged.

Knowing when I was defeated, I passed my mother's invitation on to Max this morning. To my surprise, he enthusiastically agreed.

"Really?" I asked.

"Sure. I don't get a home-cooked meal very often, it being just me and Dad. Besides, I'd like to see where you live."

"Why?"

"Because," he said, taking both my hands in his, "you are so special. You are so different from anyone I've ever met. I just want to see where you live. And I want to meet the people who made the boy I love. OK?" He squeezed my hands.

"OK."

Chapter 12

MAX

TRISTAN'S FAMILY'S HOUSE was a wonder, nestled in a wood. Sheathed in floor-to-ceiling tempered glass and cedar shingles, it had steeply pitched roofs and deep overhangs sheltering wide porches. Large cedar terraces on its upper floors poked out from numerous angles. Though I couldn't see it from where I stood at the front door, I could hear a creek gurgling as it wound its way through the trees behind the house.

Tristan, smiling, opened the door when I rang the bell. Chattering his usual nonsense, he led me into the house, a cathedral of light burning like white gold; rooms were painted white, off-white, bright white, almost-white, and damned-near-white. Grays and beiges cowered in the corners of sofas, under tables, in the shadows beside windows. Now and then, I'd catch a flash of color, faded as a childhood memory, bleeding through acid-washed fabric, surprising as blood from a finger pricked while sewing.

Elaborate paper lanterns, exquisite as origami figures, hung from ceilings above my head; at rest like giant birds in the daylight, they came to blazing life with the dusk, dashing their abundant light across the ceiling and against walls and into corners, while outside, the house was cloaked in shadow.

There was music coming out of concealed speakers—classical, Mozart or Bach—at a volume so low it was no louder than the sound of my own breathing. Tristan led me through the dazzling-white living room whose only color came from a golden-mahogany grand piano; its satin finish shimmered faintly in the brilliant light. He slid open a pair of teak-and-rice-paper Shoji screens and led me onto a deeply shadowed screened porch overlooking a creek. As my eyes adjusted to the dark, I looked back at the white living room. I found the difference between the two rooms—the juxtaposition of light and dark, shadow and sun—disconcerting, like talking to a manic depressive who was cycling mid-conversation.

TRISTAN

MY MOTHER CALLED us in to dinner. I led Max into the dining room and stopped in astonishment. He looked at my mother, then at me. My mother, inexplicably, was wearing a hanbok, a traditional Korean dress worn on semi-formal and formal occasions. The dress, in a rich purple silk taffeta embroidered at the hem with wildflowers, fell from her shoulders in a wide flare of fabric. Her shoulders were covered in a short bolero jacket of shocking pink silk whose trumpet sleeves were also embroidered with wildflowers. Her face was so heavily powdered it looked faintly blue against her red lipstick and jet-black hair. Max stood awkwardly beside me.

"Where did you get that dress?" I blurted.

"Albrecht's. They special-ordered it for me."

"It's lovely on you," Max said politely.

"Aren't you kind," my mother said. "You must be Max."

"Oh! Omma, this is Max. Max, my mother."

"It's nice to meet you, Mrs. James."

"You, too," my mother said. "Please sit down. You must tell me all about yourself—Tristan tells me nothing."

When neither of us said anything, my mother continued, "Unfortunately, my husband won't be joining us. He's at a ball game with his friend, and the game has gone into overtime or something."

"My father is obsessed with baseball," I explained, sitting opposite Max and still staring at my mother's dress.

Marta brought in a long, polished wooden platter filled with steamed rice, sautéed slivered carrots, bamboo shoots, shitake mushrooms, and seaweed strips. Another wooden bowl contained beef and kimchi.

"Have you ever had Bibimbap?" my mother asked.

"No. It smells great, though," Max said.

"It's a traditional Korean dish."

I regarded my mother with suspicion, wondering what had caused her to suddenly rediscover and claim her Korean heritage. She picked up her wine glass. Her nails were again their usual bright crimson; they looked very red against the wine, which was thick and dark red as blood.

MAX

"So, Max, is Max short for something or your actual name?" Tristan's mother asked me casually, her chopsticks clicking furiously, her blood-red nails the only color in the room.

"It's actually short for Maximilian," I said.

"Maximilian. That's quite a name. It's unusual for someone who's Chinese, isn't it?"

"I'm three-quarters Chinese. My dad is Chinese, though he was born and raised in Canada. My mom was half Jamaican and half Chinese. She was also born and raised in Canada. But yes, I suppose my name is unusual. It means 'greatest.' It was my dad's idea—he has high hopes for me."

"I hope you haven't disappointed him."

I nearly laughed. "I'll have to ask him."

"You sound like you're joking," she reprimanded. "As a mother, I can tell you there's no greater pain for a parent than a disappointing child." She glanced significantly at Tristan, then back at me.

"Oh, I can't imagine you have much experience with that," I said. "Tristan is surely an excellent son. He's an excellent friend."

"If you only knew," she sighed.

I said nothing, mesmerized by the violent movements of her chopsticks.

TRISTAN

"TELL ME, MAX," my mother asked sweetly, her blood-red fingernails, like a bird of prey's talons flashing furiously as she worked her chopsticks, "what does your father do?"

"He's a chimney sweep—that is, he owns a company that does cleaning maintenance and repair of chimneys," Max explained, struggling with his chopsticks. My head whipped toward him so hard I feared I might have given myself whiplash.

A chimney sweep? I was unsure what my own dad, who was retired, had done for a living, and questions about his career of choice were actively discouraged. I often feared he had been some kind of corporate raider, an enemy of the people, a Bain and Company automaton who routinely took over companies through means both legal and nefarious, stripping them of their assets then mortgaging them to the hilt and pocketing the proceeds, leaving them to swim or sink in the morass of debt he'd created.

"That's lovely," my mother said. "I'm sure it's an honorable profession and that he makes a good living."

"He makes enough to keep me clothed and food on the table and a roof over our heads, yes," Max retorted—rather sharply, I thought. Not that I blamed him. I was suddenly embarrassed by my surroundings, our house, the china plates which Frank Lloyd Wright had designed for the Imperial Hotel, my mother's antique Tiffany & Company sterling silver chopsticks. And I resented my mother's haughtiness—how had I not seen this side of her before? It was there, hiding in plain sight: the Cadillac in the driveway, the boutique clothing from Albrecht's, the vintage Saarinen and Noguchi furniture. I sighed and said, "May we be excused? I want to show Max the creek before it gets dark."

My mother gave me a calculating look and, bowing her head, murmured her acquiescence.

Max stood and picked up his plate. "Where—"

My mother waved her hand dismissively. "Just leave it. Marta will get it."

MAX

ONCE WE WERE outside walking along the creek, Tristan said, "Thanks for sticking up for me in there."

"Don't worry about it," I said. "I couldn't just let her put you down like that. You're the most awesome person I know. You deserve better." He hugged me as the moon peeped out at us from behind a cloud. Arms around each other's waists, we watched the creek, our blossoming love hidden by the complicit clouds.

"I'm sorry about my mother interrogating you," Tristan said, breaking the silence. "I don't know what that was about."

"Your mother doesn't think I'm good enough for you," I said, angrily skipping rocks across the broken surface of the creek. If Tristan thought it was an odd assessment of the situation, he didn't say anything.

Chapter 13

MAX

"YOUR FRIEND'S MOTHER called," my father said, pulling a beer out of the fridge. I was checking the oven to make sure the frozen pizza didn't burn.

"My friend?"

"The rich one—the one whose house you went to dinner at?"

"Tristan?" I asked, frowning.

"Yeah, him."

"What did she want?"

"She wants us to clean her chimney on Saturday."

"Us?"

"Yeah, she said she'd be especially grateful if I'd bring you along to help."

"Dad, no."

"I wasn't giving you an option."

"I hate cleaning chimneys," I said emphatically.

"Why? Because it's hard work, or because it's dirty work?" When I said nothing, my father shook his head. "I never thought I'd raise a child who was afraid to get his hands dirty."

"Afraid to get my hands dirty? Look at me. I am nothing *but* dirt. I just don't want someone I care about very much—the cleanest person I know—to look at me and just see...*dirt*."

"Is that what you see when you look at me, Max? Dirt?"

I looked at him, tried not to wince at the dirt under his nails, at the soot that smudged his forehead, forever marking him as faithfully as a cross drawn with the ink of the ashes of palm leaves on the forehead as a man of faith on Ash Wednesday. I tried not to gag on the smell of hard-earned sweat.

"No. Of course not," I said. "He's my *friend*. I don't want him to look at me and see…the person who cleans his chimney."

"If he's truly your friend, he won't confuse what you do with who you are."

"I don't want to do it," I said stubbornly.

"Being a man," my father said, "means doing hard, uncomfortable things. It means doing things you want more than anything not to have to do. I really need you on that job Saturday—we're short-handed."

I clenched my fists at my sides. "I want more than *this*!"

"Shit! You think I didn't want more than this, too? I had dreams. And I was smart—maybe smarter than you—and still look at me." His tone softened. "Look, I'm not saying I want you to be a chimney sweep—truth is I don't—but I do know that life throws crap at you, and I want to make sure you have something to fall back on if and when your dreams crumble. OK?"

I nodded.

Dad sniffed the air. "Did you burn the pizza again?"

I swiveled to the oven, stared at the wisp of smoke in dismay. "Fuck!"

"Language!"

I'd been nervous all day and had tried to hurry my father along. Now what I feared most was about to happen.

A silver Cadillac pulled into the driveway. The door swung open, and Tristan, dressed in crisp tennis shorts and a knit shirt whose collar was turned up, both white as the driven snow, popped out as immaculate and pure as the new day or a thirteen-year-old virgin at her Confirmation. Tristan glanced at the white panel truck. I imagined he was surprised. I hadn't told him we were working on his house in the hopes that we would be gone before he got home. I imagined his eyes, hidden by his mirrored aviator sunglasses, squinting at the writing on the side of the truck that right then seemed to be painted in letters ten feet tall as indelible and incriminating as DNA at a crime scene: Wong Chimney Sweep.

He pushed his sunglasses on top of his glossy black hair, which looked blacker than usual in the bright sunlight and against his gleaming white clothes. He scanned the yard. His eyes fell on me despite my prayers that God render me invisible. His face lit with a smile as I hung my head. "Max!" He strode towards me, his tennis racket bouncing against his leg. I stood rooted to the ground. "Max! What are you doing here?"

"Hey. Your mother hired us to clean your chimneys."

"Really? How very odd. Except in the last week, she's never allowed a fire in the house."

"You play tennis?" I asked, anxious to get his focus off me.

"Yes." Now he looked as embarrassed as I felt.

"Why didn't you ever tell me?"

He shrugged. "Stick out your tongue," he said.

"What?"

"You've got soot on your face. Stick out your tongue."

When I did, he rubbed his thumb back and forth across it, then like a new mother, he rubbed his thumb across my cheek.

His thumb on my cheek sent an erotic charge, so powerful I thought my knees would buckle, straight to my groin.

"There," he said at last, satisfied. "All gone."

Out of the corner of my eye, I saw my father watching us from the open door of the van. "You ready?" he called out.

"I have to go," I said.

"OK. Text me later."

As I climbed into the passenger seat, I saw Tristan's mother standing on the portico. She stepped back into the shadows, her pale fingers with their scarlet nails at her throat.

· ·

As I washed in the shower, I imagined my hands were Tristan's: brushing my nipples, trailing down my stomach... clutching, releasing, stroking.

Weak, I sat on the floor of the tub, the water cascading over me, exhausted and guilty, as if I'd borrowed something of Tristan's without first asking his permission.

Chapter 14

MAX

TRISTAN HAD A disconcerting tendency to fall suddenly asleep, often mid-sentence. I attributed this tendency to our frequent before-bed conversations that lasted well into the night. These conversations were a substitute for what we really yearned for—if we couldn't fall asleep in each other's arms, we could at least do so wrapped in the warmth of each other's voices.

Often, on the train on the ride to school, as we sat side by side, our hands entwined on the seat between us, Tristan would fall asleep. I'd concentrate on the pressure of his hand in mine and look out the window. On the other side of the glass, the downtown skyscrapers glittered and sparkled in the early morning light, as seductive and deceitful as Oz, while the rusty baroque spires of the cathedral tore through the skimming clouds and scraped in vain at the floor of heaven.

Occasionally, someone would notice our clasped hands— a conductor collecting tickets and checking passes or a strap-hanging passenger or an unusually alert rider standing in the aisle waiting to detrain.

One morning, a woman with the largest breasts I'd ever seen, and wearing a sports jersey which proclaimed across her chest—rather redundantly, I thought—*Giants*, glared down at us. Content to snort her disapproval and punish us with black looks, she said nothing. I squeezed Tristan's hand tighter.

Another time, a disembarking passenger, an older man, with a silver goatee and tired eyes, leaned over and whispered, "God bless you both. I envy you boys your freedom to be yourselves."

Even if I had had the words, I hadn't the heart to tell him that the freedom he and his generation had fought for and thought they'd won didn't really exist. Not for all of us anyway. As it was, Tristan and I existed in three different worlds, each with its own restrictions on our freedom. Alone together, we were completely free to be ourselves and express our mutual affection. At school, to a certain degree, we enjoyed similar freedom: though for the most part we enjoyed a benign acceptance, it was still a limited acceptance; mostly, we were met with derision or a tolerant indulgence which was equally infuriating. At home, both his and mine, we were mindful to be discreet, thus as teenagers, when we should have been truly free, we weren't; we were constantly monitoring our behavior, evaluating our surroundings and worrying about the consequences of both. It was unfair and exhausting, but it was the only way we could hold onto each other.

TRISTAN

"GOD BLESS YOU both. I envy you boys your freedom to be yourselves," the elegant older gentleman said before rushing off the train.

"That was so sweet," I said to Max.

"Really? I thought it was kind of sad," Max replied.

"Why sad?"

"That poor man probably dreamed his whole life of being us, and now he credits us with a freedom that we don't actually have."

"Would you tell him that?" I asked.

"No. Of course not. Hoping for freedom is what kept him going, and who knows, maybe one day we will be as free as he imagines."

"Hmmm," I murmured resting my head on his shoulder again. "He was an odd man. He looks like the sort who would wear an ascot and keep a pipe in his mouth though he would never smoke—that would be gauche—and who drinks too many pre-prandial cocktails and doesn't eat enough dinner, or any at all!"

"You're such a goon! Where do you come up with this stuff?"

I shrugged, nestling against him.

"And where do you come up with these words? What does pre-prandial even mean?"

"It means 'before dinner.' I can't believe you don't know that."

"Hey. I'm not a scholar like you—I'm just a chimney sweep."

"*Now* who's the goon?" I asked and kissed him quickly as the conductor announced our station was the next stop.

Chapter 15

TRISTAN

The school's public address system coughed and came to static life: *"We are on lockdown. Repeat, we are on lockdown."* The alarm triggered; it was deafening. I felt like it was supplanting my own beating heart. Everything became that pulsing bull horn. I wondered who among us would die this time.

Did other generations—did my parents—worry about death and destruction when they attended school each day? I wondered idly. My thoughts, as morbid as they were, had at least kept me from worrying about Max.

My phone buzzed—we'd all muted our phones as the electronic blinds descended at the window and we sought shelter on the floor under our desks while the teacher bolted the door. It was Max: *Where are you? Are you OK? I've evacuated to the church parking lot.*

We're sheltering in place in the science lab, I texted back. *Is this real or just a drill?*

IDK probably a drill. Don't be scared.

MAX

"We are on lockdown. Repeat, we are on lockdown." The message was scratchy but clear over the school's public-address system. Our coach and the school's athletic director

shouted orders and directed us to leave the track through the east gate and head to our designated meeting place in the church parking lot a block away.

The sight of dozens of us students, many barely teenagers, running with hands held high, fingers spread, is one I'll never forget. Once we arrived at the church parking lot, our coach set about calming students and taking a head count while the athletic director tried to dial into the school's emergency network. My head was pounding as I searched the crowd for Tristan. Had he been outside like me? Or had he been inside and thus forced to "shelter in place"?

None of us had any idea if this was a drill or an actual active shooter situation. Since the 1999 shootings at Columbine High School and Sandy Hook in 2012, we've had two options: shelter in place or run like hell.

I pulled out my phone and with trembling fingers texted Tristan: *Where are you? Are you OK? I've evacuated to the church parking lot.*

Is this real or a drill? Tristan replied.

IDK probably a drill, I typed even as I could see the police arrive in a fury of flashing lights and screaming sirens. A helicopter descended and hovered over the school.

Don't be scared, I texted.

. . . .

Finally, it was over. The alarms stopped blaring. We were plunged into silence like a warm bath.

Meet me in the parking lot by the bike rack, I texted Tristan. *I just want to see you.*

I threaded my way through throngs of traumatized students, officious school administrators wearing earpieces, and scores of anxious parents. I understood their anxiety because it was mine, too. The drills had never bothered me before. Before Tristan. Now I had Tristan in my life, it was different. Everything was different. I saw him politely pushing his way through the crowd towards me.

TRISTAN

I COULD SEE Max in his purple-and-aqua tracksuit. If nothing else, the school's colors made us stand out in a crowd. Max's head bobbed above the crowd as he looked around for me. I wished I was taller.

"Tristan!"

I turned, saw my mother straining towards me. I looked back at Max, who'd finally seen me. I raised a finger to my mother, *wait one second*, and pushed my way to Max. At last, we reached each other. We stood awkwardly a little apart, not touching, conscious of everyone around us, hugging, sobbing. I swear I could feel my mother's disapproval as she stood in that crowd, shocked and impatient at my dismissal.

"You OK?" Max asked.

"Yeah. You?"

"Better now that I've seen you. This is a madhouse. I didn't mean to drag you out here. I just wanted—"

"I know. I did, too. Listen, my mother is here. I'll see you after practice."

He smiled. "OK, sure." He looked around, quickly grabbed my hand and squeezed it. I squeezed back.

. . . .

"Do you want to go home?" my mother asked.

"No, I'm fine. I'll walk you back to your car. Do you know what happened?"

She sighed. "Yes. A kindergartener brought a loaded gun in for show-and-tell. When he pulled it out of his backpack, he dropped it, and it discharged. Fortunately, no one was injured. But the sound of gunshots triggered the school's active shooter protocol."

I closed my mother's door and leaned down to kiss her cheek. She patted my face. "Be careful."

As I walked away, I thought sadly: *A kindergartener. Brought a loaded gun to school.*

Chapter 16

MAX

WE PASSED A group of boys huddled in an alcove off the cafeteria courtyard—the same one where Tristan first kissed me—smoking, even though you weren't supposed to smoke on campus. I barely noticed them, as Tristan was spinning yet another fanciful tale that was no less enthralling for its wild improbability.

"Faggots!" The word snapped in the air and unfurled before us like a red carpet, bright as blood. Tristan stopped and, turning around, walked up to the boy who had spoken, a tall, gangly youth with a pockmarked face and poor posture.

Tristan poked him in the chest as he looked up at him. "Yesterday," he said, "a five-year-old boy brought a loaded gun to school and discharged it. Someone could have been killed and no one cares. Do you think *anyone*—least of all me—cares anything about some nasty little word your pea-sized brain farted out to try and hurt me? Boy, get the fuck out of here! I've seen more fearsome creatures than you in my sweetest dreams."

The other boys snickered while the one who had spoken turned bright red. Tristan, furious, turned on his heels and walked back to me like William the Conqueror stepping over the bodies of the vanquished at the Battle of Hastings.

"I can't believe you did that!" I said.

"What? I'm not putting up with that shit."

It was the first time I'd heard him curse, and I'd never seen him mad before. Hoping to calm him, I said, "What the hell prompted that? We weren't even doing anything."

"You realize gay is not an act of doing, it's a state of being, right?" he asked, effectively shutting me up.

Chapter 17

It was the first time I'd heard him curse, and I'd never seen him mad before. Trying to calm him, I said, "What the hell popping that we're supposed to be doing."

"You really guy is not an act of doing, it's an act of being, right? he asked, effectively shutting me up.

TRISTAN

"Guess what?" I asked excitedly as soon as I sat down. "What?" Max asked sleepily.

"My parents are going to a wedding this weekend."

"Are you going, too?"

"No."

"Why not?"

"Max, that's not the point."

"OK. What is the point?"

"I'll be home. Alone."

Now, he looked interested. "Home alone, you say?"

"Yes."

"What are you thinking?"

"I'm thinking," I said, lowering my voice, "You can come over Saturday afternoon and spend the night."

"Do you always have boys over when your parents aren't home?"

"What? No. Never."

"Relax. I was just teasing you." He leaned over and kissed my cheek. "Saturday," he said. "I can't wait."

Max seemed nervous. He was pacing around the living room while I watched him, amused. He stopped by the piano. "Hey," he said, "play something for me."

"Sure. What do you want me to play?"

"Surprise me."

"OK." I sat and made room for him on the bench beside me. The first song I played was Adele's "Someone Like You." I moved on to Journey's "Don't Stop Believing" and ended with the Beatles' "Let it Be."

"I love hearing you play."

"You should come to church with me sometime. I play every Sunday."

"Really?"

"Yeah. I thought you knew that."

"No, I meant that I could come to church to hear you play."

"Sure. Heck, I'll even sneak you into the organ loft."

"Cool. Hey, can you teach me to play a song on the piano?"

MAX

I asked Tristan to teach me to play a song on the piano because he plays so beautifully.

"Sure," he said. "Can you read music? Do you understand notes?"

I nodded. I'd taught myself to read music because I'd once flirted with the idea of being a guitar player in a rock band, though I was too embarrassed to tell him this.

"OK, good. I can start you playing scales."

"No, no," I said. "I want to play a song."

"You'll get there, but first—"

"No, you don't understand. I just want you to teach me to play one song."

"And what song is that?"

"The theme song from *Mission Impossible*."

"The theme song from *Mission Impossible*? That's it? That's all you want to learn how to play?"

"Yes."

"OK. It's in two sections. First section is easy. It's one hand, your left hand. That section is a five-four rhythm, ten beats in all. To make it easier, we'll divide each measure in two. So, one-two-three, one-two, one-two-three, one-two. The notes are G, G, B flat, C, then G, G, F, F sharp. OK, you try it."

I did. It took some practice, but I got it, and then we moved into the second part, which was more difficult. By dinner, I could play the entire theme song by myself.

TRISTAN

WE WERE SITTING under the willow tree in my backyard. Max sat with his back against the tree's trunk while I lay with my head in his lap, looking up at the sky. He was stroking my hair.

"Thanks for teaching me to play that song," he said.

"Mmmm," I murmured, trying not to drift off to sleep. He stopped stroking my hair. "Don't stop," I said. He started again.

"I can't believe I used to hate myself," he said.

I propped up on one elbow. "You used to hate yourself? Why?"

He shrugged and guided my head back to his lap. He began stroking my hair again. "For wanting *this*."

"That's no reason to hate yourself."

"I know that. *Now*. But back then, I thought I wasn't supposed to be like this. I wasn't supposed to want this. Just like I wasn't supposed to notice how handsome you are. Because I *liked* you, and that was supposed to be wrong. And I didn't think you'd ever like me back."

"Are you saying you hated yourself because you're gay?"

"Yes. No. Oh, this is so hard. Look, I always knew I was gay, but I didn't really want to be. But then I met you, and more than anything I wanted to be gay because I wanted to be with you. I didn't care if it was wrong anymore."

"Well, I'm glad we cleared that up."

He looked at me so solemnly that it was almost comical. "Do you think I'm an idiot?"

"Well, yeah."

He looked at the slow-moving creek.

Hey," I said, "I only think you're an idiot because you hated yourself."

"I don't really," he said.

"Good. I'm glad you don't hate yourself."

"Why?"

"Because if you hate yourself, you'd have to hate me, too. And I don't want you to hate me."

"Why would I hate you?" He looked confused and alarmed.

"Because I think you're handsome, too. Because I'm gay."

"Really? I didn't mean what I said. I don't hate myself, but I think I'm in love with you—"

"You can't love me if you don't love yourself," I interrupted softly.

"OK, maybe I didn't mean it like that. I didn't mind being... *different*...until I met you, and then I thought maybe you wouldn't be my friend if you knew how I felt about you, how I *was*..."

"I know and I do, but see, the thing is, I want to be *more* than your friend." I paused for breath. I'd just told him more than I'd ever told anyone about myself. I'd certainly never said the words, *I'm gay* out loud before.

"When did you know you were gay?" I asked Max.

"Oh, I think I always knew on some level. I was always attracted to guys who were younger, or smaller, but when I was young, I figured it was because I was an only child and lonely and wanted a little brother I could teach and protect. And then—even before puberty hit—I would have these dreams, and I realized that little bro/big bro thing—yeah, that wasn't what I wanted. At all." He laughed.

MAX

MARTIN. HE LIVED across the street from us, our ancient neighbor's wild, overgrown grandson. Every Saturday morning, from the first breath of spring to summer's last gasp in late September, he'd appear like clockwork, pushing an old hand mower across the lawn just beyond my bedroom window.

In the summer, he'd often strip off, beads of sweat clotting like curdled milk in the tangle of blond hair that spread across his chest from shoulder to shoulder, then narrowed to a magical trail that disappeared under the waistband of his low-slung jeans.

His heavy, greasy, sandy-blond hair lay on his head in moribund profusion. It needed cutting, as did his not inconsiderable beard. His startling, crystal-blue eyes were sunk deep in his weathered aesthete's face. When he wasn't shirtless, he wore a grimy, torn tank top that clung to his abdomen; he was lean but ripped. He looked like a homeless Jesus. And like Jesus, he possessed a magnetic aura that cloaked him in attractiveness. Looking at him, I was painfully aware of my erection straining against my jeans. It was in that moment so many summers before that I first truly *knew* myself. And in that moment, I thought I understood religious fervor. Like Christ on the cross, he inspired a lust so pure, so *new*…it was impossible to recognize it as simply lust, thus it was easy to ascribe the feeling to a higher more noble emotion—to sublimate and codify it into pious devotion that called one to conscription into an army of people straining to achieve saintly behavior.

Christ on the cross, I was sure, was responsible for thousands of gay men—horrified at their desire for their Lord and Savior—joining the priesthood and signing on to a lifetime of celibacy in penance for such impure thoughts.

My attraction to him scared me. With Tristan I wasn't afraid.

TRISTAN

"IF YOU COULD live anywhere in the world, where would you live?" I asked.

"Why would I want to live anywhere else?" Max asked. "Everything I need is here. *You're* here."

"Let's try this again—where would you be happy?"

"Wherever you are."

I was still lying with my head in his lap, and I closed my eyes so he wouldn't see the tears that pricked at the corners. I believed him. He was an excellent son, and excellent sons never lie.

"How about you?" he asked. "Where would you live?"

"Paris," I said without hesitation.

"Paris. OK. Paris is cool. We could visit the Arc de Triomphe and the Louvre—I've always wanted to see the *Mona Lisa*—"

"Really?"

"Yeah. When I was little, I decided I wanted to shave off my eyebrows like her. Fortunately, Dad talked me out of it." He laughed. "Is that terribly gay?"

"No," I said, with great gravity, a physician making a difficult diagnosis. "But it *is* very strange."

He lunged at me and proceeded to tickle me. "Take that back!"

"Not until you kiss me," I choked out between giggles.

He kissed me.

"I'm sorry you're so strange."

"You scoundrel."

"How dare you, good sir! I must remind you I am an excellent son!"

The tickling continued.

"We should go," I said when the tickling and laughter finally subsided.

"Where?"

"Paris."

"When?"

"I don't know. Next summer after we graduate before we go off to college."

"OK," he said. "I'm in."

I closed my eyes and dreamed of us, alone together, in Paris.

MAX

GETTING READY FOR bed was awkward. We were both suddenly shy. We'd kissed and even made out some, but we'd never seen each other fully naked. I'd always avoided getting naked in the locker room. I'd almost convinced myself that it was modesty, but at some point, I'd had to admit it was more than that. I did not want other boys to look at me naked. I suppose on some level, part of my fucked-up rationale was that if they did not look at me, I wouldn't have to look at them and admit to myself what looking at them did to me.

Tristan, naked, looked at me puzzled. I felt ridiculous as he stood there completely naked while I stood fully clothed, blushing and trembling like a sixteen-year-old virgin on her wedding night in a Victorian romance. I quickly disrobed and, screwing up my courage, looked at him. He was grinning at me. His hands moved to cover his erection. And I felt...validated. I moved to the bed and sat. He did the same. He reached for the bedside lamp. "Wait," I said. "Leave it on?"

Chapter 18

TRISTAN

MAX WAS STANDING, leaning against the living room's glass wall, looking at the relentless rain. I stepped gingerly, feeling self-conscious. Sex had changed everything, making us shy with each other, yet I felt myself assuming a proprietary air when I looked at him.

He turned around. "You OK?"

"Fine," I lied. "What are you doing?"

"Watching the rain. It's really warm outside. Do you want to go for a walk?"

"In the rain?"

"Yeah, in the rain."

"OK. I can probably find a rain slicker that will fit you—"

"No. Let's go like we are?"

"Um, OK."

He opened the door and dashed out into the pouring rain. "I'll race you," he called over his shoulder.

"Race me where?" I ran after him. He ran across the back lawn, past the weeping willow to the creek's edge. Then, hopping barefoot across the rocks that formed a rough-hewn bridge, he crossed to the other side, where he flopped down on his back in the tall grasses. Catching up, I threw myself down on top of him. Our chests rapidly rose and fell with our rushed breath. I propped up on my elbows and, looking down into his face, tried to shake the rain out of my eyes. He smiled and gently stroked my wet hair then leaned up to kiss me. It was a kiss without beginning, without end. Lips still pressed together, we pulled at each other's wet clothes, his breath skating past my lips in a damp rush. His name tangled in my throat.

MAX

AFTER, WE LAY on our backs, spent, as the rain sluiced away the evidence of what we'd done.

"I used to hate rain," Tristan said.

"Used to?"

He sat up and, looking at me, nodded.

"And now you don't?"

"And now I don't."

"Why not?"

"Because before, I just thought about all the things the rain was keeping me from doing. And now, well, now it will remind me of you...of our first night together."

I reached for his hand. After a few minutes of lying like that, he said, "We'd better get back inside and clean up and get you out of here before my parents get back."

"Noooo," I groaned childishly. He rolled onto his side and gazed at me.

"Noooo," I pleaded.

"Yes." He kissed me and, standing, picked up our discarded clothes.

"Race you back."

TRISTAN

MY PARENTS RETURNED a little before dinner time. Even as she hugged me, I could feel my mother scanning the room for untold damage and perhaps a clue to what I'd been up to.

"Well, good to see the house is still standing," my father said with uncharacteristic humor. Perhaps he was just channeling my mother's thoughts.

"How are you?" my mother asked.

"Fine. How was the wedding?"

"Fine. Everyone asked for you."

Evidently satisfied that I hadn't burnt down the house, my father moved to take their suitcases upstairs. "Here," I said, "I can do that." I took the suitcases out of his hand. "Oomph," I gasped as the air went out of my lungs. "What do you have in here?"

"Your mother's shoes," my father said.

"Shoes," my mother echoed.

"Shoes? How many pairs did you need? You were gone a day and a half!"

My father rolled his eyes.

"Just take those upstairs," my mother said.

When I returned to the kitchen, they were seated at the island, drinking Scotch. "Well, I guess I'll start dinner," my mother said with a sigh.

"I'll help," I said. My parents exchanged a look but said nothing, and I set about gathering and chopping vegetables and humming.

Over dinner, my mother suddenly put down her chopsticks and stared at me. "You look different."

"Since yesterday, you mean?" I asked sarcastically around a mouth full of stir-fried vegetables.

"Your mother is right," my father said, putting down his fork and looking at me more intently. "You *do* look different. Like we were away for a year, and you grew up in that time."

I rolled my eyes. "I think the mimosas you two had at the post-wedding brunch combined with your pre-prandial Scotch is making you hallucinate."

My mother picked up her chopsticks. "Perhaps," she said cheerfully. "If you were a girl, I would think you were pregnant."

I choked on my ginger ale, and my father got up to pound me on the back. "Thanks," I coughed out. "Wrong pipe." And hoped they would attribute my sudden flush of color to choking.

Chapter 19

MAX

Tristan groaned against my shoulder. "What's wrong, babe?" I asked him.

"I don't want to go to school today."

"Why not? You sick?"

"No, I just want to play hooky." He sat up. "I'm a junior in high school and I've never played hooky. I've never even pretended to be sick so I didn't have to go to school."

"I think you may have spring fever."

"Yeah, maybe."

Just then, the conductor announced the Chinatown stop.

"Chinatown," Tristan said wistfully. "What's that like?"

"You've never been to Chinatown?"

"No. Have you?"

"Yeah."

"You're full of surprises, aren't you?"

"Who hasn't been to Chinatown?"

"Me."

"Get up," I said, pushing him out of the seat.

"What?"

"Get up. We're getting off. Hurry."

We made it to the platform just before the doors closed. As the train pulled away, Tristan looked confused. "What are we doing? Why'd we get off?"

61

"We're playing hooky," I shouted. I grabbed his hand. "We're going to Chinatown."

"We are?"

"We are. C'mon."

. . . .

We emerged from the train station and paused on the corner as Tristan gazed in wonder at the Chinatown Friendship Gate. The brightly painted portal done in the traditional Qing Dynasty style had been built by Chinese engineers and artisans and acted as the formal entry into Chinatown.

TRISTAN

THE FRIENDSHIP GATE was unlike anything I'd ever seen before. I could have spent hours examining its intricate, brightly colored tiles that had been imported from Tianjin, China, but Max was impatient to show me around. We stepped through the portal and into another world, a world pulsing with mystery and every imaginable sensory pleasure: fantastic foods, raw and cooked, exotic smells, the loud buzz of conversation in unfathomable languages and frenetic movement. Cheek-to-jowl were restaurants and shops and stands representing Hong Kong, Cantonese, Fujianese, Northern Sichuan, and Taiwanese cultures, all sprinkled with Korean, Thai, Malaysian, Burmese, and Vietnamese influences.

I don't like crowds. The crush of people, the unfamiliar smells, the cacophony of a dozen languages and dialects all being spoken at once, the often-jarring sights, and the prospect of eating foods I'd never tasted before generally would have made me anxious, but this day something about the sun on my face and the weight of Max's hand in mine stilled my anxiety. I felt like I could do anything—even fly—with this handsome sturdy boy who was so confident in his feelings for me, beside me.

We passed a fruit and vegetable market that skirted an entire corner. On the sidewalk, under a narrow awning covered in Chinese characters, were cardboard boxes full of fruits I'd seldom or never seen before and certainly had never tasted. These were attended by a swarm of flies. Shoppers exiting the market released into the street the smell of seaweed, fresh-caught fish on ice, and lobsters floating in murky tanks.

MAX

As WE WOVE our way, hand in hand, through the throngs of early morning shoppers and strollers, we passed a multitude of elderly women, fragile and white-haired, attended by a legion of excellent sons, patient, dutiful, devoted. These sons carried their mother's packages and helped them cross the street and offered them sunglasses to protect their cataract-clouded eyes from the sun's glare. I watched them with interest; Tristan did not. If he saw himself in these excellent sons, he gave no indication of recognition.

Tristan seemed reluctant to try any of the foods the stands and stores offered, so when I saw an ice cream truck, I asked, "Want an ice cream cone?"

"There's ice cream?"

I pointed to the aqua truck playing a tinny, old-fashioned tune through a mangled bullhorn mounted to its roof.

"I don't know..." he said, following my finger and seeing the truck.

"Oh, come on. It's got to be good—it matches your shirt," I said pointing to his aqua polo shirt with its purple, oversized silhouette of a horse and jockey.

"OK, sure."

I flagged down the truck, which rattled to a precarious stop at the curb.

The driver was a burly, bearded man in a too-tight T-shirt that read *The Bike Stop*. The sleeves were cut off to reveal his bulging, tattooed biceps. "Do you want sprinkles on that?" he asked.

"Yes."

"Chocolate, vanilla, or..." He hesitated and, leering suggestively, offered, "Rainbows?" His leer, though, wasn't hostile or challenging but friendly, supportively questioning what he already knew.

"Rainbows," Tristan said.

The man nodded approvingly and handed the cone to Tristan. When I attempted to pay him, he barked, "No charge," and, smiling, slammed the window and made his way to the driver's seat.

....

Tristan's mindless chatter was soothing, and soon I found myself drowsing as the spires and glass towers of downtown rising from the rubble of decaying streets and collapsing tenements of the slums that encroached on the railroad tracks raced past us.

"Hey!" he said suddenly. "Are you sleeping?"

He looked so indignant I couldn't help smiling. "No," I said, stretching and yawning conspicuously.

"You were!"

I shrugged. "I can't help it if your voice is so soothing it lulls me to sleep."

He pursed his lips, feigning annoyance.

"Did you have fun today?"

"I did," he said, then after a moment asked, "Do you suppose school called our parents?"

"Probably."

"Damn it. There's going to be hell to pay."

"I'm sorry."

"Don't be. It was worth it."

I put my arm around him and pulled him against me, ignoring the curious stares we drew.

TRISTAN

"SHOW ME YOUR company, and I'll tell you who you are," my mother said, slamming plates down on the table. It was Marta's day off.

I'd had about enough of my mother nagging me about playing hooky and the company I was keeping, so I said I had a headache and went upstairs. As my parents sat down to eat alone, I sat at the top of the stairs listening.

"He seems changed," my mother said.

"Changed? Changed how?" my father asked.

My mother's sterling silver chopsticks grew furious in their movements, and I had trouble hearing her.

"I don't know. Before, he approached everything with a kind of grim determination, as if he was committed to giving it his best shot but was resigned to failure. And now...now..."

"Now, *what*?"

The chopsticks paused in their furious clicking. "Now, he seems happy all the time."

"You're upset because he seems happy? You'd prefer he was unhappy?" The incredulity in my father's voice was unmistakable. Curious about her answer, I took a chance and moved farther down the stairs.

"No, John. I want to know what he has to be so happy about."

"Do you ever listen to yourself?"

The click of my mother's chopsticks began again. "He seems different."

"He's seventeen. He's growing up. If anything, he seems more confident—less scared."

My mother pounced. "So, you *have* noticed a difference!"

"Yes, but *I* don't think it's a bad thing."

"It's that boy he won't stop talking about."

"Max? So, he has a friend. Again, I don't think that's a bad thing."

My mother didn't respond, but the movement of her chopsticks grew louder, frantic. I heard my father sigh. His chair scraped against the floor, then I heard ice being added to a glass and the unmistakable slur of bourbon being poured. Their conversation, I knew, was over; I went to my room.

Chapter 20

TRISTAN

MY MOTHER WAS in the kitchen washing and polishing apples.

"I'm heading over to Max's," I said.

She nodded. "Do you need a ride?"

"No. Max is picking me up." As I turned to leave, she said, "Judy stopped by yesterday."

"Yesterday? Why?"

"To see you—she said she never sees you anymore."

"Odd. She knew I was at the library, that I was meeting Max after practice."

"She likes you. She's turned into such an attractive young lady. I don't understand why you're not dating her." My mother began inspecting an apple.

"I thought you were against high schoolers dating—you know, nose to the grindstone and all that."

She ignored my outburst. "She's a nice girl," she continued.

"Then why don't *you* date her?"

"Tristan, I'm warning you." She dropped apples into a white melamine bowl. When she spoke again, her tone had softened, and she repeated, "She *likes* you."

"I like someone else."

Her eyes narrowed with contempt. "Who?" she sneered. "That boy Max?"

The obvious truth lay between us. Her hands were shaking when she lifted her white bowl full of yellow apples. She waited, not moving, her bowl of apples held in her hands like a communal offering.

Excellent sons don't lie, lest their noses grow long like Pinocchio's and they bring shame to their mothers. I took two apples out of the bowl. "Thanks. I have to go."

. . . .

Max was waiting on his motorcycle at the foot of our driveway. When he saw me, he got off his bike and handed me my helmet. "Is that all you're wearing? he asked me, looking at my long-sleeved Oxford shirt.

"Yeah. Why?"

"You'll be cold."

"I can run back and get a jacket if you think—"

"No. Wear this. I brought it for you." He handed me his letterman's jacket. It was then that I noticed he was wearing an old leather jacket.

"Thanks. I'll give return it when we get back."

"No, I want you to keep it and wear it."

"Really?"

"Yeah. I know it's kind of ugly," he said apologetically, "but I'd really like you to have it and wear it."

I looked at the jacket. Its body was teal boiled wool, and its sleeves were purple leather. Our school initial was over the left breast in purple, and his name was inscribed in small script on the right breast.

"Ugly? Are you kidding? I think it's the most beautiful jacket I've ever seen."

Smiling, he said, "Well, go ahead—put it on."

Chapter 21

MAX

B'WOY, WHERE YOU going so early on a Sunday morning?" Aunt Kaleisha, who was busy frying bacon at the stove, demanded as I attempted to slip out the door to the garage.

"Church," I answered.

"Church!" When she was agitated, her Jamaican accent thickened. "Why? You suddenly fin' God? Why you suddenly going to church alla time?"

"Leave him be," Aunt Tianara chided. "Maybe he's getting religion."

"He bes' not be," Aunt Tashelle added. "You know what they say back home—the church and the rum shop join together to keep we in ignorance!"

"I'm not getting religious. I go to hear Tristan play."

"Ah-ha," Aunt Kaleisha said. "I shouldna know it—he goin' see that b'woy—"

"What boy?" Aunt Tashelle asked.

"The one he bring here to the house—the Korean."

"Mine what you doing, nuh?" Aunt Tianara said. "You burning the bacon."

"I not! What you know?"

I slipped out the door leaving The Aunts to argue among themselves.

When I slid onto the bench beside Tristan, who was playing the processional hymn, he glanced at me and smiled. I forgot about my badgering aunts.

TRISTAN

CHURCH HAD ENDED, and I was standing with my mother, waiting for my father to bring the car around so my mother wouldn't have to walk across the damp grass in her light-colored, silk heels. She was greeting fellow parishioners as if she was the first lady of the church or campaigning for political office. I was scanning the congregation for Max. Judy walked up to us. I halfheartedly murmured a greeting, still looking for Max, who'd gone off to the men's room.

My mother took Judy's arm. "Judy—so good to see you."

Max walked up to me just then. "Good morning," he said with impeccable good manners.

"Max!" Judy cried. She seemed delighted to see him, which shocked me. "Did I see you in the choir loft with our Tristan?"

"You did," Max said curtly.

My mother looked at her in surprise. "Judy," my mother said, "we haven't seen you in so long. You must come by the house— like you used to."

"Oh, you know," Judy said to my mother, "Tristan doesn't have time for me anymore. His interests lie…elsewhere." She looked pointedly at Max. My mother followed her gaze and frowned.

I started to say something, but Max stopped me by touching my arm.

"Hey, we still on for breakfast?" There was an unmistakable intimacy in his voice. If I could hear it, I was sure my mother and Judy could.

"Of course," I said, then, turning to my mother, "Mom, Max and I are going to breakfast, OK?"

She looked from me to him and back to me. I was suddenly self-conscious about how closely Max and I were standing to each other, his hand on my arm. My mother said nothing but waved her hand dismissively. I could feel her eyes on us as we walked away, Judy speaking to her softly, her voice like the hiss of a viper.

· ·

We were waiting for our order when Max reached across the table and took my hand in his. "Hey," he said. "You OK?"

"Yeah, fine. Why?"

"You've been quiet."

"I've been thinking."

"About what?"

"Us—this—how nice it is to be out alone with you, just the two of us and *this*." I squeezed his hand.

He smiled and stroked my knuckles with his thumb, triggering another round of my desire for him.

"I—"

"Hello, son."

We both looked up at the same moment to see his father, holding a cup of takeout coffee, standing at our table. His gaze moved from Max's face to the spot on the table where our hands lay entwined. Instinctively, I started to pull away, but Max tightened his grip.

"Hey, Dad."

"You boys getting breakfast?"

"Yes."

"How was church?"

"OK. Tristan played brilliantly as usual."

"I don't doubt it," his father said, then turned to me. "Tristan, good seeing you."

"You, too, sir."

"Max, I'll see you at home." He glanced again at our clasped hands, took a sip of his coffee, then walked away.

Chapter 22

MAX

DAD SAT AT the kitchen table where I was eating cereal and trying to finish the homework I'd neglected over the weekend to spend time with Tristan.

"So...how was breakfast yesterday?" he asked.

"Good. Afterwards, we went to the zoo because Tristan wanted to see the new baby koalas."

"Is Tristan your boyfriend?"

My heart started to race. "He is," I said, not looking up but watching him from my lowered eyes. He nodded but said nothing. I rushed to fill the silence. "I—I should have told you."

Dad laughed, causing me to look at him. "You never tell me anything," he said. "If I want to learn something about you, I have to watch you. That's always been the truth of you. This is no different."

"Are you—are you OK with it?"

"I don't have to be OK with it. You—and Tristan—have to be OK with it. I just have to accept it. It's not my choice—"

"It's not a choice!"

He held up his hand. "We don't need to have that discussion. It doesn't matter whether you chose this or not. You don't have to defend your life—or who you are—to me. Or anyone else for that matter. But since you asked, yes, I am OK with it. I don't fully understand it, but I don't have to."

"Are you surprised?"

He laughed again. "I'm guessing for rather twisted reasons—probably all tied up in your internalized homophobia," he said, surprising me again, "you're hoping I'll say I'm shocked, but no, I'm not surprised. You're seventeen. You've never brought a girl home or particularly talked about one. When we're out, you never even *look* at girls, but I've noticed a boy or two turn your head."

I said nothing, only stared at the open book in front of me, my cheeks aflame.

"I told you, if I want to know something about you, all I have to do is watch you. You play at being inscrutable, but you're not. Anyway," he stood and picked up a bag I hadn't noticed when he came in, "I assume you and Tristan are having sex—or will have sex—"

"Dad!"

"Relax. I'm not asking for details or confirmation. But you need to have this." He upended the bag, and to my horror, out tumbled packets of condoms in rainbow colors no less, several tubes of something called Gun Oil, and a pamphlet on safer sex practices.

"Dad. Where did you get this...stuff?"

"I stopped by the queer—the *gay*—center in town and talked to them. They said if you're gay and sexually active, you need these."

"Dad—I—"

"I'm not saying Tristan isn't a good boy or not to be trusted, I'm just saying you need to protect yourself—*both* of you need protection."

"Dad, I—"

"I know, son, I know. I love you, too. OK, I'm off to work. Don't be late for school." He kissed me on top of my head like he used to do when I was a little kid. Picking up his keys, he said, "Maybe you and I and Tristan can go out to dinner or something soon."

"I think he'd like that. *I'd* like that."

He nodded and was gone.

Chapter 23

TRISTAN

I WAS SITTING ON the ground, reading *Pinocchio* for the umpteenth time and waiting for Max to finish practice. Judy walked by with her girlfriends, a quintet of gossipy, stylish girls. None of them seemed to have a boyfriend; whether they wanted one or not, their feminine harmony seemed to preclude the incursion of testosterone.

She said something to them, and they all turned to look at me. She broke away and approached me.

"Hey."

"Hey," I said without getting up.

"What are you doing?"

"Waiting for Max."

"Max! What is it with you two?" She crossed her arms and pouted.

"What do you mean?" I asked, wary.

"Suddenly everything is Max. Max this and Max that. And the way you look at him. And him always *touching* you. If I didn't know better, I'd think—"

"You don't know shit! And, by the way, it *is* what you think," I snapped, too mad and too in love with Max to care what I'd just confessed. She stared at me with furious burning eyes. If she thought those red-rimmed coals could burn holes in my enmity, she was sadly mistaken.

"You should go now," I said in the iciest tones I could muster. "The Hydra is waiting." I nodded to her restless quintet of martinets.

When she stormed off, I picked up my book and began reading again, trying to calm myself.

· · · · · · · · · · · · · · · · · · · ·

Feeling like I was being watched, I glanced up from my book to find Max looking at me, his gym bag over his shoulder.

"What are you doing?" I asked.

"Looking at you."

"I can see that. Why are you looking at me?"

"Because you're handsome and you're my boyfriend."

I grinned up at him.

"What are you reading?" he asked.

"*Pinocchio*."

"Isn't that a children's book?"

"Well, sort of. It was written as a serial for children, but to me, it's more than a children's story. It's brutal and fun. I suppose my mother started reading it to me because its only premise is that bad things happen to bad children. It's also a universal metaphor for the human condition. It's a canonical piece of children's literature that has had an enormous impact on world culture. It's been translated into more than three hundred languages, which makes it the most translated non-religious book in the world and one of the best-selling books ever published. I read somewhere that only the bible has been more widely read."

"Really? I'll have to read it sometime," he said, taking the book out of my hand and staring at the wooden child/puppet on its cover.

"You've never read it?"

"Nope."

"It was my favorite story as a kid. Finally, my mother refused to read it anymore. She told me if I wanted to hear the story, I'd have to learn to read it. So, I got my dad to teach me. One night, when she asked me what book I wanted her to read, I said, '*Pinocchio*,' and she said, 'I told you, you would have to read that one yourself.'

"'OK,' I told her, 'I'll read it to you.' And I did."

"How old were you?"

"Three."

I stretched out my hand, and he pulled me to my feet.

"I saw your friend," Max said as we started to walk.

"You mean Judy?"

"Yeah."

"Why is Judy always hanging around you?"

"I don't know. Because we're friends?"

Even as I said it, I wondered if it was true. Judy was my oldest friend. Until I met Max, she'd been my only friend. Some people assumed Judy and I were best friends, while others wondered if we were nursing secret crushes on each other. But the truth was we had nothing in common and neither of us shared much about ourselves with the other. We'd met in third grade when I was a refugee from homeschooling and she was a chubby girl in need of braces. We were like two neutral countries at opposite sides of the Earth with nothing in common outside of a shared enemy—in our case, it was schoolyard bullies, though now we were in high school, that shared enemy was more likely to be a disgruntled classmate with access to ammunition and a semi-automatic weapon—and a heartfelt desire to live in peace. We'd seen strength in allyship, in keeping company.

As vicious and innocent as they are, children are masters at identifying the weak or different among them and move to separate them from the rest of the herd. An early outcast from the herds, I was bullied for the usual things: carrying my books pressed against my chest with my two arms crossed over them; always knowing the answer, though I did learn to stop raising my hand. When teachers, exasperated by a series of wrong, sometimes wildly absurd answers, would call on me, I would be torn between giving the answer and ending the teacher's pain or feigning ignorance and preventing my own. And I was bullied for wearing glasses.

I'd worn glasses until I was fourteen, when a particularly nasty classmate threw a ball at my head during a game of dodgeball, breaking my glasses. I realized my vision without glasses was no different than my vision had been with them perched on the edge of my nose. This was a revelation; I'd been wearing classes since first grade when I'd brought home a series of B+s. My mother had insisted it was because I couldn't see the lessons on the board. She took me to three different ophthalmologists before she found one who agreed with her assessment. She dismissed the other two as quacks.

When my mother's friends commented on the sudden absence of my glasses, my mother shrugged and boldly claimed my ophthalmologist had declared my vision had been restored to perfection by some sort of near-miracle—rare but known to happen in exceptional cases. My father merely laughed at the miracle and said I'd never needed them, that the lenses had been plain glass.

MAX

WHEN I ASKED Tristan why Judy was always hanging around him, he said it was because they were friends, though he made his answer seem more like a question, so I pressed him.

"Are you—*friends*?"

"I guess." He shrugged.

"Is that what she thinks?"

"What do you mean, Max?"

"You know what I mean."

"Actually, I don't."

"She wants to be your girlfriend!"

"Well, *I* don't want a girlfriend."

"Why not?"

"Because I have a boyfriend."

"You do?"

"Yeah, I do."

"Who?"

"You, knucklehead. You're my boyfriend."

"Am I?" I teased, suddenly relieved, jealousy like a burden lifted from my shoulders.

"Well, you said you were two minutes ago. Have you changed your mind? Did you just dump me?"

"My dad asked if you were my boyfriend."

"What did you say?"

"I said, yeah, you were."

Tristan grinned. I could tell he wasn't mad at me anymore. That made me happy for some reason I can't explain. "You look happy," I said.

"I am. You make me happy, Max."

"I could kiss you," I said.

"So, kiss me," he said.

"There are people around."

"Not that many."

I hugged him, too quickly. Then, despite myself, I looked around guiltily. "We should probably be careful, though. Especially around Judy…and your mother."

"I don't care," he said. "I don't want to hide anymore. Do you?"

By now, we had somehow attracted the attention of our classmates, who were unabashedly observing us, poking the inattentive among them in the ribs and pointing at us.

I decided Tristan deserved better than a rushed hug—*we* deserved better. "No, neither do I," I said. I pulled him to me and full-on kissed him on the lips, with tongue; my hands wandered over his body. He kissed me back, hard.

That first kiss within sight of our classmates changed everything. The surprised gasps of our classmates were like the sound of shackles falling. The snickers and giggles like the sound of a prison door creaking open. Their shocked looks like a match being struck in the dark. The popular narrative holds that being gay but not out is like living in a closet. I can tell you it isn't. It's more like living in a prison cell, or maybe a windowless, mirrorless box; you can't see anyone, not even yourself, and no one can see you. Maybe the joy in that first public kiss was the joy of seeing and being seen.

Chapter 24

TRISTAN

"HEY, GUESS WHAT?" Judy asked, walking up to me in the hall. She was smiling. I hadn't seen her smile much lately.

I closed my locker, spun the combination on the lock. "What?"

She tickled me under my chin and danced around me. "I am taking you to dinner tomorrow night."

"I can't tomorrow night."

"But it's your birthday. I always take you out on your birthday."

She was right. She always did. I had completely forgotten.

"I can't. Really. I'm going to dinner with Max."

"But it's your birthday."

"I know. But it's Max's birthday, too."

"You have the same birthday?"

I nodded.

"It's not fair. Why can't I have something that's just mine?" She looked as if she was about to cry.

"Look, I have to go. You can take me to dinner Saturday if you want."

Max walked up to us. "Hi," he said. "You ready?"

"Where are you going?" Judy demanded suspiciously.

"I'm walking Tristan to class," Max said, putting his arm around my shoulders.

Chapter 25

TRISTAN

MAX AND I were walking into the cafeteria as Judy and her crew were exiting. "Hello, Thunder and Lightning," one of her coterie, indistinguishable from the others, said. The others stared at us and giggled.

The kids at school, noticing us, had taken to referring to Max and me as Thunder and Lightning because they say where there's one, there's soon the other. I think it's kind of funny that we have a couple's nickname. Most of the kids refer to us that way offhandedly, an easy way to acknowledge our coupledom. Others spit the nickname out like phlegm, dripping with contempt and sometimes confusion.

Max put his arm around my shoulder. "Ladies, Judy," he said. "Nice to see you."

The girls, seeming shocked he'd addressed them, mumbled, "You, too."

Judy, however, chose to ignore him, instead glaring at the spot where his hand rested on my shoulder. She turned to her friends. "Don't call them that. I hate nicknames. I think they're stupid!"

"Actually, it's not a nickname," Max said. "I think it's more a couple name—you know, like Brad Pitt and Angelina Jolie are known collectively as Brangelina."

This, apparently, was a bridge too far, for Judy now acknowledged him in fury. "I hate you, Max."

"You hate me? Or you want to *be* me?" Max squeezed my shoulder. Her eyes followed his hand.

"Let's go!" Judy ordered; her friends closed ranks, and they marched off.

MAX

OF EVERYTHING THAT happened this term between me and Tristan, what surprised me most was the bestowing of a nickname on us. Tristan calls it our "couple name," with his irrepressible glee. I suppose it was meant to be our couple name, but it didn't combine our two names, so it wasn't anything as sickeningly cute as "Brangelina." Instead, kids at school dubbed us Thunder and Lightning.

Oh, we had other nicknames, too: Mutt and Jeff, the less imaginative of our peers called us. My elderly West Indian neighbor, insisting where you saw one, you saw the other, named us Bam Bam and Poe. On what she considered the rare occasion she saw one of us without the other, she'd call out, "Hey, Bam Bam, where's Poe?" or "Poe, where's your Bam Bam?" To get the joke, you need to know Bam Bam is West Indian slang for your butt. Poe is slang for a chamber pot. Even my dad started calling us Bam Bam and Poe.

I liked that all the nicknames recognized us as individuals but also acknowledged our partnership. And I suppose I should admit I rather liked Thunder and Lightning. I was thunder, they said, because I'm always scowling, dark and stormy. And Tristan is Lightning because he is all smiles and glittering light.

Chapter 26

TRISTAN

MAX AND I were standing next to my mother after church, waiting for my dad to bring the car around. It had rained the night before, and the grass was wet; this time, it was my mother's *peau de soie* pumps in danger of ruin.

Judy came from around the side of the church and headed for where I stood next to Max. Stopping in front of me, she stretched on her tiptoes and kissed first my cheek and then Max's. "Good morning, Thunder and Lightning," she said a little too brightly, a little too loudly. Beside me, I could feel Max recoil from her touch, her words, both gesture and words hinting as they did at an understanding, an intimacy, that did not exist between us. She turned swiftly to my mother. "Good morning, Mrs. James. You look stunning as ever." She leaned forward and kissed my mother on both cheeks.

My father drove up. I opened the passenger door for my mother out of habit.

"Judy, do come to breakfast with us," my mother said.

"Are you sure?"

My mother nodded, ducking in the open door. "Max," she called over her shoulder, "be a gentleman and open the door for Judy."

My father lowered the convertible roof. "Sure you boys don't want a ride somewhere?"

"They'll be fine," my mother said impatiently, tugging on his arm. "John, put that roof back up. The wind will absolutely ruin my hair."

My father, disappointed, did as he was told and they drove off.

"I don't like her," Max said.

"Who?"

"Judy."

"Oh, I thought you may have been talking about my mother."

"I don't know that I dislike your mother," he replied. He seemed to think for a moment, then added, "But I'm not sure I like her either."

I nodded but said nothing. I envied him his luxury of indecision. I'd been raised to believe my only option was to love my mother.

"It's like you're gay Jesus and she's your disciple."

"Who?"

"Judy."

"Oh, I thought you were talking about my mother."

"Well, I suppose I can see how that statement could apply to either of them."

I laughed. "Let's not waste the rest of our Sunday talking about them."

Max threw his arm across my shoulder. "What do you want to do today?"

As we walked away, I could hear the sibilant whispers of The Church Saints who had finally emerged from the shadowed depths of the church, with its low-hanging cloud of incense, into the morning sun, birthing their latest scandalized judgments against the young organist and his heathen companion.

Chapter 27

TRISTAN

WHAT ARE YOU doing? Don't you care? People are talking about you and that boy—"

"His name is Max."

"Don't smart-mouth me! They are laughing at you behind your back. They've nicknamed the two of you Thunder and Lightning."

Damn Judy!

"Thunder and Lightning," she repeated, her voice full of contempt. "It's a joke—and you're the punchline!"

When I remained silent, she repeated, "Don't you care?"

I made a show of pulling my wallet out of my pocket. I looked inside for a moment, then turned it inside out and upside down. "Just as I suspected," I said. "I have no fucks to give—"

My mother slapped me fast and hard. She had never hit me before; I don't know which of us was more surprised. My cheek stung, but I refused to cry in front of her.

"Grace! Stop it!" my father said sharply from the kitchen door. I had no idea how long he'd been standing there. I pushed past him. He grabbed my arm. I yanked it away and stormed out, letting the screen door slam behind me.

Under the shade of the weeping willow in the backyard, I let the tears fall. Through the screen door, I could hear their raised voices, the opening volley in what would explode into one of their rare arguments.

"It feels like I'm losing him!" my mother shouted.

"It feels like you're pushing him away."

"What has gotten into him?" my mother asked before answering her own question, "It's that school!"

"It is not that school," my father shot back. "And may I remind you that *that school*, which costs a bloody fortune, is one of the best in the state."

"Pftt!" A dismissive sound.

"Need I also remind you that *you* chose that school?"

"I wanted to homeschool him!"

"And that worked out well, didn't it?"

Shortly after quitting her job as a patent attorney with both an engineering and a law degree, my mother had undertaken homeschooling me. It was a failure, begun in September and abandoned before Christmas. I'd refused to learn. When she tried to force me, I'd put down my pencils and cried until I threw up. I'd stopped playing the piano. Eventually, my father and our housekeeper, Marta, in a rare show of resistance, approached my mother to point out the futility of her quest and the folly of paying Marta to mop up vomit an hour a day.

My mother hated failure, and while her failures were few and far between, she despised being reminded of them. I heard the screen door open and bang shut. My mother stood on our preternaturally green lawn and, straining to see in the dusk, called my name. I stepped farther under the tree. She gave up and stomped back into the house. The screen door banged shut again.

Like all excellent sons, I'd kept my nose to the grindstone—what an awful phrase that is—and as I should have expected, I'd found myself ground down to dust, a pale, lifeless powder. Then Max came along and like a warm spring rain reconstituted me, and now I knew joy and color. My grades hadn't dropped; the Earth hadn't stopped in its rotation.

Remember, my mother had routinely threatened me: *I am the mother. Together, you and I are a knife, but I have the handle and you have the blade. If I draw, you're bound to get cut.* Standing under the weeping willow in our backyard, I discovered I was no longer afraid to get cut, no longer afraid to bleed, and I had Max to thank for that.

Sliding down the trunk, I pulled out my phone and texted Max: *I think I love you.*

He texted back almost immediately: *Good, because I KNOW I love you.*

And there it was: I was in love with a boy who loved me. As the thought sank in, I began to cry again.

MAX

TRISTAN JUST TEXTED me: *I think I love you.*

Good, I texted back, *because I KNOW I love you.* And just like that, I told Tristan I loved him. Although it wasn't in the way I'd imagined I would. But he needed to hear it and I needed to say it.

That I'd found Tristan was a miracle. That he loved me, as special and handsome as he was, was astonishing. He was my Hail Mary; my last and only chance.

Keep your nose in your books and your head out of the clouds, my father used to tell me. *Dreams are for other people.* Now, most unexpectedly, I found myself walking among the clouds, my dream a living, breathing person who said he loved me.

TRISTAN

"THIS IS SO new. I hate to see you and your mother fighting," my father said.

"It's not my fault."

"You provoke her—"

"How? By being myself? By standing up for myself and the boy I love?"

My father winced as if I'd slapped him. "You're too young to know you're in love—or that you're...*that way*."

"You were sixty when you met Omma and then had me. How many people told you that you were too old for love, too old to father a child?"

My father stared at me in silence for a long time. He sighed and said, "Discounting your feelings—your understanding of yourself because of your age—is wrong. I apologize for that. But you have to understand, all of this is so new. It's kind of a shock—"

I cocked my head and looked at him without saying anything.

"OK," he laughed, "maybe not so much a shock. But it does disrupt the vision your mother had of you—of what your life would be like."

"But her vision can't supersede my own."

"Look, I get that. But you know your mother."

Now it was my turn to sigh.

"When we brought you home from the hospital, the first thing your mother did was create a spreadsheet. She logged your every behavior and the solution that resolved each of your complaints—and you being an infant, your complaints were many and ceaseless. If you woke up crying at three a.m. and she gave you a bottle and walked you around for twenty minutes and you fell asleep, she logged that, and the next time you got up at three a.m., she would repeat her previous. The problem was you weren't a machine with built-in logic. The same action didn't always deliver the same result. This terrified and frustrated your mother—while she is a lawyer, she is also an engineer. And engineers know every problem has a solution, and any action when applied uniformly under the same circumstances should deliver the same result.

LARRY BENJAMIN

"Your whole life, your mother has operated in consultation with this 'boy' spreadsheet so that she could anticipate and predict your behavior and take proactive steps to course-correct any aberrations or undesirable outcomes. Your falling in love with another boy wasn't an expected outcome, and none of her efforts to course-correct you based on her previous successes are working. You have, in short, thrown a monkey wrench into the works. As an engineer and a lawyer, she *hates* unexpected outcomes."

"So, I'm an unexpected outcome? Gee, thanks."

"Well, in a way you are."

"Seriously?"

"OK, I admit that your being gay isn't quite the shock she is making it out to be, but that's not the point."

"So, what *is* the point?"

"Look, what matters is that your mother loves you very much. She loves us both, but her heart has teeth."

Chapter 28

TRISTAN

MRS. C WAS away visiting relatives, and I was tasked with walking and feeding her many dogs and the immortal Pablo, as I'd been doing since I was ten. This time, Max was helping me. Actually, at the moment, he was more of a hindrance, kissing my neck, tickling me, while I tried to pour out kibble.

"Will you *stop*?" I asked, exasperated.

"Only if you kiss me. I feel neglected."

"If I kiss you, will you let me finish feeding the dogs?"

"Yes. Scout's honor."

I turned and kissed him, more passionately than I'd intended. I loved kissing him, touching him. The dogs, restless, waiting to be fed, threaded around our legs. Pablo sat in the kitchen sink watching us curiously. Max slipped his hands under my T-shirt and brushed my nipples. Just then, the screen door banged shut. We sprang apart guiltily and swung around to face the door. Mrs. C stood there. She watched us for a second before setting down a heavy-looking black nylon suitcase. She laid her handbag on it.

"Oh! Hello, Mrs. C," I stammered brightly.

"Tristan." She nodded at Max. "Who's this?"

"Um…this is Max. He's my friend. We were just—"

She looked at us. "It's OK," she said after a moment. "I know. I've heard the gossip. You're safe here."

"I— We—"

"I admire your courage," Mrs. C interrupted. "I wish I'd been as courageous when I had the chance. I would have made different choices. I wish I had. I could have been happy."

Max and I looked at each other.

"Evelyn," she continued, talking to herself. "Evelyn, forgive my cowardice."

"Who's Evelyn?" Max asked.

She held up her hand. "Ask me no questions, I'll tell you no lies. In exchange for your discretion, I promise you my home will always be a safe place for you both."

"Mrs. C, thank you."

"It's hot," she said. "Would you boys like to join me for a Coca-Cola?"

She indicated we should sit at the cheerful enameled table which took up a good bit of the kitchen.

"The guest room is always made up. If you make a mess, all I ask is that you throw the sheets in the washer. I'll take care of the rest."

Mrs. C set down her Coke and said, "I'm sorry."

"Sorry for what? We were in your house—"

"No, not for interrupting you. For outing you to your mother when you were still a little kid. I'm sorry if that caused you pain or somehow made your young life harder. I think in my own ill-advised way, I was trying to smooth the path for you."

"It's OK," I said. "At the time, I didn't understand what you were saying, or why. But, once I did, it was helpful to know that there was a name for it, that there was a path to get me where I needed to go."

Pablo, exhausted, climbed into my lap and lay still. I knew how he felt; I was so tired.

She leaned over and stroked Pablo's head. "Poor, tired kitty. Listen, boys, I'm going away for the weekend week after next. Tristan, will you take care of the animals?"

"Of course."

"I've dug a grave for Pablo. It's in the backyard by the rear gate. You can't miss it. If he dies while I'm gone, can you bury him?"

Max and I looked at each other.

"Absolutely," Max said.

"Thank you. Now drink up. I'm sure you boys have better things to do than spend the afternoon with an old lady." Her eyes twinkled.

MAX

"WELL, THAT WAS...UNEXPECTED."

"What was?"

"Mrs. C's reaction."

"Yes. The world, it's changing."

Tristan sounded pensive. I stopped walking and, catching his hand, asked, "What's wrong?"

"Nothing." He looked at the ground and kicked at some loose gravel. With my finger, I lifted his chin until our eyes were level. "Tell me what's wrong. I can tell something is bothering you."

"Mrs. C..." he said then stopped.

"What about her?"

"What she just said, made me think. Maybe things really are changing. It got me thinking that maybe—that is, I was thinking. I—Max, I want to go to prom—"

"Prom?"

"Yeah. I really, really want to go. With you."

"You want to go to prom together?"

"Yeah."

"I'm being stupid, aren't I?"

"No, no, you're not. Prom. Wow! Are two guys even allowed to go together?"

"Yep. I already checked. We can. So, what do you say?"

"I say we're going to prom." I kissed him. "Hey, we'll need tuxes."

"We can get them at Albrecht's. Want to go Saturday?"

"It's a date."

Chapter 29

MAX

ALBRECHT'S WAS WORLDS away from any store I'd ever been in. It was different from the Sears and Walmart my father favored and even more different from the Chinatown shops where I bought most of my clothes. It was less crowded; the lighting was softer; instead of blue-light special announcements, there was a mix of contemporary jazz and moody blues coming out of hidden speakers. It even smelled different. Sandalwood, Tristan said when I commented. Here too, was a different Tristan. He was more at ease and self-assured than I'd ever seen him. He ran the gauntlet of overeager salesmen easily, turning down their offers of assistance with charm and disarming firmness. He was definitely his mother's child.

"Formal wear is over here," Tristan said.

Predictably, I moved towards the wall with black tuxedos while Tristan wandered away to look at the lighter colored and pastel offerings. A suit caught my eye. I looked for my size and pulled it from the rack.

It was black velvet; the jacket was embroidered with dragonflies in black slubbed silk; the pants had a slubbed silk stripe down each leg. "I'm going to go try this on," I said.

"OK," Tristan said, barely looking at me.

TRISTAN

WHILE MAX WAS trying on his suit, I found a white silk tuxedo embroidered with silvery sequined dragonflies. Instead of a silk stripe up each pant leg, there was a line of sequined dragonflies. I stepped into a dressing room and quickly tried it on.

"Hey, Tristan where did you go?" Max called.

"I'm trying something on. Be out in a second."

I stepped out of the dressing room to find Max standing on a tailor's pedestal and scrutinizing himself in the triple mirror. When he saw me in the mirror, he turned around. He took my breath away. While I'd only ever seen him dressed in black, this black looked different somehow; elegant, sophisticated, as if he'd grown up in five minutes. "You look amazing," I said, meaning it.

"You look stunning," he responded. "That tux is perfect for you. Come stand next to me."

I did, and we stood admiring ourselves in the mirror, grinning with helpless delight.

"Tristan? Tristan, is that you?" Judy appeared in the archway between the men's and women's showrooms. "I thought that was your voice." When she saw Max next to me, she stopped talking.

"Hey, Judy."

"What—what are you doing?"

"Trying on suits for prom."

"You're going to prom?"

"Yup."

"Oh. Do you want to go together?"

Max and I glanced at each other. He stepped off the pedestal. Now I did, too. "I'm going with Max," I said, taking his hand in mine.

"You're going with Max? Like together? Like a *couple*?"

"We *are* a couple," I said.

"You can't do that!"

"Yes, we can," Max said. "Tristan checked the rules, and they don't say we can't. And I got our tickets yesterday."

"Tristan, you can't be serious."

"I can be. I am."

"You!" she yelled at Max. "You've ruined everything!" She burst into tears and ran back into the women's showroom.

MAX

TRISTAN LOOKED AFTER Judy then turned to look at himself in the mirror. "Do you really like this? Or should I try something else on?"

Tristan looked beyond perfect. He was gorgeous. I liked that we had both chosen dragonflies. "No, you look perfect," I said because I didn't have the words to tell him how fantastic and magical he looked, how much I loved him.

"So do you," he said. "Let's go find the tailor, then we can look for shirts and ties."

TRISTAN

MISS DOROTHY STUCK her head in the archway between the two showrooms. "Tristan, you decent?"

"Miss Dorothy, yes, come on in."

She stepped through the doorway. She looked me up and down then Max. "You two look very smart. So, Tristan, you going to introduce me to your young man?"

"Um, sure. Miss Dorothy, this is Max. Max meet Miss Dorothy—saleswoman to the stars! I've known her since I was, what…three?"

She laughed. "At least."

"Nice to meet you," Max said. "I've never been here before."

"Well, you must come back." Turning to me, she asked, "You boys find everything you need?"

"Yes. We just need shirts and ties now."

She cocked her head and thought for a minute. "Those suits have so much detail, I'd keep accessories simple. Plain white, classic pleated formal shirts and simple bow ties. Max, I'd say white for you, and Tristan, you wear black. Those will contrast nicely but also make it clear that you coordinated outfits."

"I like that—a lot," Max said.

"Good. Have Victor help you with that. When you're finished, come up front to me and I'll ring you up. Tristan, your father called. He said to put both your outfits on his account."

When I looked at her in surprise, she added, "I think he was afraid you were going to pay in nickels and dimes."

I giggled. Sobering, I asked, "My father called? How'd he—"

"Your little friend out there called your house. Your mother wasn't home, so she told your father that you and Max were here buying tuxes because you were going to prom together."

I stared at her, dumbfounded. She touched my arm. "Tristan, I wouldn't trust that friend of yours." She looked at Max for a moment. "Max, nice to meet you."

When she continued looking at him, I asked her, "What do you see?"

She smiled and said, "Black velvet and a little boy's smile. What do you see?"

I cocked my head. "I see my yesterday, my today, and my tomorrow."

She touched my arm again. "Don't forget to come see me when you're done." She disappeared back through the arch into the heated pastels, pop music, and whispers of the women's showroom.

Chapter 30

TRISTAN

WHAT DO YOU want?" I asked Judy when the convex mirror above my head showed her easing into the unused music room I'd come to think of as my place. I instantly regretted having once told her that this was my hideout when things got to be too much. I thought of it as my *hatbox* where, like a seldom worn hat, I could rest until I was needed as a talisman against the March winds or the preacher's words during a particularly aggressive sermon.

"I just want to talk," she answered, moving a music stand and sliding into a chair next to me.

"About what?"

"About yesterday—what—what happened at Albrecht's."

"I don't know what there is to talk about. I don't even understand why you were so upset."

"Please don't be dense. I had plans for us—for you!"

"How could *you* have plans for *me*?"

"Because I thought I knew you. Now I find out you're not the person I thought you were."

"Oh, my God—"

"Don't take the Lord's name in vain," she chided reflexively.

"To be clear, you *never* knew me. You only knew who you wanted me to be."

"I knew you in the context of our church, of the world we were raised in."

99

I got up and wrote on the chalkboard: *There was a farmer who had a dog, and Bingo was his name.*

"What—what are you doing?" she was practically yelling through her tears.

"Read that."

She frowned, sniffled, and wiped her eyes. She turned from the board and crossing her arms demanded, "What's a stupid nursery rhyme got to do with anything?"

"Who was named Bingo?" I asked. "The farmer or the dog?"

"What? The dog, of course."

"Are you sure? Read it again. It's ambiguous—"

"Don't be ridiculous. The *dog* is named Bingo. Everyone knows that. But tell me how you think it's ambiguous." She uncrossed, then recrossed her arms and jutted her chin out a little.

"He could have written 'There was a farmer who had a dog named Bingo,' or 'There was a farmer who had a dog whose name was Bingo.' Do you see? But he didn't. Do you see my point?"

"I don't see anything except, my whole life I believed one thing, and now you want me to suddenly believe something else. What's your point, Tristan? I'm not seeing it."

"That is precisely my point. The point is you thought you knew something about me—thought you knew *me*—because you ignored the most obvious thing about me. That at best, *I* am *ambiguous*. And your reaction is to get mad and cry and blame me for *your* self-centered, myopic version of me—"

"I don't know you anymore—"

"You never knew me, and now that you have the chance to, you don't want to. You can't accept who I am—you can't accept that Max is who I want—any more than you can accept the idea that the farmer may actually have been the one named Bingo!"

I had nothing left to say to her, so I picked up my backpack and walked out of the room, leaving her with her tears and her sense that the universe had dealt her a terrible injustice.

. . . .

"Judy is heartbroken," my mother said. "She thought you'd ask her to prom."

"Why would she think that?" I asked.

"Because I told her you would."

"You told her I would?"

"Yes, and now I find out that instead of taking her, you're going *stag* in the company of that boy—"

"I'm not going stag. Max is my—"

My mother held up her hand warningly. As a lawyer, she knew not to ask questions to which she did not already know the answers.

"I've agreed to be a prom chaperone," she said.

"You've *what*?"

She turned to the sink and turning on the faucet full force proceeded to attack, with a soapy sponge, a stack of dishes that were already surgically clean.

"It's already been decided," she said, her back to me. "I'll need you to go with me to Albrecht's to pick out a suitable dress to wear."

"Fine," I shot at her back. "But Max and I are still going to prom together. And, by the way, Max and I already got our tuxes at Albrecht's."

In response, she slammed the stack of dishes into the sink with such force, I *felt*, before I heard, them break in two.

Chapter 31

TRISTAN

YOU THINK I'M stupid," my mother accused, raging. "You think I don't see what's going on with you and that...*boy*. Well, I'm not stupid. I see it. If I can see it, everyone can see it. It's disgusting."

"What's so disgusting about it?"

"It's not normal—"

"When you say normal, you mean common—you confuse the two. When you define normal as common, then I am normal in more ways than I can count. The color of my skin, the shape of my eyes—they're not common, yet everyone has skin and eyes—"

"Don't you get smart with me. That's your problem— you think you know more, are smarter than everyone else. Maybe that's my fault. I raised you to be better, smarter than everyone else."

"Yes, you did," I said quietly. "You also raised me to think for myself, to not follow the crowd."

"People are talking."

"So? Let them. I don't care."

My mother moved to slap me for the second time in my life. This time, I caught her hand in midair. I think we both realized with the same degree of surprise that I was stronger than she was.

"I'm not an animal or an imbecile. There is no need to hit me to make your point."

She sat heavily on the sofa, with an air almost of defeat. "What happened to you?"

"I grew up. Oh, my God—"

"Don't take the Lord's name in vain. The Tristan I knew didn't swear. I feel like I don't know you anymore—"

"I am so tired of everyone saying they thought they knew me."

"Well, I did—"

"You never knew me. You only knew your idea of me—that's all you ever wanted to know. Do you know how lonely I was before Max? Do you know how alone and strange I've felt my whole life? Do you know every day I struggled with feeling I wasn't smart enough or good enough? That I wasn't an excellent son?"

"I know you *were* an excellent son. And then that boy came along and turned your head."

"You know what? I don't care about being an excellent son anymore."

My mother rose suddenly to her feet and leaned in towards me until our noses were practically touching. "I will not let that boy ruin you."

"I have to go upstairs and change," I said. "I'm meeting Max."

"Well, I hope you don't expect me to drive you to him."

"I don't. He's picking me up."

MAX

I was sitting on my bike at the end of their driveway waiting for Tristan. We were going for the final fitting of our tuxes. I saw his mother come around the side of their house carrying a basket of cut roses. She glanced at the house and quickly made her way towards me. I braced myself and removed my helmet. "Hello, Mrs. James."

"I want you to stay away from my son," she said.

"You can't make me stay away from Tristan any more than you can make him stay away from me," I said, trying to keep my voice steady.

"Of course I can. I am the mother!"

"If you could, you wouldn't be here talking to me."

"I'm warning you. I won't have you ruining Tristan's life with your dirt and Americanized ideas and your perversions."

"Perversions? Who even uses that word anymore?"

"I won't have it, I tell you." She leaned in so close to me, I could smell ginseng on her breath. "I'll not see all my hard work thrown away. I will lay down in my grave before I allow that."

"My father once told me being a man means doing hard, uncomfortable things. It means doing things you want more than anything not to have to do." My father's words—built on a pile of ashes, transformed into ridges and steps and finally a mountain on which I could stand—showed me a mark at which to aim my arrow.

"Standing up for my right to love Tristan means I have to do the thing I want more than anything not to have to do. This world—people like *you*—have forced me to grow up sooner than I may have otherwise. I had to become a man at seventeen to find and hold on to the love of my life, simply because he is a *he*, because we are *both* hes.

"Having people question our relationship, whisper about, and yes, laugh at us means I have to do hard, uncomfortable things, but I will do these hard, uncomfortable things every day until I don't have to, to make sure I remain worthy of Tristan's love."

I did not draw this battle line, but I saw it, and I stepped up to it.

Tristan's mother reached in the basket, grabbed her roses and flung them in my face, then turned on her heels and stalked off, disappearing so quickly I wondered if she had been there at all. And then I felt the blood on my face. The roses' thorns had pricked my skin and tore at it as they fell to the ground. My eyes stung. Tristan walked up to me carrying his helmet. "Hey," he said.

"Hey." I blinked away tears.

"You're bleeding. Max, what happened?"

"I collided with your rosebush," I said.

"Do you want to go up to the house and wash your face?"

"No. I'll be fine."

He pulled out his handkerchief and dabbed at my wounds. After he dried the blood from each spot, he kissed it.

My face covered with the memory of his tiny fluttering kisses, he asked, "Better?"

"Better," I said, putting on my helmet.

Chapter 32

TRISTAN

I WAS LATE GETTING to the track. In the distance, I could see Max, in his purple crew-neck singlet and aqua track shorts, rounding the curve, head held high, chest thrust out, shoulders thrown back. I dropped my backpack on the ground and ran to the low chain-link fence surrounding the track so he'd see me when he ran by. A woman on my right caught my eye. "Omma?"

She turned towards me, her coal-black eyes blazing with love and hatred, as if I was both beloved and enemy.

"Omma? Omma, what are you doing here?"

"Tristan, what are you doing here? You're not supposed to be here." She sounded desperate and distracted.

"What are you doing here?" I asked again.

"I will save you from that...*devil*!"

Out of the corner of my eye, I saw Max moving down the track towards us; he was so fast, and his uniform so bright, it hurt my eyes. My mother, following my gaze, spun around. Her arm shot out, something silver and cylindrical clasped in her slender fingers. I noticed that her nails were once again lacquered a dreadful reddish brown. I tried to make sense of what she held in her hand, of the crisp, determined movement of her thumb and forefinger.

There was a sound like a whistle on the wind.

"She's got a gun."

"Drop your weapon!"

In my peripheral vision, rapid movement, an advancing dark blue like nightfall.

I reached for my mother. "Omma!" The word seeped from my constricted throat, an exhortation and a last breath.

I fell with all the chaos and confusion of a passenger train crossing a bridge, jumping its track and tumbling slowly, agonizingly to the crowded roadway below; the still air became heavy with the scream of metal ripping from metal. The staticky voice screeched, "*We are on lockdown. Attention, we are on lockdown,*" as the shrill cry of the sirens rose, announcing yet another school in crisis, another act of violence. The ground rose to meet me; the cool fescue grass swallowing my panic. Green shadows replaced bright sunlight. Then that, too, faded away.

MAX

I FELT A searing pain and then it faded, and my leg felt weak, and then I was spinning, falling. I heard screams and sirens. Pain and color erupted, a kaleidoscope of purple and aqua and red as I spun violently. Everything went black, like the sun falling from the sky, or the lid of a coffin slamming shut.

I awoke abruptly. The room I found myself in was strange: fawn-colored fluorescent lighting buzzed so loudly, I feared I'd stumbled into a beehive. I sat up to swat at my noisy assailants. Pain engulfed me; an obliterating white heat shot up from my leg, and I fell backward with a bewildered cry. What had happened? What was happening?

A woman in white emerged into the fawn-colored light, admonished me loudly in some sort of medical gibberish, then stabbed me in my arm. Everything—my pain, the buzzing muddy light, the woman's chastising white presence—disappeared.

When I woke again—hours? days?—later, my father, surrounded by my aunts, was staring at me anxiously. I strained to see them in the weak light, understanding finally that the buzzing was caused by the fluorescent bulbs overhead, trying, and failing, to cast out the gloom that was unimpeachable, sovereign.

Chapter 33

JOHN

THE POLICE REPORTS, the credit card receipts I'd found for a gun and target practice at a shooting range two towns over—it was all too much. I had to talk to someone. I know this need to share the burden of my knowledge was weakness, but I am only a man. I called Salt.

"That's a lot," she said when I told her everything I knew.

I poured her a Scotch neat. She tossed it back.

"Thanks for listening."

"Any time."

"Would you like another drink—for the road?"

"Maybe…OK. Just two fingers. Though you know," she said putting down her glass, "I could stay…"

I swallowed my drink. "No," I said. "I'll call an Uber. That way, I'll know you got home safely."

TRISTAN

I HAVE NO recollection of what happened, no memory of anybody—most likely my father—sitting me down and telling me tragedy had struck. My mother had lost her mind and tried to kill my boyfriend, then had been killed herself and my boyfriend wounded in some way that would change both of us forever.

Even years later, I am unable to remember the exact moment I found out what had happened or who told me. All I remember is that one minute I didn't know, and the next I knew, and the minute after that I wished I didn't know; I wish I still didn't know.

I still awake frantically from dreams, which I am unable to recall on waking. I can remember only my mother's voice, a flash of light, and a feeling of devastation. I lie in bed shaking and disoriented for some time after waking. Day after day.

MAX

I TRIED TO make sense of the doctor's words: "You were shot in the leg. The bullet severed the femoral artery in your left leg and fractured your femur." He went on to explain I'd had one six-hour surgery and would likely require two more before I went home. Also, I'd never run again. "You were lucky," he said.

"Lucky? How is this—any of this—emblematic of luck?"

The doctor took off his glasses and pulled a chair closer to the bed. He sat. "Look, you may not feel lucky, but trust me, you were. I've treated a lot of gunshot wounds. The person who shot you used full-metal-jacket bullets rather than hollow points, which explode into flesh-tearing shrapnel and do unbelievable damage. The second point in your favor was she wasn't an experienced shooter. From my understanding, she had a clear shot at you as you rounded a curve in the track—head, chest—but because she was inexperienced with guns, she tried to compensate for the expected kickback of the gun by lowering her aim. It will likely be three to six months before you can walk normally again. You'll never run competitively, but you will walk, and you'll live. I call that lucky. Now, before I leave, do you have any questions?"

"Yes. You said she was an inexperienced shooter. Who is *she*? Who shot me?"

The doctor looked from me to my father. "If you don't have any medical questions, I'll leave you with your family now. I'll be back later."

"Dad?"

"Tristan's mother shot you."

I closed my eyes.

"I'm so sorry," my father said.

"For what?"

"For failing you."

"Dad, you didn't fail me. This isn't your fault—"

He continued talking as if he hadn't heard me. "Tristan's mother came to me and asked me if I knew what was going on with you and Tristan. I said I did. She said we had to stop it. I told her to leave you boys alone, that that train was on its track, and she owned neither train nor track. She left saying she would stop you without my help. Max, I had no idea—no idea—she meant to harm you, that she meant to—" He covered his face with his hands and wept. I'd never seen my father cry before.

"Where is she? Is she in jail?"

"No, son. She's dead. A school security guard shot and killed her."

I tried to sit up. "Where's Tristan? Is he OK? I need to see him."

Aunt Kaleisha stretched over me and pressed the buzzer at my side. A nurse appeared. After a brief exchange, the nurse left only to return and jab me in the arm with a needle.

. . . .

I woke up to hear Aunt Kaleisha say, "It's God's will." She laid her hand on my father's shoulder.

"God's will? For some crazy woman to shoot me and shatter my leg and ruin my chances for a track scholarship. My boyfriend's mother tried to kill me and instead was killed. Now he's an orphan and I'm crippled. You call *that* God's will?" I shouted.

"God moves in mysterious ways, His wonders to perform," Aunt Tianara said.

"It was a wake-up call—"

"A wake-up call? For what?"

"To get your life back on track. I'm sure that boy will leave town and then you can start your life over—"

"What life? Tristan *is* my life!"

"No, he isn't. You can't see that now because you're young and upset, but that boy—well, I don't like to speak ill of anyone, but—"

"That boy led you astray," Aunt Kaleisha interrupted. "I understand he was probably very sweet, and he was good-looking, but he was the devil—"

"Get out!" I rang the buzzer for the nurse.

The nurse arrived. "Do you need something?"

"Yes. I need you to make them leave. My father can stay, but I want those two gone."

The nurse looked at my father.

"Pay him no mind," Aunt Kaleisha said in her imperious tones. "He's just upset."

"Yes, he's upset," Aunt Tianara added. "This has been hard on him. On all of us really, as you can imagine—"

"Stop talking about me as if I'm not lying right here!"

"I'm afraid I'm going to have to ask you all to leave. It's important Max get his rest and avoid becoming upset."

"But—"

My father said something in a tense whisper to The Aunts, and they filed out after tossing me pitying glances.

"I'll be back later, Max," my father said, touching my arm.

"Fine. Just don't bring them with you."

The nurse followed them out, then returned and offered me a paper cup of water and a white pill. I swallowed the pill with a gulp of water. Handing the cup back, I lay down with my back to her and pulled the covers over my head.

Chapter 34

TRISTAN

JUDY LEANED IN to kiss me. The Klonopin the doctor had prescribed must have slowed my reflexes for I was too slow to avoid her kiss; her lips skated across my cheek.

"How are you?" she asked.

"They won't let me see Max," I said.

"That's probably just as well," she said with oddly dismissive brusqueness. "You've been through a lot—"

"*I've* been through a lot? My mother tried to kill my boyfriend."

Judy winced.

"She probably crippled him for life."

"You need to focus on you—"

"There is no me without him."

"Tristan!"

Her hands jangled. When I looked over, I saw a bracelet around her wrist: small rubies trapped in delicate cages of pink gold, each bound together by strands of yellow and white gold. I recognized it as my mother's. When she'd left Korea as a child, an old neighbor had secreted it on her in case the family, prosperous at home, fell on hard times in America. "Sell it if and when you need to," the woman had told her.

"Where did you get that?" I asked, pointing to the bracelet.

"This?" She spun it around her wrist. "Your mother gave it to me."

"What else did she give you?"

"Oh, just a few other pieces," she answered vaguely.

"A few other pieces? How many exactly is a few?"

"Oh, thirty."

"My mother gave you her jewelry? Why?"

"Well, she liked me, and she said she'd never have a daughter, and now she'd never have a daughter-in-law either, so she wanted me to have them. She *liked* me."

"Unlike me, you mean?"

"Tristan."

"When did she give it to you?"

Now, she squirmed. "Um…ummm…the day…it happened."

"You saw her that day?"

When Judy said nothing, I continued. "You know, I have always wondered how she knew where I was and how she came to be at the track that day. I keep going over it in my mind, and I just don't understand. How did she know where I was—that Max was at practice?"

"She didn't. You weren't supposed to be there. You were supposed to be rehearsing with the band for prom!"

"How did you know about that?"

"Volkman told me. He thought we were friends. He swore me to secrecy, of course, but he told me. He was so proud, thought what you were planning—to surprise Max with a serenade—was so cute and romantic—"

"And you told my mother."

Judy looked down. In her lap, her hands leapt and danced restlessly. She jiggled her foot. "I—I may have told her."

"You *may* have told her?" I repeated. I wondered if I sounded as dull, as dead, as I felt.

"She called my house looking for you. You were supposed to go with her to Albrecht's to pick out the dress she was going to wear to chaperone prom. She was upset, so I went over."

I looked at her unable to speak; I had no words.

"She thought you were with Max. I told her you were rehearsing and that not only were you going to prom with Max as your date, but you planned to surprise him with a love song." She practically spat the last words.

"You *told* her that?"

"I did! I had to. You weren't being fair. She was going to be there, and she was sure to be surprised and embarrassed. I wanted to warn her! Besides, I was so mad." Her anger gathered speed. "I felt like I was losing you."

"Losing me? You never had me. There was no future for you and me—not like that."

"I just wanted you to take me to prom. I just wanted her to break you two up. I didn't know she was going to…was going to…" She put her face in her hands and wept. "I didn't know."

"You didn't know."

"Tristan, I didn't. I swear I didn't. You have to believe me. Please."

I stood and walked to the window overlooking the creek. I suddenly remembered that Sunday after church when she had inexplicably, in front of my mother, kissed me then Max and called us Thunder and Lightning.

"Tristan?"

"Get out," I said without turning around. "Get out."

"Tristan, you can't mean—"

"Go."

I could hear her start to shuffle out of the room. I turned from the window. "Judy?"

She stopped and turned around looking hopeful.

"My mother's jewelry is quite valuable. When did she give it to you? Before or after you told her about me and Max?"

She hesitated, took a step towards me.

"Get out, Judy," I said, turning back to the window. "I never want to see or hear from you again."

Chapter 35

TRISTAN

M Y FATHER, HELPLESS, clueless, devastated, asked me to help him pick out a dress to bury my mother in.

Once when I was seven, over my objections, my mother had bought two sun dresses: a bright-yellow one with white polka dots and a green lace collar, and an apple-green one with white polka dots and a white lace collar. I'd retaliated by refusing to leave the house with her if she was wearing either dress. Weeks later, I was gratified to see the hated yellow dress stuffed in a basket of items my family no longer wanted and which my mother was collecting for the church rummage sale.

At the back of the closet, I found the apple-green dress with the polka dots and white lace collar. I pulled it from the closet. If my father was surprised at my choice, he didn't show it.

Just before Mother's Day one year when I was seven or eight, I asked my father to take me to Albrecht's to buy a present for my mother. As we drove in Dad's dark-blue 1961 Lincoln Continental with the top down, I informed him proudly that I merely needed a ride; I'd be paying for my mother's present myself. I'd been saving feverishly since the previous fall when I'd beheld the magnificent brooch in the glass case for the first time.

At the store, I held the beloved brooch in my hand while my father and Miss Dorothy tried to interest me in other things. But I, enchanted by the brooch's bulbous petals—enameled sky blue and grass green, and anchored to a gold-plated stem and leaves—unable to imagine anything more beautiful, more perfect, wouldn't be swayed.

"Well, Salt," my father said with dismay, "it looks like his mind is made up."

Miss Dorothy wrapped the brooch and laid it in a bed of corrugated cotton, then covered it with a lid that had "Albrecht's" spelled out in fanciful script on its glossy lime-green surface. When she rang up the sale, I proudly emptied both my pockets of their burden of savings; the glass counter screamed under the assault of quarters and dimes and nickels and pennies. My father shuffled his feet and swore under his breath. Miss Dorothy smiled at him disarmingly over the half-moon glasses she had donned to count my bounty and murmured, "It's all right."

My mother had accepted the brooch with a kind of doting indulgence, even as she gazed at the thing in horror.

Now, as I examined my mother in her casket, I pulled the brooch, the only remaining piece of her jewelry, out of my pocket and pinned it to her apple-green dress, just over her heart.

. . . .

I could hear my father arguing in a low whisper with The Church Saints.

"Please understand we simply think it would be best if he remained down here in the pew with you—"

"It is his *mother's* funeral. He wants to play. You will not stop him."

. . . .

I played like a boy demented. My grief ran from me and galloped around the nave below as I beat the keys like they were a flesh-and-blood sinner to be flogged. The pastor had to shout his eulogy—that epistle of deceits and equivocation—to be heard above the cacophony of my mourning. I sent the last chords of the hymn crashing down, and let the organ fall silent.

As the echoes faded, I charged into the next hymn, allowing little time for Mrs. C to squeeze in the final words from her reading. When I paused to catch my breath and rest my hands, she looked up to me and recited Psalm 34:18 into the silence: "The Lord is close to the brokenhearted and saves those who are crushed in spirit."

I brought the organ screaming to life.

"Yea, though I walk through the valley of the shadow of death, I will fear no evil, for thou art with me…"

As the echoes of their empty prayers hung in the air above our heads, I leapt into another hymn. The choir glanced at each other then up at me in increasing alarm as their voices strained to keep up with the impossible frenetic music; their nerves, frayed as their patience with my antics, ran out.

Attendants from the funeral home moved to the transept where my mother lay. I leaned over the balcony and stared at my mother in her satin-lined casket. She had never looked more beautiful or malignant. My father sat alone, squeezed into a corner of the first pew, his face and hands as ashen as his suit, his shoulders shaking.

When the attendants lowered the lid of my mother's casket and she disappeared forever, her image was replaced by the sight of Max, stumbling, falling in an explosion of blood. For years, whenever I thought of her, I'd see Max, stumbling, falling, bleeding.

As they turned my mother's casket, I returned to the organ and began to play the recessional hymn, the ordered, stately

"Morning Has Broken." The choir relieved, on familiar ground, began to sing. Quickly, unexpectedly, I segued into the theme song from *Mission Impossible*, then back to "Morning Has Broken." And back again. Eventually, the theme song from *Mission Impossible* won out. The unmistakable, cataclysmic energy of its 5/4 rhythm filled the church, making everyone frantic. *Max's left hand played the opening, his right arm tight around me while with my right I played the second part.*

The choir, defeated, stopped singing. People turned their heads to glare up at me. I wondered what they'd wanted from me. Had they expected me to play hymns full of joy and freedom and celebration, of angels dancing miraculously on the heads of pins?

I'd clearly lost my mind or finally gone too far. My hands fell from the keys; Max's arm dropped from my shoulder, and he faded away. Tears poured down my face. My father stood and looked up at me. He looked both defeated and resigned to his defeat.

As my mother's casket passed out the church doors, the congregation sank, exhausted and broken, against the pews like the storm-tossed survivors of some great disaster.

I stood next to my father as the congregants filed out of the church and stopped to offer their condolences. They took our hands and belched rancid platitudes into our grief-etched faces, their hollow words meant to console the inconsolable. Failing to comfort, they moved on and away.

Miss Dorothy, followed by Miss Minnie, came up to us. Their eyes were swollen and red from crying. Miss Dorothy embraced my father and held him too long, breathing deeply. My father, nearing eighty, was still extremely handsome. Women seemed to melt in his presence, yet he appeared oblivious to the power of his good looks. I'd always known Miss Dorothy had a crush on him; her faint flirtations over the years were easy enough to ignore but almost impossible not to see. I wondered what my life would have been like if she'd been my mother. I sniffled loudly. Miss Dorothy released my father and rushed over to me. "Oh, you poor, poor child…"

My father and I waited outside the church while they loaded my mother's casket into the hearse which would take her back to the funeral home and in the morning deliver her to the airport where the three of us would board a flight for Korea.

The priest came up to my father and murmured, "Again, Mr. James, my deepest sympathies for your loss. Your wife was a good woman and a pillar of this church." Glancing at me and perhaps remembering the more lurid of the headlines, he paused. "I hate to trouble you at this time, but seeing as you're leaving the country in the morning…"

"Yes. Yes?" My father prodded with uncharacteristic impatience.

"A young lady of the congregation—Judith Iscariot…"

"Yes. Yes?"

"She brought me this jewelry the other day," The priest took the lid off a jewelry box I had given to my mother when I was twelve. Inside was my mother's jewelry, including the ruby bracelet. "She asked me to take it and sell it and use the money for the church."

"Yes. Yes?"

"You see, it was your wife's jewelry."

"My wife's—"

"Omma gave it to Judy," I said, looking away.

My father looked at me, then back at the priest. "Well, then I suppose it is the young lady's to dispose of as she wishes."

"Then you don't…object?"

"No. Sell it to fund your good works. Come, Tristan, we must go." My father took me by the crook of my arm and guided me away. As I ducked to get in the car, I realized it was prom day. I should have been getting into a different limo, dressed in a white tuxedo embroidered with dragonflies instead of a plain black suit, Max beside me instead of my father.

JOHN

IF TRISTAN WONDERED at my abrupt plans for us, he at least didn't question them. He tumbled blindly in my wake. Now he handed his passport and boarding pass to the TSA agent.

TRISTAN

THE TSA AGENT handed me back my boarding pass and my passport. When I simply stood there, Dad took my hand and pulled me along. I stumbled after him like a blind child; I had no idea where I was or where I was going. Without Max at my side, I was lost. He was my North Star as I was his.

I found myself standing on a precipice, a step in any direction as likely as not to lead to a fatal tumble into the abyss. Thus, I was unable to step forward or backward; I was doomed to remain standing tensely in place retracing, in my mind, the steps I had taken that had led me into this paralyzing darkness, this world without end. I'd been in a hopeless place before and found love; now I found myself again in a hopeless place. Only this time I couldn't see what could be, other than this enduring darkness, this cold, this...*hopelessness*. Sightless, aimless. Death would not have been a worse fate.

Chapter 36

TRISTAN

IT WAS AS if I'd been asleep for the last two weeks and was now suddenly wide awake. Too awake. And cranky. I squirmed in my seat. My father glanced at me over his reading glasses. "Aren't you hot?" he asked me, gesturing at Max's purple-and-aqua letterman's jacket.

I pulled the jacket more tightly around me. "No."

My father shrugged. "Want some peanuts?" He pushed an open bag of Planter's nuts towards me.

"No." Forgetting that excellent sons are always cheerful, I snapped, "How can you be so...perky...when we've been trapped in this tin box for hours?"

"Oh, this isn't so bad," Dad said. "There's movies and food, and these seats are pretty comfortable."

"They are not."

"Well, compared to the last trip I made to Korea, this is pretty nice."

"When were you last in Korea?"

"When they shipped us over for the war."

"How did you get there?"

"They flew us to Japan in a military transport jet. Then we took a ship to Korea. The thing was, the transport had no seats, so we were strapped to the plane's fuselage."

As he spoke, his voice grew hazy and crackled as if he was being broadcast over a ham radio from 1953 Korea. I missed some of his words, as if the winds had stolen his breath, or maybe some of his words weren't meant for my ears. He paused, looked out the plane's window, then began speaking again.

As I listened to my father's words, it struck me that this was the first time we'd ever really talked without my mother between us, either as physical presence or thought. My mother with her thirst for attention and her demands for my singular devotion had squeezed my father out, relegating him to the role of a prisoner of war, hostage to her proprietary feeling over me; I was hers and hers alone.

The day my mother shot Max, and had herself been killed, had been my personal D-Day, liberating me from my place under her thumb, a liberation that had started the day I met Max.

"What was Korea like?" I asked.

"Cold. It was so cold. And it stank. They have this native food—kimchi. They eat it at every meal every day from the cradle to the grave, boiled, fried, and stewed. It smells awful. The smell was everywhere. It really stank. It's an odor I will never forget. Once, when your mother was mad at me, she made kimchi." He chuckled.

I wasn't yet ready to talk about my mother, so I closed my eyes. When I opened them again, we had landed.

JOHN

As I watched Tristan turn his head and pretend to fall asleep in Max's letterman's jacket, I felt sad. But I was grateful for our conversation on this fool's errand to bury his mother. For this conversation, even more than his mother's final act of desperation, more than her death itself, served as my invasion of Normandy after which I intended to establish a beachhead on which our relationship as father and son would flourish.

Chapter 37

MAX

CRUTCHES PROPPED AWKWARDLY under my arms, I hobbled into the dining room. The Aunts and my father fell silent. "I want to see Tristan."

The Aunts started to speak at once, but my father held up his hand warningly. "Come and sit down. Do you want something to eat?"

I shook my head. "I want to see Tristan," I repeated stubbornly. "I don't understand why he hasn't come to see me."

"Max, try to understand how difficult this is. His mother tried to kill you. And now she's dead."

"He loves me."

"I'm sure he does, but put yourself in his shoes."

"I'm sure he wants to see me."

"I'm sure he doesn't," Aunt Tianara, the cruelest of The Aunts, said. "He doesn't want to see you. His family doesn't want him to see you. You tore his family apart, and now he's an orphan and his poor father is a widower. And his mother died a criminal. Surely even *you* can understand how he would, on some level, blame you for all that."

"That's enough, Tianara," my father said.

"You need to stop babying him, Neville," Kaleisha said. "He needs to learn from the mistakes of others. Look at Tashelle—God rest her soul—"

"What about Aunt Tashelle?" I asked.

125

"How you mean? She die, nuh?"

"I know that." Aunt Tashelle had been hit by a car and died during the twelve days I was in the hospital.

"She went chasing after some man. Then she fin' out he was married! She gave in to the devil heself and went drinking at the speakeasy. All sad and drunk up, she staggered out in the fore day morning into traffic. A tractor trailer lick she down."

"By the time they scraped her off the pavement," Aunt Tianara finished with glee, "there was barely enough left to fill a casket."

My legs buckled as if under the weight of her assault. My dad caught me.

"I want to go back to my room," I said.

"I'll help you, son."

Back in my room, I sat on my bed until it was dark and I'd heard The Aunts leave and my dad go to bed. He'd knocked on my door, but I hadn't answered.

I tried to sleep but couldn't. I kept hearing Aunt Tianara's words, tearing into me like a pack of rabid dogs. No matter how often they repeated themselves in my head, I refused to believe them, *couldn't* believe them. Tristan wouldn't hate me.

I got up and dressed and made my way through the dark house and outside. My motorcycle stood abandoned in the driveway. No way could I ride it with a cast on my leg. So, adjusting the crutches under my arms, I began to walk to Tristan's house.

I stopped in their driveway to catch my breath and give my aching arms a rest. Hobbling to the front door, I rang the bell incessantly. When I tired of its hollow sound, I beat on the door with my fists. It started to rain. I stepped off the porch, and looking up at Tristan's dark window, I yelled his name. He *had* to be there. He wouldn't just leave without saying anything to me. It started to rain harder. It was almost summer, yet it was a cold, driving rain. Then it began to hail.

The hail fell, twisting, spinning, somersaulting, dancing. The biting cold gnawed on my toes, the tips of my fingers, the tops of my ears, but still I stood there calling his name. I grew hoarse and the hail fell around me, catching like diamond chips clutching white light, and through its strange alchemy releasing rainbows of color. The hail assailed my flesh, glowing, and grew in clumps around my feet, iridescent, misshapen, unseemly as freshwater pearls. Each hailstone resembled its brothers, yet each was unique, alone, tumbling through the dark air, as cold and lost as I was.

My father opened the door. He didn't ask me where I'd been; perhaps he didn't need to. Saying nothing at all, he helped me strip off my wet clothing and led me, shivering and crying, to the bathroom where he filled the tub with warm water. He added bubble bath and helped me into the sudsy water, being careful to keep my leg in its cast out of the tub. He left briefly and returned with a tumbler of water and a white pill, which he offered me.

Dad lifted me out of the tub and briskly toweled me dry. I could barely stand, probably from a combination of exhaustion and the sedative effects of the Valium. He gathered me in his arms and carried me to my bedroom, where he gently laid me among the fresh sheets and blankets and a mountain of pillows. Fragile as I was, having lost my boyfriend and the future I'd dared imagine, his infinite tenderness threatened to break me.

TRISTAN

MY MOTHER'S KOREAN family received us with faultless hospitality, yet every courtesy, every meal, every murmured word of condolence was delivered reluctantly, as if to say: *We do this not for you but because it is our obligation, and you have a right to expect at least this.*

My mother's implacable granite tombstone, her name chiseled into it in delicate but emphatic Hangul script, stood cold and unyielding in the pockmarked earth beneath a flowering cherry blossom tree in a far corner of the family cemetery behind the house.

I had a roof over my head, but I was homeless. I was alive, but my reason for living was gone. To avoid their punishing politeness and inscrutable judgment, I spent a lot of time away from the house. I wandered aimlessly through sun-dappled fields, untouched by anything but the icy fingers of grief and loneliness.

One Sunday out of the blue, my dad packed our bags and called a taxi. We left the pink-and-green countryside behind.

MAX

I SWEAR IT rained every day that spring and summer. It was as if the earth and the heavens were conspiring to wash away my grief. But I wouldn't let it go. It was all I had left of Tristan. Losing that sadness meant losing him and what he meant to me. Losing that was equal to losing *myself.*

I began physical therapy. We would start with strengthening exercises and move on to resistance training using resistance bands, free weights, and weight machines. It wasn't easy, and there were times when I wanted to give up, but if I wanted to return to school in September, I had to do it.

Because Dad had to work, Kaleisha and Tianara drove me to my appointments. They would sit in the reception area in their black clothing, their dripping umbrellas at their sides, waiting for me like death. I was barely speaking to either of them. I hated them both and stopped just short of wishing violence upon them. I missed Tashelle. I missed Tristan.

Chapter 38

TRISTAN

W E MOVED TO Paris. Dad enrolled me in the American School of Paris. Learning French supplanted the study of music.

We rented a furnished fifth-floor flat in an apartment block on the Rue Raynouard, in the 16th arrondissement. The building's exterior was limestone with elaborately corniced windows and wrought iron balconies. Worn marble steps led into a grand lobby. An oval staircase, buttressed by an ornate brass balustrade and carpeted in a densely patterned red rug anchored by heavy brass rods, swept upwards and curved over itself for five stories. A humming art deco chandelier of etched glass and black enamel, like an inverted skyscraper, caused the pale-pink, felt-lined walls to shimmer faintly. All in all, it was like stepping into a snail's shell.

Inside, the apartment was the complete antithesis of our mid-century modern house back home. Everything there was worn and warm and comfortable. There was not a Saarinen table or a Noguchi lamp to be seen.

There were marble fireplaces in narrow, dark rooms, whose high ceilings were painted dark colors: blues and grays. There was a salon with purple velvet walls and a high banquet covered in the same purple velvet. Hanging on the walls were enormous, gilt-framed paintings of storm-lashed landscapes and scowling French men and women dressed in black. We would come to spend most of our time in the salon like the storm-lashed survivors of the room's paintings.

Bronze chandeliers, their bulbs shod in fragile, amber slippers, marshalling their faint light, did their best to defeat the darkness. Thick Persian carpets covered the parquet floors. You could see the Eiffel Tower across the river, from the kitchen window. I avoided looking at it. It was one of the places Max and I had dreamed we would one day see together. Seeing it now, alone, without him, was impossible.

At night, when I heard my father pacing through the quiet empty rooms of our Paris flat, I wondered if he, like me, was grieving for what we had lost. I didn't ask him, though, for to do so would have seemed like an invasion of privacy or an aggressive assertion that I had some inalienable right to examine his grief so I could pronounce judgment on its validity. Other times, I assumed he was merely reviewing past events, looking for ways the catastrophe might have been avoided.

．．．．．．．．．．．．．．．．．．．．．．．．．．．．

I was lying on the green of the quad, trying to read a French translation of *Pinocchio*, when, first his shadow, then the boy himself fell over me. Literally fell over me. Tripping on the uneven cobblestones in the quad, he fell face first, sprawling over me like a splash of sunlight falling through a break in the clouds, or perhaps, given the flamboyance of his manner and dress, his appearance was more like the arrival of a rainbow after a long spring rain. I scrambled to my feet, dragging him up with me. I glared up at him and spluttered, "What the hell?"

"Sorry! I'm Javier, and I'm clumsy," he said.

There didn't seem to be anything clumsy about him. He was striking, with hooded eyes and an aristocratic nose. His skin was smooth and brown as a brazil nut. His jet-black hair was spiked on top of his head, defying both gravity and humidity, each spike bleached a wild, improbable platinum. He was as exotic and unreal as a Disney prince.

"Tristan James," I said.

He snapped his fingers. "I knew you looked familiar. You're him."

"Him?"

"Your mum tried to kill your mate."

I turned away.

JAVIER

I MET THE new student today. That is such an innocuous description. In truth, I stumbled over him in the quad this morning. Literally stumbled over him. Sent him sprawling arse over tit and the book he was reading flying. I landed awkwardly on top of his flailing body. He looked so bewildered and hurt, I wondered if he'd imagined I'd knocked him over on purpose.

I'd seen him before: slender and delicate, Asian. I'd never heard him speak, but I assumed from his dress and the speed with which he careened around campus, that he was American. He jumped to his feet and pulled me to mine. Embarrassed, I apologized and introduced myself. Brushing off his backside, he told me his name. As soon as he said it, I recognized him from the social media reports. "Your mum tried to kill your mate," I said. Like falling over him wasn't enough, I had to go and make it worse.

I'm a bloody fool, I decided. I couldn't believe I'd just blurted out what I did. He turned away. I reached out to touch him in reassurance but stopped because he looked as fragile as a pile of ashes or a sandcastle that would crumble if touched.

"I'm sorry," I said. "That was indiscreet. Listen, I didn't mean to embarrass you. I just think what happened was awful. I'm so glad to see you're OK."

He said nothing, so I tried again. "Look, it can be our secret—I'm sure the others don't know."

"Do you have many secrets?" he asked me.

I shrugged. "Maybe. But listen, this campus is absolutely *polluted* with secrets."

"It is?"

"Oh, yeah," I said. "The closets are *full*. You have closet Jews, and closet aristocrats, and closet alcoholics, and, of course, the closet gays. My dear, everyone seems to be in the closet. It's so bad that each morning one yanks open one's wardrobe expecting to find clothes and hatboxes and finds instead everyone and everything *except* clothes and hat boxes."

He laughed. "But...not you?"

"No, not me. Nor you. I don't get the point. How is one to get laid if one hides one's preferences? Nasty public lavatories and city parks crawling with poison ivy and nosy spinsters are *so not my style*. I prefer a feather bed and Champagne on ice!"

He laughed again.

"Ah—there! See, you *can* laugh."

TRISTAN

JAVIER AND I have become fast friends, if not each other's only friend. Thick as thieves, my mother would have said. Oh, Javier has lots of what he calls acquaintances and boyfriends by the dozen, each of whom lasts a week or two in his orbit before being discharged into deep space and despair, but mostly it's just him and me. And occasionally my father.

Despite Javier's enticements and entreaties, I have managed to avoid the tourist destinations—the Eiffel Tower, the Louvre,

Versailles. He keeps asking me why, but I can't bring myself to tell him. He says, "For better or for worse, Paris *is* the Eiffel Tower and the Arc de Triomphe and the Louvre and Versailles." Exasperated by my implacability, he curses in French, and we do something else.

We hunt for out-of-the-way bistros and patisseries. We've gone shopping for hats at Eux dans l'Eau on place des Vosges and Borsalino on rue de Grenelle. Once, he drove us four and a half hours in his Citroën to Chapellerie Traclet on rue de Cadore in Roanne, where he bought a heather-colored patchwork cap with a leather brim and a custom-made rabbit-and-hare-mix fur felt Campaign hat by HUFVUD. I bought a made-to-order deerstalker in purple and aqua.

"You know," Javier remarked, "that hat will make you look like a gay Sherlock Holmes in a letterman's jacket?"

Ignoring him, I asked the clerk how soon they'd ship me my cap.

JAVIER

I REALLY WANTED to show Tristan around Paris, but he refused to go to any of the places Americans were usually keen on visiting.

Versailles?

No.

The Louvre?

No.

The Eiffel Tower?

I can see it from my kitchen window.

"What do you have against landmarks?" I finally asked in exasperation.

"They're tourist traps!"

"Tourist traps?"

He just smiled. Mysterious and sad, he kept his secret hurt to himself. So we did other things. I took him to the Paris Sewer Museum; we went for ice cream at Berthillon and wandered around the Île de la Cité; on Sunday, he, his father, and I went for a hot air balloon ride in Parc André-Citroën.

TRISTAN

DESPITE ITS BRILLIANCE, for me, Paris was immutably dimmed by the absence of Max. His absence was like a shadow on me all of the time; I stumbled through the city of light as if it were a dead zone. Yet on Sunday, when Javier took my father and me on a hot air balloon ride in Parc André-Citroën, 150 meters in the air, hearing their chatter, hearing my father's occasional excited exclamations as Javier pointed out first one landmark then another—seeing the city of Paris laid out before me like an intricately woven carpet—I finally saw light. It was faint and distant, but it was there, both beacon and warning.

That light I felt was likely a train. I also knew I had two choices: I could stay where I was and let that train run over me, swallowing me in darkness, or I could jump out of the way and swing on board and let it carry me out of the darkness.

My father put his hand on my shoulder. "Magnificent, no?" he asked in his cheerfully bad French.

"Yes, Papa." Sometimes, to tease him, I call Dad "papa" in the manner of the French.

Chapter 39

TRISTAN

JAVIER CALLED ME from halfway up the stairs. I stepped onto the landing. He was moving at a snail's pace and carrying an enormous hatbox. "What is that?" I asked when he finally reached our door.

"A hatbox."

"I can see that. What's in it?"

"Why, a hat," he remarked, astonished.

"You bought another hat? I've never even seen you wear a hat."

"I don't. With hair this glorious, why would I wear a hat?"

"Then why do you keep buying hats?"

"Because I *love* hats. And because I expect one day my glorious locks will be gone, or I'll turn old at thirty, and I will be prepared with a hat for every occasion."

I tried not to roll my eyes. "Why are you bringing it here?"

"I need you to store it for me. There is no more room in those *broom closets* at school they call wardrobes."

Javier and I were sitting on the purple velvet banquet in the salon while he helped me decline French verbs.

"Does your father know you're gay?" he asked me in French.

"Of course. Why?"

"I think he thinks we're an item."

"Why would you think that?"

"Just the way he looks at me, and he's always excusing himself from our company so we can be alone. And God knows I spend enough time with you."

"He probably just doesn't want me to be lonely."

He corrected my pronunciation and then said, "He's a remarkable man—our papa." I'd noticed Javier had stopped calling Dad "Mr. James" in favor of "Papa," but this was the first time he'd referred to him as "our papa."

"That he is. Is your father anything like him?" I asked, switching back to English.

JAVIER

I TRY so hard not to talk about my parents. Now, I said, "No. The opposite. Quite the homophobe, he is."

"Really?"

"Oh, yes. When I was four or five, I loved to dance. I asked if I could take dance classes, and my father said no. He said it would make me gay."

"He actually said that?"

"Yes. I didn't even know what gay was back then. Anyway, fast forward to the other year when I actually *saw* my parents. I must have pranced a bit too much because my father looked disgusted, and my mother said, 'Given the outcome was the same, we should probably have let you take dance classes when you were five. It would have kept you out of my hair, and you would have been a happier kid.'"

"Oh, Javier—"

"Anyway," I said, changing the subject, "we should get you a proper boyfriend."

TRISTAN

A PROPER BOYFRIEND? Who could there be after Max? I wondered. After the perfection of his love for me—and mine for him—there could be no other. I remained devoted to him even in his absence, or maybe his is an exile, because I could not be otherwise.

Still teenagers, we had started to build the foundation of an eternal love, one kiss, one smile, one caress at a time. And in my youthful arrogance, I'd been sure the house of love we were building would be impervious to the world's disapprobation, no matter how mightily it huffed and puffed and blew.

Chapter 40

MAX

GRADUATION WAS YESTERDAY. I felt both finished and stalled. I hadn't expected to graduate from a new school, hadn't expected to graduate without Tristan.

"You seem so sad," my father said.

"I am," I replied. "I miss Tristan."

And I did. Tristan, in the short time we'd been together, had become my locus, marking my place in the world. My place was at the end of his hand, in the center of his heart. With his sudden and seemingly irrevocable absence, I was lost, blind, unable to place myself in the world, unable to see a path forward.

I found myself trying to explain this to my father. He nodded, lost in his own thoughts. I felt stupid because he'd lost my mother when he'd still been young. I'd never stopped to consider, had never wondered what that had been like for him, to lose his love, how he'd coped. He hadn't remarried, had never even had a girlfriend in the years since my mother died, as far as I knew.

"I understand how you're feeling," he said gently, "but I want you to remember this. You are both still alive. Where there is life, there is hope. If your relationship was meant to be—and before you ask, I believe it was—you will find each other again."

TRISTAN

"Can you believe we're graduating next week?" Javier asked.

"No. Hey, do I get to meet your parents?" I asked.

"They're not coming," Javier said, picking up a sweater and holding it against his chest. He pivoted to look at himself in the mirror.

"They're not coming? But why?" I watched him in the mirror.

"They're on holiday, or Dad's got a business trip—I can't remember. It's usually one or the other."

"But it's your graduation—"

"Oh, don't start. They're not like other parents. I was an accidental child, inconvenient and unsuitable for the life they intended to live." He said this without the slightest trace of resentment or self-pity.

"No matter," I said with a brightness I did not feel, trying to match his tone. "I'll be there and so will Dad."

"Yes," he said. "You and Papa will be there." He turned toward me. "This sweater—yay or nay?"

"Nay," I said.

"I think you're right." He dropped the sweater in a crumpled heap on the table. "I'm hungry. Let's get something to eat at that café you like so much. We can pick up croissants for Papa, too."

He turned to leave. I quickly picked up the sweater he'd discarded and, folding it neatly, placed it back on the pile on the table because excellent sons leave things as they find them.

· ·

As he bit into his croissant, Dad asked, "What do you want for graduation?"

"I want to go home."

139

I hadn't made any plans for college or figured out what I wanted to study, and Dad hadn't pressed me, so most likely returning home meant I'd attend community college until I did.

A week later, I found myself on a flight to New York, my father in the window seat, Javier, who would be attending Princeton in the fall, on the aisle. I sat in the middle in Max's letterman's jacket and my deerstalker cap. All I could think about was seeing Max again.

Chapter 41

MAX

I WAS MISERABLE. I missed Tristan so much. No matter what anyone said, I couldn't imagine loving anyone else. Not after losing the one whose heart I had captured, and who had captured mine in turn. Yet even as guilt at what my selfishness had wrought clawed my nerve endings, loneliness screamed in equal measure.

"You need to go back to living," Aunt Kaleisha had said the last time I saw her. "You need to live for yourself." Having once lived for Tristan, I found it impossible to live for myself.

I had to find Tristan. *If you were meant to be, you will find each other again.*

I reread my note:

> *I love you, Dad. I do, but I can't live in this town after they ripped out my heart and stomped on it. Not without him. I can't sit across the table from The Aunts one more night, knowing they despise me because I love him and suspecting, as I do, their complicity and treachery in everything that happened.*
>
> *Thank you for your patience and for being the best dad I could have asked for, but I have to find Tristan. I have to find myself.*
>
> *I'm sorry.*
>
> *I love you.*
>
> *Max*

Satisfied this was the best I could do, I attached it to the refrigerator door with a magnet. Inside was a six-pack of my dad's favorite stout beer.

I grabbed my stuff and headed out to the garage. I lifted my helmet off its shelf and got on my motorcycle. I had only the vaguest plan, but I was ready. As I walked the bike out the garage, I glanced back at the shelf where Tristan's matching helmet sat, looking as forlorn and alone as I felt. I adjusted the kickstand and walked back to the shelf. I took his helmet and strapped it to the bike.

At the end of our street, I stopped and looked back. The houses, painted pastel colors so faded it was hard to tell they were ever cheerful and bright and lit by hope, surrounded by hardscrabble lawns that were mostly dirt and weeds, all leaned to one side.

. . . .

I got off my bike and looked up at Tristan's house. I hadn't meant to come but found to my chagrin that I couldn't leave without seeing it, if not *him*, one last time.

The house, clearly empty, sat silent and brooding, deep in shadows, like a childhood friend who, tired of your antics, turns his back on you. I strapped on my helmet and climbed back on my bike. This time, I did not call his name.

As I backed down the driveway, his helmet banged against my leg. It was probably foolish to bring it, but when I found him, he would need it, wouldn't he?

Act 2:
The Adventures of
Testa di Cazzo

I take no responsibility for what happens in this tale you are about to read. I will tell you only that it happened not so long ago. Nor will I attempt to explain what is set down in these pages. I leave it to you to believe...or not.

I

A DILDO, MY FRIEND, A DILDO
(JOSEPH GETS ADVICE FROM CHERRY)

JOSEPH HAD A predilection for unlit pipes, smoking jackets, and pre-prandial cocktails, which some found pretentious, while others, more charitable, chose to find it charming and eccentric. The truth was probably somewhere in the middle. Though it may also have been simply who he was. As for the pre-prandial cocktail, those who knew him best knew it was often dinner itself. However, it wasn't as clear why he never lit his pipe. He was seldom to be seen without it gripped firmly in his mouth until one night, over pre-prandial cocktails, one of his youngish guests, an arrogant little fop, quite a bit too full of himself, asked, "Why don't you ever light that blasted pipe?"

"Light my pipe?" Joseph replied, astonished. "But I don't smoke. Smoking is gauche. I suppose I just have an oral fixation. I am too old for a pacifier, and sucking on a pipe is safer and more socially acceptable than sucking on a cock—especially in front of one's guests. Don't you think?"

"You are," the arrogant little fop ill-advisedly said, "like a character in a Noel Coward play."

Joseph set down his lobster brioche roll and picked up his Champagne flute, which contained his pre-prandial Le Grand Fizz—a blend of Grey Goose vodka, St~Germain liqueur and soda water with a squeeze, just a squeeze, of lime juice—and said, "My darling boy, I aspire not to be a character in a Noel Coward play nor an actor in a Noel Coward play. No! *I aspire to be the play itself!*"

Joseph was a poor playwright, though his plays were seen and well-reviewed, and he was considered a *playwright with promise*. That promise, like the promise of Love, receded each year until now it was more probable he would be struck by lightning than author a hit play. He'd survived in the theatre on the largess of his supporters—a significant conglomeration of movers and shakers and influencers—an inability to accept failure, and a modest trust fund.

Part of Joseph's cachet and thus the popularity of his cocktail parties was his ability to pair Titans of Broadway of a Certain Age with desirable young men who were available by the hour, the night, or the week: young men who could pass as besotted boyfriends; young men who could be relied on not to be nonplussed when confronted with a snail fork or peach knife at brunch in the Hamptons.

Later that evening, after the last rent boy had departed with his evening's *patron*, Joseph found himself sitting across from his lone remaining guest, the irritating fop. Devouring the last lobster brioche roll in two bites and eyeing the fop's impressive basket, he asked him his name for the fourth time that night, then invited him to disrobe. The fop had obligingly stripped and, sprawling on top of Joseph, had attacked his rectum like he was drilling for oil on a city street; that is to say, with a certain absence of passion and a bored resignation that this drilling, this *coupling*, would come to nothing. But as the fop pounded away and Joseph considered asking him to stop, he'd felt a brightening growing within himself, steadily growing lighter, rising, rising, until he delightfully, unexpectedly, crested, flooding the depression in his linen sheets until it was slippery as an iceberg.

The fop—he *must* stop thinking of him that way, only what *was* his name? He could not remember, though Damon came to mind—proved more irritating in sleep than awake: he snored loudly and took up most of the king-size bed, thrashing about and balling the imported linen sheets in his fists. Joseph, clinging to the edge of the bed, tried to sleep. Now, Damon— Joseph was *sure* that was his name—stretched in his sleep and kicked him. Hard.

··

Joseph's was a world of hierarchy and order: uptown and downtown; rich and poor; up-and-coming and has-been with the occasional never-was and never-gonna-be thrown in; patron and artist; john and hustler; top and bottom; pickpocket and mark. Damon existed outside of this world; he was from South Jersey, of all places. He'd grown up not rich but not poor; he was educated but without ambition; versatile—either top or bottom, as the mood or the man moved him. Bold, recklessly affectionate with little regard for the context in which that affection was displayed, and even less for the reactions his indiscretion elicited in those around them, dismissing them as reactionary, out-of-touch, *closeted*, homophobic, and cowardly. Damon questioned *everything*, including the order of Joseph's world.

It was altogether too much, Joseph decided. It was too disruptive. He ended it.

"By the way," Damon had snapped before he left, "my name is Michael, not Damon."

"But why didn't you correct me before?"

Damon/Michael shrugged. "It didn't seem particularly important."

"But now it does?"

"Yes. If you're going to think of me bitterly and talk disparagingly about me, you ought to get my bloody name right."

Now without Damon—*Michael*, Joseph realized he missed his outrageous cock, his abrasion, the *frisson* created by their opposing perspectives.

He found himself confessing all of this to one of his closest friends—if one can be said to have friends in the theatre. His name was Antonio, but everyone called him Cherry. A carpenter by trade, he'd started out as a builder of Broadway sets, then penned a play which had been singularly successful. He was now one of the most revered playwrights in the last quarter century, a Titan of Broadway. And of a Certain Age.

"Cherry, why did you stop coming to my parties?" Joseph asked him suddenly.

"The point of your parties, Joseph, was the boys. I finally asked myself why rent a whole boy when I was only interested in one part of him?"

"But what could replace a young man's attention?" Joseph spluttered.

"A dildo, my friend, a dildo."

"That seems kind of...*lonely*." He'd almost said "pathetic" but caught himself in time.

"Maybe, but I don't have to share my bed or my attention. I don't have to make introductions or excuses. My life is simply my own."

"Where does one even get a dildo?" Joseph asked, half to himself.

"I know a wonderful...*boutique*. Wait, I have a card," Cherry added, digging in the carryall he was never without. He placed the card, a glossy black square embossed in metallic silver, discreetly on the coffee table.

"A dildo," Joseph mused.

"Not just *a* dildo. Several! You can have one for each day of the week—perhaps *two*—if you're up to it!"

Joseph stared at the glossy black card lying on the mahogany table but did not reach for it. Cherry drained his cocktail and, setting down the empty glass, said, "Well, I really must be going. Thanks for the drink and the chat." Then, like a devil knowing his seduction is complete, he rose and faded away.

Alone in his king-size bed, plagued by an itch his hand alone could not scratch, the glossy black square embossed in metallic silver, still lying on his coffee table, took over Joseph's slumbering mind. Eventually, it overtook his dreams, becoming a holy grail demanding a quest. Waking exhausted, he knew he'd get no rest until he found his grail.

YOU SEEM LIKE AN ARTIST WHO WANTS
TO CREATE A UNIQUE EXPERIENCE.
(JOSEPH VISITS AN ADULT BOOKSTORE
AND A CHINESE HERBALIST)

JOSEPH MARVELED AT the name Adult Book Store, since as far as he could tell, the store sold every salacious thing *but* books. The clerk behind the counter looked over at him and smiled encouragingly. Embarrassed, Joseph went and stood in front of a magazine rack that was as tall as a man and six times as wide. He'd intended to stand there only long enough for the clerk's attention to drift so he could dart over to what he had really come for, but the magazines snared his attention.

The titles in large, gritty fonts, disturbing as graffiti, were lurid: *Rod, Stallion, Steel*. And sometimes starkly frank: *Holes*. Beneath their titles, a myriad of men in all shades and musculatures sprawled suggestively in professionally lit, airbrushed glory: a bulging bicep here, a perfect swirl of chest hair ringing a plump, swollen nipple there; a stunning uncircumcised cock. Joseph, after a moment, turned his gaze away. After all, he was through with men—their demands and quirks and messiness; there was only one part of them he needed.

He stepped through an open metal gate and was instantly confronted by a wall of dildos and butt plugs of all sizes: thick and thin; long and short; curving upward and downward; with balls; without balls; with suction cups at one end; harness or strap-on ready; in black and brown and that surreal "flesh" color of a Band-Aid; and pastels, too—pinks and greens and watery blues; in glass and stainless steel and latex and silicone.

There were so many options. How could he choose? And then he saw it: The Jeff Stryker—ten and a half inches of thick silicone molded from a cast of the porn star's own cock—a salami of Heaven on Earth, the Holy Grail of dildoes.

"Molded after Stryker's wondrous cock, this signature dildo, measuring ten and one-half inches in length, is equipped with veins, balls and a smooth tip," the writing on the package proclaimed. *"The added suction cup provides endless possibilities, and for all you true Jeff Stryker fans, an autographed photo is included."* He picked up the dildo, the solid weight of it heavy in his hands. He ran his fingers caressingly along its length; it was like taking the first steps into the promised land. He looked at the autographed photo: Jeff in his prime, forever beautiful and unchanging, trapped in the same moment in time as his erect cock replicated in silicone. The autograph was clearly as much a facsimile as the dildo.

Joseph's eyes fell on a mold kit that one could presumably use to create a mold on one's own dick—or someone else's. He hesitated a moment, torn by a new idea. But no, his need was too great, too immediate, The Jeff Stryker too present, calling him.

Joseph grabbed his prize and, striding to the counter, plunked down sixty-five dollars in cash for his Jeff Stryker cast Silagel replica.

The clerk—at least he'd assumed he was the clerk, but now up close, Joseph decided he was probably the owner, given his guarded proprietary air—was a tall, misshapen man with a lazy eye and an avuncular air. "Ah, The Jeff Stryker—good choice," he said, ringing up Joseph's purchase and placing it in a discreet, unmarked, brown bag.

It took Joseph less than a week to grow dissatisfied with The Jeff Stryker. Unable to define his dissatisfaction, he blamed it on the toy itself and began to look at ways he would improve it. He would make the balls bigger, heavier so that, suspended in his mouth, he would feel as if he were gargling two soft-boiled eggs. As for the phallus itself: he would make the shaft thicker, the head slightly more bulbous and curved.

Adjusting himself to hide his growing excitement, Joseph picked up his wallet, straightened his ascot, and quickly made his way back to the adult bookstore.

"Ah, you've come back," the proprietor said, his air more avuncular than before.

"Yes, I…" Joseph stammered.

The man furrowed his hideous brow in thought. "You bought The Jeff Stryker."

"Yes—I—"

"And what have you decided on today?"

"Well, this."

The proprietor regarded the mold kit in his hand. "Ah, the Make-a-Willy kit. A fine product. And you know, customized cock is always the best." He winked horribly.

"Yes, well…"

"Make sure you read the instructions and follow them to the tee. But it's pretty simple, really. First, you'll mix the molding powder with water. Then you'll pour it into the molding tube and insert your erect penis and balls—you'll have to stay hard while the mold sets. Many men find using a cock ring helpful—for, you know, *maintaining*—"

"I'm not making a mold of my own," Joseph said, shocked. "What would be the point of that? I'm creating the perfect dildo—just for me."

"Ah," the proprietor said. "After you've made your mold, you'll have to let it rest until it sets. It takes about two hours to set, if I recall correctly. Again, make sure you read the instructions. Once it's set, mix the liquid silicone rubber that comes with the kit and pour it into the mold. After twenty-four hours, you can take it out and *voilà*!"

Joseph nodded.

"You know," the proprietor said, after studying him for a moment, "you seem like you're an artist who wants to create a unique...experience."

Joseph's chest puffed out slightly. "I am."

"Well then, may I suggest you don't use the rubber silicone that comes with the kit?"

"What should I use then?"

"Well, there is a similar silicone product made by a gentleman in Chinatown. He customizes his silicone product with a mix of ancient herbs and spices to create a silicone that is singularly lifelike—it even warms to your body temperature, so it feels less like a toy and more like a man."

Joseph's breath quickened. "Where can I find this gentleman?"

"Here." The proprietor handed him a business card. This one was also black with raised metallic gold lettering, but it was shaped like an octagon.

....

Anxious to get started, Joseph boarded the trolley early—early for him, anyway; he usually slept till noon—so he'd get to Chinatown just as it was awakening from its evening slumbers.

When he'd first moved to The City, the trolley had scared the bejesus out of him with its shuddering and rumbling. Now the yellow-and-black trolley arrived like a benevolent bumblebee. It paused, trembling, and its doors yawned open to welcome him. Once he boarded, it streaked off with a bone-rattling roar, the electric cable above humming and buzzing with the charged effort of locomotion.

Joseph tried to sit still on the uncomfortable yellow-and-black straw seat, but he was too excited, too full of anticipation. The trolley, despite its racket and great rushing speed, seemed too slow to him. At last, the driver announced the Chinatown stop.

As he exited the trolley, Joseph spotted two young men seated side by side; one appeared to be asleep on the other's shoulder. On the seat between them, discreetly hidden, lay their clasped hands. Joseph leaned over and said softly to the one who was awake, "God bless you both. I envy you boys your freedom to be yourselves."

Once Joseph emerged from the subterranean trolley station, he made a right turn and passed through the Chinatown Friendship Gate—and into a kind of multicultural chaos that was welcoming to the familiar but intimidating to the uninitiated.

Following the directions on the back of the black octagonal card with the raised gold lettering, Joseph quickly made his way down the crowded streets until he came upon a litter-strewn alley around the corner from a storefront advertising Chinese natural herbs and promising long life. Walking down the alley, he descended some decaying steps to a shadowed doorway with a large glass pane and no discernable lock. He checked the address against his card and pushed the door open, calling out, "Hello?"

"May I help you?" the man asked politely in English shaded with a faint Chinese accent and just a trace of English boarding school.

Joseph handed him the black card with the gold lettering.

"Ah. That is I," the man said, bowing slightly. "How may I help you?"

Joseph looked at him in surprise. He'd expected someone older, wizened and wise-looking. Instead, he was confronted by a very handsome young Chinese man, skin as smooth and white as porcelain, who looked like an Ivy League chemist in a white lab coat. His hands, when he folded them and bowed, were small and efficient with immaculate polished nails. His eyes, beneath eyebrows that had been waxed into arches of surprise, seemed to see everything and revealed nothing.

At home, Joseph took off his jacket, discarded his ascot, and rolled up his shirt sleeves. Oh, his Make-a-Willy would be grand, he told himself, more perfect than any boy, for it would come with no needs, no demands. And with those thoughts dancing in his head, he set to work, adjusting the mold.

He mixed the molding solution and poured it into the molding tube, then after ten minutes, he plunged in The Jeff Stryker. Two minutes later, he removed it as the instructions ordered. Now working quickly, he sliced the tube in half and removed some of the mold so the finished product would be thicker. Next, he adjusted the head so it would be more bulbous, and finally, holding the tube over the gas jet until it softened slightly, he twisted it so it would curve. Satisfied, he quickly restored the split mold to wholeness and set it aside to finish hardening.

Once the mold was ready, he carefully poured in the silicone he'd gotten from the Chinese herbalist. He made himself a cocktail, then a second, then a third.

When he awoke, it was midafternoon and his Make-a-Willy was ready. Not even pausing to brush his teeth, he freed it from the mold and immediately launched it on its maiden voyage.

WHOLE MEN ARE MORE TROUBLE THAN THEY ARE WORTH
(JOSEPH CONTEMPLATES GETTING A COMPANION)

I T HAD BEEN more than a week, yet neither Joseph's desire nor his satisfaction with his Make-a-Willy had diminished. Once again satisfied, Joseph threw the dildo into its usual drawer. As he started to close the drawer, to his astonishment he heard weeping. He looked all around but could not find the source of the ungodly wailing. He started to push the drawer closed again, and the wailing increased. This time, he heard a small squeaky voice.

"Why do you do this to me? I am nothing but an object to you. You wring your pleasure from me, then rinse me with that foul disinfectant and lock me up until your nasty desires rise again as faithful as a fever. It's not fair, I tell you! I spend half my time in this smelly drawer and the other half in you! It's dark and stuffy in you, too. Oh, it's not fair."

Joseph listened to this soliloquy in stunned silence. After a few moments, he regained himself and asked, "How is it that you can speak?"

"You will have to ask the herbalist from whom you got the silicone you used to create me."

"You say I use you as an object, but what can I do? You are but an object—an object I created for one purpose—a purpose for which, I must tell you, I suited you well."

"I want to be more than *this*. I want to be a whole man."

"But why should *I* want a whole man? Whole men are more trouble than they are worth. They're costly to keep—they lie, and they cheat—"

"If you made me a whole man, I would be no trouble to you. I'd never lie to you or cheat, and you know already I'm the best lover you've ever had. Imagine how happy I'd make you if I could be your companion, too."

"But how— Even if I wanted to do as you say, I cannot. I have no silicone left."

"Then pray go and find the wizard you bought it from and buy more. Go now, and hurry."

"No," Joseph said firmly and closed the drawer with a crash.

. . . .

Sipping his pre-prandial cocktail, Joseph leaned back against the cracked leather of his ancient chesterfield sofa and moodily contemplated his lone self and the reflection of the room behind him in the antique gilt-framed pier glass that leaned casually against the opposite wall. In fact, the mirror was firmly attached to the wall by an elaborate mechanism of anchors and bolts, as immovable as the room's other architectural features: the crown molding, dark oak paneling, and plaster ceiling medallions. Perhaps, he thought reluctantly, his miraculously talkative Make-a-Willy was right: it wouldn't be so bad to have a man to keep him company on the evenings there was no play to attend or cocktail party to host.

Joseph drifted off to sleep, his would-be companion playing with him at the edges of his consciousness.

IV

THE SUNLIGHT SLANTING IN THE TALL EAST-FACING
WINDOWS CLAWED AT JOSEPH'S EYELIDS
(JOSEPH RETURNS TO CHINATOWN)

THE SUNLIGHT SLANTING in the tall east-facing windows clawed at Joseph's eyelids, prying them open. His hangover faded, and his fingers burned with the artistic urge to create. His throbbing erection told him what he must do. He threw off the covers and, rushing about his room, performed his toilet and dressed.

This time, it being later in the day, instead of dashing through throngs of child laborers and delivery men carrying fresh-caught fish and ugly exotic fruits, he had to thread his way among elderly white-haired women and the excellent sons who attended them.

Feeling he'd rushed his first errand, Joseph was determined to take his time and enjoy the experience. At the grocery on the corner, he lingered over the displays of exotic ugly-beautiful fruits he'd never seen before: curious lychee with its odd, spiky, red skin; waxy, yellow-green star fruit; purple-and-yellow-skinned passion fruit; dragon fruit dressed in its inedible leathery pink-and-bright-red skin and sporting green talons that looked like fleshy hangnails; pawpaw; kumquats; bulbous Asian pears; Buddha's Hand; heart-shaped rose apples; Rambutan with its spiky, hair-like rinds.

An aqua ice cream truck, blaring a repetitive, juvenile melody, strummed his taut nerves like a remarkably untalented second cousin playing guitar at his first recital. Frowning, he glared at the truck.

It was then that he noticed the two young men standing on the corner. One was plain, dressed all in black, and sported a short ponytail springing from the top of his head; the other one, smaller, browner with a beautiful mouth, gazed up at the one in black adoringly. Joseph recognized them as the two boys he'd seen on the trolley discreetly holding hands the other morning.

They were walking with their arms about each other and sharing an ice cream cone. When they stopped at the red light at the corner, the one dressed all in black stole a kiss. There was such a purity in the gesture, an unconscious claiming of their birthright, that Joseph was touched. He feared he might weep and, lowering his head, hurried past them, crossing against the light and earning a prolonged honking and a stream of verbal obscenity from the ice cream truck driver, who was making a right turn and had nearly run him over. Joseph glanced back at the two young men. They seemed so happy and so in love, Joseph allowed himself to imagine that nothing would ever separate them from each other. He quickened his step with a new determination to create for himself a life companion.

Joseph walked to the alley behind the Chinese herbal shop. Its sign still offered long life, but Joseph knew its herbs offered more: endless satisfaction. The alley was more littered than last time, if that were possible.

· · · · · · · · · · · · · · · ·

The Chinese herbalist didn't seem surprised to see him. He assured Joseph he could deliver one hundred seventy-five pounds of the herb-infused silicone, and together, they settled on an olive tone that would complement the brick color of the Make-a-Willy.

When he'd first met him, Joseph had thought under the flawless English he'd heard a slight Chinese accent combined with a British one, as if he'd been born in China and educated at Eton and Oxford. Now he thought it had been the herbalist's extreme erudition and the genteel courtliness of his manner that had made Joseph fancy he'd heard a British accent.

BUILD A WHOLE MAN? JOSEPH WONDERED.
COULD HE? DID HE DARE?
(JOSEPH MAKES A MAN)

JOSEPH'S BIGGEST AND earliest success had been a play called *The Seven*, in which the seven princes of hell, led by Lucifer, and each representing one of the seven deadly sins, battled the seven archangels, each of whom represented a virtue of heaven. Unfortunately, he'd been unable to raise the money to hire fourteen actors, so he'd fallen back on his early interest in artistic pursuits and made...*puppets*. He'd outdone Dr. Frank N. Furter by creating, in just seven days, not just one but *fourteen* men, though they lacked the grace and beauty of Frank's Rocky.

All this came back to him now, as he, a pre-prandial cocktail in his hand, contemplated a bathtub full of Chinese herb-infused silicone putty. Surely the idea was crazy. Build a whole man? Joseph wondered. Could he? Did he dare?

He slowly warmed to the idea of having a companion, a dream stud cast to his own specifications, and soon forgot the idea hadn't been his at all. He set aside his drink, determined to work hard, eager to create his new companion.

He shaped his creation's hairline and brow. When he got to the eyes, he remembered his childhood collection of cat's eye marbles and went to retrieve them from their wooden casket in the den, where he'd buried them, along with his childhood, when his parents died. He almost forgot to give him ears, which his man would need for hearing and boxing.

He lovingly shaped the mouth, making it generous and pouty. No sooner had he finished the newly formed mouth than it began issuing complaints and suggestions and urging him to hurry that he might sooner stand and admire himself. Looking at his face, Joseph grew irritated with its whining petulance and had to remind himself that if his creation looked petulant, it was because he'd given him a pouty mouth, and if he talked too much, it was because he'd given him too big a mouth. It was his own fault.

Joseph smiled. Petulant or not, his new companion was handsome, with the cutest nose which was sexily crooked, and he would be well hung. He returned to work: the shoulders, the arms, the curvaceous but muscular buttocks, the cradle where his prodigious manhood would lie.

At last, he was finished. "Finito!" Rocking back on his heels, he leaned over the tub for a final inspection. His creation leapt from the tub.

"I'm your boy, and you're my Daddy!" he declared, dancing around the room on his new legs.

Joseph bristled, a frown corrugating his forehead, at the appellation, for some men do not wish to be daddies of any kind, and Joseph counted himself among their ranks. Still, this "son" was temptingly naked and willing to do as his Daddy bid him, so, swallowing his objection, Joseph smiled and cooed, "Come to Daddy!"

"Wait—what's my name?"

"What?"

"My name. As my Daddy, you have to give me a name."

Joseph, focused on his groin, offered the first name that popped into his head. "Cazzo."

"Cazzo."

"Yes, now come to Daddy, Cazzo!"

Cazzo paused in his attentions. Joseph opened his eyes. "What is it?"

"What's my full name?"

"Huh?"

"What's my full name? I can't have just one name. Who am I? Cher? I need a first and a last name. My name should be dignified, elegant—"

"Testa di Cazzo!" Joseph spat, annoyed.

"Testa di Cazzo. I like it. It's dignified and elegant. It's me."

"Yes," Joseph agreed, wilting and trying not to roll his eyes. "Now, can we please get on with it?"

Cazzo obliged.

"Say my name, say my name, say my name," Cazzo urged as he worked, annoying Joseph, who believed sex was like a symphony and thus best enjoyed in silence.

"Testa di Cazzo!"

WHAT DID YOU DO?
(CAZZO GETS COLD AND SLEEPS TOO CLOSE TO THE FIRE)

C AZZO WAS NOW more than just a dildo, but he had one last challenge to overcome: he had no clothes. How could he go out and explore the world—which would surely be his oyster now that he had legs—unclothed? Joseph was asleep, and Cazzo was impatient.

Determined to cover his nakedness, Cazzo went into the closet and, finding a pair of tuxedo trousers with a fine satin stripe down each side, slipped them on. Next, he pulled one of Joseph's smoking jackets off its hanger and slipped that on, too. Then he fastened an ascot about his neck as he'd seen Joseph do. Thus dressed, he set out into the gayborhood. He entered the first bar he saw, where a gaggle of queens stopped gossiping and, pointing at him, laughed. They mocked him and insulted his clothes. Though there were only seven of them, their derision was so violent that, to Cazzo, they felt like a mob.

Embarrassed by their remarks, he pulled the ascot from his neck and threw it to the floor, then he removed his jacket. The tuxedo pants were slightly too small for him and clearly revealed what hung between his legs. One queen, quicker than the other six, jumped off his stool and, rushing to Cazzo's side, slipped an arm through his. "Why don't we," he cooed in Cazzo's ear, "leave these silly queens and go back to my place?"

Relieved to finally not be the object of their ridicule, Cazzo readily agreed.

"What's your name?" Cazzo asked the queen.

"Lucifer, but my friends call me Luci."

"Hi, Luci."

"What's your name, stranger?" the queen asked, squeezing Cazzo's massive bicep.

"Cazzo."

"Cazzo what? Or are you telling me you only have one name? Who are you? Cher?"

"Oh! No, sorry. I misunderstood. My Daddy calls me Cazzo, but my full name is Testa di Cazzo."

"Your name is Testa di Cazzo?" the queen, whose grandparents were from a small village in Italy, asked in disbelief and started to laugh.

Cazzo flushed with a combination of confusion and embarrassment. Joseph had named him. His name was obviously some kind of joke, something else for him to be mocked for. He started to pull away from the queen's grasp.

....

Feeling the massive bicep flex in his grasp, Luci became weak and feared losing him. "Testa di Cazzo is a fine name," he cooed and led him farther towards his lair under the railroad tracks just steps from the Bucket of Blood. "In here, Cazzo," he whispered. "Quickly."

The apartment was cold, and Luci set a few large pots of water to boil. Soon the old plaster walls started sweating from the effort of keeping the cold out and the warmth in. Luci led Cazzo to a bearskin rug and turned on the electric heater which, simulating a wood-burning fire, glowed orange-red-orange.

Naked and slightly warmed, they rolled over each other, tangled in the bearskin rug.

. . . .

After, when Luci fell asleep, Cazzo became cold because his silicone body took on the ambient temperature wherever he was. He crawled over Luci to be closer to the simulated wood fire still glowing orange-red-orange and, naked, fell into an exhausted sleep.

When Cazzo woke the next morning, he couldn't believe his eyes. His magnificent silicone cock, too close to the fire all night, had softened and become misshapen. He was too embarrassed to be seen and so stole into his clothes quickly and quit the now-cold-again room, his former companion sound asleep and apparently impervious to the room's rattling cold.

. . . .

"What did you do?" Joseph cried, seeing the misshapen cock.

"I went home with my friend to see his own dear Daddy. His Daddy was hungry, but my friend can't cook, so I attempted to scramble some eggs, only it took me a long time and the stove was very hot, and I stood too close."

(Now you and I know better, but poor Joseph, half besotted and half swollen with pride at what he had created, could countenance no other explanation.)

"Oh, you poor, dear, sweet boy!"

"Will you fix it?" Cazzo asked pitifully. "So it's like it was before?"

"But what does it matter?" Joseph asked. "Who will see it besides me? And I don't mind."

"I have decided to become a stage actor," Cazzo said, "and star in a great Broadway play, but what if there is a nude scene?

I should be too embarrassed to take the role. For if I did, not only would they laugh at me, but they would also whisper that you, the great playwright, Joseph Collodi, had made me, and look what a poor job you'd made of me."

Joseph nodded knowingly. The old Broadway gossips *would* talk and say surely he'd made Cazzo after too many pre-prandial cocktails. Joseph set down his pre-prandial cocktail and went off in search of his mold.

Joseph carefully detached Cazzo's manhood so he could heat it and recast it to its earlier perfection. As he worked, he remarked aloud to himself, "It really is a miracle that Cazzo rises and walks and talks and feels and fails like a real man." As those words trembled on the air and faded, he couldn't help but feel proud at the dream he'd made reality.

Repaired, Cazzo immediately set to work making love to Joseph, not in gratitude as one might expect, but to free himself from Joseph's company so he could begin his next adventure. Joseph drifted into sleep, and Cazzo, admiring his restored perfection in the pier glass leaning against the wall, slipped into his clothes and out the door.

VII

IT LOOKS EVEN BIGGER THAN BEFORE
(CAZZO DISCOVERS THE BATHS)

WHEN CAZZO RETURNED to Joseph's, he found him agitated. His eyes were glistening and red, his face more wrinkled than usual.

"Why, Daddy, what's wrong? Have you been crying?"

"What is wrong? Have I been crying? I woke up to find you missing with no idea where you'd gone or where to look for you."

"Why, how extraordinary! I simply went for a walk."

"A walk? You've been gone three days."

Three days? Surely it hadn't been three days. Cazzo tried to think. It had been just twilight when he'd arrived at the baths and dark when he'd left. He'd assumed it had been the same night, just later.

There had been the first man, slim and beautiful with a shaved head and a massive ass. He'd been an Olympic gold medalist—a swimmer, Cazzo recalled. There had followed a darkly furred man in a sling who'd been offering himself to a line of men whose towels had been dropped to the floor as they stood naked in erect anticipation. He'd pushed them aside when he'd glimpsed Cazzo, naked, at the back of the line. After him, there had been the couple: one flat on his stomach on a white-sheeted cot, his hands and feet shackled, while the other, his "master," invited men in from the hall to have a go at his defenseless raw-looking hole. Then there had been—

"Where have you been?" Joseph roared, interrupting Cazzo's thoughts.

"I made a friend."

"A friend? Where?"

"At the baths."

"The baths!"

Now afraid of Joseph's rage, Cazzo said, "It doesn't matter. I'm back now. Would you like to make love?"

Before Joseph could spit out a response, Cazzo stepped out of his clothes. Joseph spluttered as his anger died abruptly. "Why, how can this be? It looks even bigger than before."

"*Does* it?" Cazzo asked seductively, carelessly. "Would you like to try it out and see if it *feels* bigger, too?"

Joseph climbed off Cazzo and lay back with a satisfied smile.

Cazzo chuckled and pinched a nipple and waited patiently for Joseph to fall into a deep sleep as he inevitably did after sex, so he could go out and make more new friends. He was enjoying his sudden popularity.

VIII

CAREFUL YOU DON'T GET TOO BIG FOR YOUR BRITCHES
(CAZZO RECEIVES A WARNING)

As Cazzo ran down the stairs, the door to the first-floor apartment opened a crack. The face that revealed itself was simultaneously impossibly young and impossibly old. Thigh-length hair, sometimes silver, sometimes blue, glowed. It was widely rumored the apartment's occupant was a fairy. Now words floated through the crack: "Beware what you do, Cazzo. You promised to be true to poor Joseph. There is a cost for breaking that promise."

"Hush, fairy," Cazzo commanded arrogantly.

"I'm not a fairy."

"What are you then?" Cazzo asked, stopping and looking more closely.

"I'm a Magical."

"What's a Magical?"

"A Magical is exactly what you mean by 'fairy,' but you, like your human counterparts, use fairy to assign us a gender that is female when we are nonbinary—neither male nor female. Just as we are neither human nor angel but something in between. We are not either, not both, not at the intersection of the two but standing firmly in the middle.

"Humans assigned us the female gender because they think we are weaker, less than men. Because we choose to help humans does not mean we are subservient to them. Our assistance does not make us your chattel."

"Where do Magicals come from?"

"We don't have sex, so we're not born. We come about through not pollination exactly, but rather like how mushrooms appear suddenly in shadowy places after a heavy spring rain, or as moss grows on rocks on the shaded side of a mountain. We're like that. We spring up in the right circumstances. We're ninety percent imagination and ten percent self-determination."

"Why are you troubling me, fai—Magical?"

"Have you noticed each time you cheat on Joseph, your penis grows?"

"What of it? Joseph—and every other man in this city for that matter—doesn't seem to mind. Besides, your dick can never be too big, so what does it matter?"

"Take heed of my words, my child."

Cazzo waved his hand in their general direction dismissively and continued down the stairs.

"Careful you don't get too big for your britches," the Magical whispered. Their words, falling short of Cazzo's ears, lingered on the air half warning, half prophesy. The Magical's door closed with a faint click like a sigh.

IX

I'LL DEDUCT THE COST OF THOSE ORANGES
AND POMEGRANATES FROM YOUR LAST PAY
(CAZZO FINDS AND LOSES A JOB)

JOSEPH WAS IN a tizzy, a fever of anxiety.

"Daddy, what is it?" Cazzo asked.

"We are broke. We are broke. It's all gone."

"What is?"

"Our money."

"How is that possible?"

"The market—the market—it *crashed*!"

Cazzo wondered how this could be. He'd just passed the all-night grocery, and it was open and bustling with activity. Its crates of oranges and apples and pomegranates were brightly lit under the pretty green awning that sheltered the fruits and vegetables and bags of corn chips from the sun and the rain and the thieving hands of strolling brats.

"We're going to starve! We'll be evicted!" Joseph was pacing back and forth and ripping at his hair. "Oh," Joseph wailed, "we are ruined!"

"You'll make more money, Daddy."

"How? I am too old and sick and frail to work."

Now, Joseph *was* old—he was nearly sixty—but he was a *playwright*. He was healthy and strong as an ox. Surely, he could still wield a pen and summon words to fill its tip.

Nonetheless, Cazzo gallantly offered, "Don't worry, Daddy. I'll get a job. You took care of me. Now I'll take care of you."

"You? Get a job? How? Where?"

"I don't know, I'll figure it out," Cazzo said and kissed Joseph on the top of his head before flying down the stairs, full of enthusiasm and determination.

Outside, in the cool evening, his enthusiasm waned, and he leaned against the building's brownstones to think. *I know. I will go to the market and apply for a job selling oranges and apples and pomegranates. I have bought so many, surely, I can sell them, too.*

The grocer, a dour henpecked man possessed of a wife and seven daughters—all short and all named after a day of the week—and a starving soul in search of something he dared not name, was only too happy to hire Cazzo. With a quickness, he gave him a striped apron and a cap and set him to work.

He sent Cazzo to work in the storeroom, uncrating oranges and pomegranates. The grocer came in and said to Cazzo, "You've been working very hard. You should take a break," even though Cazzo had only been working five or ten minutes. Cazzo, who really was very lazy, agreed, and the grocer sat on a pickle barrel and watched Cazzo intently. Cazzo knew he was staring at the place where his apron bowed out. He leaned back a little to show his bulge to better advantage. "I've never had a break before," Cazzo said, stretching. "What does one do on a break?"

"Why, we can do anything you want," the grocer said, smiling.

Cazzo slipped off his apron and, pushing back his cap, said, "Why don't you lean over that pickle barrel, and I'll see what we can do?"

And that is how the grocer's missus found them: the grocer bent over the pickle barrel, his arms plunged into the pickle juice and each hand holding a pickle, while the biggest pickle of all was buried deep in his ass.

Cazzo was busy with the task at hand when he felt a cool breeze across his buttocks. A smell of frying fish rose on the air. The grocer's wife had entered, carrying a live chicken in each hand; she'd intended to wring their necks then butcher them for sale. Now, she swung them like nunchaku at her husband and Cazzo. When the chickens objected at being so abused, she dropped them and began boxing the poor grocer about his ears.

"So instead of fish for lunch you wanted pickles?" she asked and recommenced boxing the poor grocer's ears.

Cazzo pulled up his pants and, grabbing his apron off the floor, gave the grocer a pitying glance then turned to leave. A squadron of little girls in striped and polka-dotted pinafores— the seven daughters, all short and named after the days of the week—gave chase, pelting Cazzo with oranges and apples and pomegranates. The chickens ran ahead of him, squawking and lifting into the air briefly, only to fall to the ground and begin running again.

"I'll deduct the cost of those oranges and pomegranates from your last pay," the grocer's wife shouted, pausing in her abuse of her husband. "And the cost of those two escaped chickens, too!"

The get-up-and-go Cazzo had shown in such abundance earlier now got up and went. He was a failure. With nowhere else to go, he returned to the stoop of the brownstone where he lived with Joseph. He hid in the shadows so that Joseph, looking out the window or stepping onto the balcony, might not see him.

He sat in a corner of the lowest step nearest the wrought iron gate and fence that imprisoned the super's basement apartment. The super was a belligerent, secretive man, and Cazzo was sure he'd have dug a moat around his basement apartment if he could have—rather than erecting a merely formidable fence—

to discourage residents from making service requests and UPS from attempting to deliver residents' packages to him.

Looking up, Cazzo saw light in the Magical's apartment and thought about knocking on their door and asking for advice. He had almost resolved to do just that when the Magical's window opened slowly and a shimmering blue light rained down on the portion of the steps where he sat crouched and moody.

"Poor Cazzo," the Magical began. "How I pity you."

"You pity me?" Cazzo shot back. "Why, the nerve! I am a man and human. Why would *you* pity *me*?"

"Because you are not a man. You are just a dick," the Magical returned. "And worse, you have no heart and a hard head full of silicone."

At these words, Cazzo flew into a passion. He dug a fragment of brick out of the weed-choked garden at his feet and threw it at the Magical's window. The window closed as suddenly and silently as it had opened. The brick struck the glass and bounced off it, landing at Cazzo's feet in a shiver of pinky-red dust.

Despite his agitation and wounded pride, a pale young man barely dressed under a purple-and-aqua-letterman's jacket emerging from the apartment building across the street caught Cazzo's attention. Upon seeing Cazzo, the young man dismissed the town car that had been waiting at the curb. Cazzo watched with amusement as the young man leaned against a streetlamp and pretended to wait for a bus they both knew wasn't coming.

The young man tried not to look as if he was staring at Cazzo. Cazzo stood and, pretending to stretch, pushed his hips forward. He stroked his crotch casually and called out, "Hey."

The man eyed him with a mix of hunger and embarrassment. Cazzo continued stroking himself absentmindedly. The man licked his cracked lips and said in a voice as cracked as his lips, "I haven't money to pay you."

With a start, Cazzo realized the man thought he was a prostitute. He was incensed, but then, sensing opportunity knocking, smiled. The man bashfully smiled back but said nothing further. He turned away in defeat, and as he did, Cazzo caught a glimpse of his ass which, cradled in snug-fitting shorts, promised secrets deep and tight. "We can trade," Cazzo called out. "I'll take that jacket." He pointed to the letterman's jacket the man was wearing, "In exchange for this." He grabbed his crotch again and rotated his hips in a burlesque of copulation.

The man smiled uncertainly, revealing crooked, stained teeth.

"What's your name?" Cazzo asked, crossing the street.

The man seemed startled by the question. "Umm…Gad."

"Gad, I'm Cazzo."

Gad glanced at his crotch. "Yes, I can see that."

"Can we go back to your place?" Cazzo asked, taking his arm.

Gad lay prone with his head turned to the side on a pillow. His eyes fluttered in rhythm with his ragged, excited breathing. His longish, dark hair, slick with sweat, clung about his ears and neck; a pillow under his stomach raised his ass in the air.

Watching the yawning hole suckling his juices, Cazzo felt himself grow still bigger and hornier. "Want to go again?" he asked.

Gad's eyes rolled back in his head; his yawning hole puckered and opened, both answer and invitation. A delicate gold cross dangled from a thin gold chain around his neck.

As he pulled out of Gad for the second time, Cazzo's withdrawal seemed to take longer. When he was finally free, to his astonishment he'd grown longer, thicker still. Alarmed at first, he shrugged off his fright. While he could pound the willing, welcoming holes of men like this one, he didn't care if he never stopped growing.

Unable to get all of himself into his jeans, Cazzo asked Gad if he could borrow a pair of sweatpants. Gad, who was in a near coma of ecstasy, could only point feebly at the closet.

"Can I see you again?" Gad asked hopefully, seductively, looking over his shoulder from where he lay. When Cazzo made no comment, he wiggled his ass, pushed out his rosebud, then retracted it.

Cazzo watched him but said nothing as he struggled to fit himself into the borrowed sweatpants.

Gad sat up. "You know, you might find wearing a kilt easier."

"A kilt?"

"Yes."

"And where would I find a kilt?" Cazzo asked with an edge of sarcasm.

"In the closet behind you. On the left."

Cazzo pulled a worsted wool kilt in a traditional tartan pattern in red, black, and yellow off the shelf. It unfolded, and he stared at the length of fabric in dismay.

"How do I put it on?"

"Wrap it around your waist with the pleats at the back. Now wrap it around you and insert the strap in the slit on your left side."

Cazzo, frowning with effort, did as he was instructed.

"OK, buckle it. Now, wrap the other piece around you and buckle it on your right side. There you go."

Cazzo looked at himself in the mirror. The kilt fit well and showed his muscular legs to great advantage. Better still, it covered his enormous dick without the pain of confinement pants brought.

"You look great," Gad said enthusiastically. "Hot."

Cazzo still said nothing but pulled on the letterman's jacket and without a backward glance or a thank-you moved towards the door.

"Wait! If you'll see me again, I'll pay you."

"Pay me? How? You're as poor as a church mouse," Cazzo said, looking around the ramshackle room with its peeling paint, crumbling vaulted ceiling and stained-glass windows which were missing panes. "You told me so yourself."

"I am, but I know people—men who will pay me for what you just got for free. And then I will pay you."

Cazzo sat on the only furniture in the room besides the bed—a church pew whose shellac was dark and cracked with age. Gad leaned back and folded his legs over his head, holding them in place by locking his arms behind his knees. Cazzo stared at his exposed, ravaged pink hole, opening and closing.

"Tell me more about these men who would pay you," Cazzo said.

"No. Why should I?"

Cazzo moved and sat on the edge of the bed. "Because." He dragged his fingers along the cleft in Gad's ass. "C'mon, tell me."

"Why should I?"

Cazzo's fingers continued their journey, then circled Gad's hole. He slowly worked a finger, then two inside. "Tell me."

Gad tightened his hole, trapping Cazzo's fingers inside. Cazzo wiggled his fingers, inserting a third, then a fourth. He whispered, "Open sesame." The mouth of the cave yawned, and Cazzo added his thumb. Gad let out a helpless, ecstatic groan. Cazzo quickly knelt and, lifting up his kilt, plunged into him for the third time in as many hours.

Both hand and cock inside him, Gad sighed. "Oh. Oh. Ohhh!"

"Tell me about these men who would pay you? Where can I find them? Would they pay me, too? Would they pay us double together?"

Cazzo, his cock in his hand, began to jerk himself off inside Gad. At this, Gad bucked up, clenching and releasing Cazzo, clenching and releasing. "Maybe…Maybe…"

Cazzo stroked faster.

"Yes, definitely…ohhh…ohhh…"

Cazzo sat against the headboard. Gad, his head in Cazzo's lap, nuzzled his cock. "Are you in love with me?" Cazzo asked casually.

"Maybe—if being in love means being too sore to be fucked again."

Cazzo laughed. "Are there really men who would pay for… this?" He ran his hand along the impossible length of his cock, dislodging Gad's face.

"Yes."

. . . .

Cazzo had left Gad fully intending to return to Joseph to show him his new jacket, but seeing the bright lights of a nearby bar where Gad had told him men willing to pay for sex gathered, he forgot about poor, broke Joseph and his promise. He pulled the bar's door open and stepped inside.

×

THESE WERE WILD AND STORMY NIGHTS
(CAZZO FALLS IN WITH RENT BOYS)

A RRIVING LATE TO the production, Cazzo took center stage, relegating the incumbent rent boys to the chorus where they had no choice but to lap at his leftovers and wait for his reign to end. In the meantime, to while away the increasingly long hours between tricks, the rent boys indulged in a game of bickering one-upmanship: who was the tallest; who was the handsomest; who had the biggest dick; who turned the most tricks; who had the biggest profit margin when you evaluated time spent versus dollars earned; what was the best marketing strategy—hiding one's goods and counting on the allure of the mystery of conquering the unknown, or putting one's merchandise on full display; who was most likely to leave this life behind and for how long, for many had escaped only to return months, or weeks, later when the Daddy ran out of sugar.

Cazzo entered the trade of hustling like a great locomotive pulling into a dark, rarely visited, country station. There was great excitement on both sides, and much shouting and whispering in wonder, and whistling in abject pleasure at the beauty and raw power of the driving engine. There were great white plumes of satisfaction being expelled at startling intervals; lust satisfied pealed like old church bells, and his partners like overexcited railway conductors shouted instructions—*this way, watch your step, harder, faster, all aboard!*

These were wild and stormy nights. The sex was tremendous and their shared orgasms so vivid and bright that the world seemed on fire. Together, Cazzo and his clients cried out and whistled lustily, inciting each other into creaking and groaning as satisfaction arrived and moved into contentment then exhaustion.

For all his efforts, he was rewarded with fists full of dollars and purses filled with coin of the realm. It had never been like this with Daddy, and this was why he thought, forgetting his early rash promise to Joseph, one should never settle for sex with just one's lover.

Bored with waiting for his reign to end, each night, the rent boys gathered and demanded to know the secret of Cazzo's popularity. He haughtily ignored them, only to have his secret revealed one evening when he heedlessly stood on the grate vent that aerated the underground tunnels through which the trolley ran. A trolley running late sent up a gust of air so strong, it blew his kilt into the air in the style of Marilyn Monroe. "Oh!" the rent boys said in unison and admiration.

THE REPTILIAN MOUTH, HANGING WIDE OPEN,
CAME AT CAZZO WITH THE VELOCITY OF A BULLET
(CAZZO MEETS A SERPENT)

H E HAD COARSE, rather reptilian features adorning a large head, which was capped with a towering yellow pompadour that had been moussed into cresting waves so violent it made Cazzo slightly seasick while the color reminded him of a particularly vivid corn pudding.

The man pulled from his purse five gold coins. "I'll pay you in these," he said, placing the coins in a small stack on the floor. Leaning back on the bed, he beckoned Cazzo closer. Cazzo dropped his kilt, freeing his erection, and caressed it lightly.

The man tumbled off the bed onto his knees and grasped Cazzo's hips. Cazzo leaned back and playfully slapped his cock against the man's cheek. The man released his hips and rocked back on his haunches. Without taking his round, black eyes off Cazzo, he opened his mouth and removed his teeth, which apparently were false. Then he shook his head until his mouth waggled open. Next, he slammed his fist into his jaw; his jaw unhinged.

The reptilian mouth, hanging wide open, came at Cazzo with the velocity of a bullet. In sudden terror, Cazzo touched the man's head to delay the consummation. The yellow pompadour slipped and fell to the floor. Cazzo's caressing fingers massaged a scalp that was slightly scaly and cool in the hot room.

With a drawing of his breath, the man sucked Cazzo in like a mongoose would have sucked a hen's egg; he swallowed him with such violence and avidity that Cazzo felt faint, growing dizzy with sensation as the man's mouth engulfed him. The head of his cock brushed against the man's tonsils as it slid down his throat. The man's tongue tickled his scrotum.

Cazzo became suddenly alarmed and pulled out of the man's mouth. When his cock popped free, he fell backwards. His hands, at his sides and behind him, broke his fall.

The man's flat, unblinking eyes bulged from their sockets as he fell with a sinuous grace from his kneeling position to a prone one. His mouth, which still hung open as if about to receive communion, hissed at him. Drool pooled on the floor. His feet, crossed at the ankles, seemed to merge into a bifurcated tail; he now appeared more serpent than man. Cazzo recoiled and on his hands and feet scuttled sideways like a crab towards the front door. He reached for the pile of gold coins he'd been promised and was shocked when his hand closed on a fistful of scales. Reaching the hall, he kicked the apartment's door closed and collapsed on the landing.

I'M AFRAID MY EYE WAS BIGGER THAN MY ASSHOLE
(CAZZO GETS REJECTED)

O H, STOP. PLEASE, stop!" the man squealed, and when Cazzo did not, lamented, "You're hurting me."

"What?" Cazzo asked, puzzled.

"Stop! You're too big. You're tearing me apart."

"I'm too big now, am I? You saw how big I was, and you wanted me still. You begged your boyfriend to rent me for you—"

"I did. I'm afraid, though, that my eye was bigger than my asshole…"

"C'mon," his boyfriend cajoled. "You can do it—I want to see you take it all. Show me how open you can get. You know I want to see your hole wrecked in a way I can't with my own small penis."

"No, please."

"You promised!"

"No, I tell you. He's too big!"

"You'd break your promise? But it's my birthday. You said I could do anything I wanted with you." The boyfriend wailed with a disappointed child's petulance. "I want you to do this for me."

"We can try again—with someone else. Someone smaller."

They began to fight, and Cazzo slipped off the bed unnoticed, wrapped his kilt—now so long it practically reached his ankles—around his waist and, stepping into his boots, palmed the stack of twenties on the dresser and left the lovers to their arguing and negotiating.

XIII

CRY ME A FUCKING RIVER
(CAZZO RETURNS TO JOSEPH)

PERHAPS PREDICTABLY, CAZZO'S popularity began to wane as his kilt lengthened. He came to be regarded as a freak, a kind of circus sideshow with his outsized cock, long kilt, and black lace-up boots. He was rejected more and more often.

Finally, the train had reached its destination, and exhausted, his pockets bulging with gold coins and dollar bills, Cazzo made his way back to Joseph.

To derail Joseph's anger, as he did so often in the past, Cazzo moved to reveal his nakedness. He unbuckled his kilt and let it fall to the floor in a puddle of fabric that reached the top of his boots. Joseph stared at him in disbelief.

"What?! What is this that I see? You are...deformed..."

"I'm not deformed. I've merely grown—"

"Into a monstrosity—to match the monstrosity of what you have done."

"I did nothing."

"You sold what was not yours to sell. Oh, how could you do this to me?" Joseph wailed. "After everything I have done— I gave you life!"

"You gave me nothing. You used me like a toy."

"I loved you."

"I gave you—and every other man I came across—what you wanted, what you cared about most—"

"I wanted you to love me—only me. You said you'd love only me. You said you wouldn't lie and cheat, but all you *do* is lie and cheat!"

"Oh, cry me a fucking river, why don't you?"

Joseph did as he was bid. And Cazzo, being made of lifelike, lightweight silicone, floated to safety, while Joseph, flesh and bone and weighed down with grief, was washed by the relentless torrent of his tears into The Great River, and lost.

XIV

SHOW ME WHAT YOU'VE GOT, BIG BOY
(CAZZO GETS CAREER ADVICE)

SHOW ME WHAT you've got, Big Boy," the man with a Southern accent and golden eyes growled drunkenly.

Cazzo, by this time feeling the sting of rejection too often, had stopped receiving propositions so that the man had to repeat his demand.

"Me?" Cazzo asked, surprised.

"You. Look around. Do you see anyone else?"

It was true. Cazzo was alone. The man folded a hundred-dollar bill and slipped it into the waistband of Cazzo's kilt. "You'll get the rest after. Now follow me."

Cazzo dropped his kilt. The man stared at him open-mouthed for a long moment, then looked around the room at everything but Cazzo and what dangled tantalizingly and alarmingly large between his legs.

Watching the man's eyes through his own cat's eyes, Cazzo imagined he was watching a school of intoxicated goldfish swimming in tequila. Finally, looking at him, the man drawled, his accent somehow more pronounced than before, "What do you expect me to do with that? Throw it over my shoulder and burp it?"

Cazzo, confused by the sudden rejection, felt his face grow hot, and his sizable appendage seemed to shrink ever so slightly. He put his kilt back on. "Why did you pick me up?" he demanded.

"You have that look I like—completely artificial. As if God decided to remake man after a lost weekend watching too many pornos and reading Tom of Finland."

"You still owe me a hundred," Cazzo said.

"Indeed, I do." The man handed him the money. Now he offered him an additional fifty. "With my apologies. I was unnecessarily cruel in my rejection."

"It's OK," Cazzo said. "I'm used to it."

"Look. *Cazzo*—is it?" The man chuckled. "Look, you're too much for real men like me, but you could totally do movies."

"Movies? I always wanted to be an actor."

The man laughed drunkenly but not unkindly. "I'm not talking Hollywood. I'm talking porn."

"Porn?"

He sighed. "Porn. Sex movies. God, your head is as thick as your cock, isn't it?" Before Cazzo could take offense, he continued, "There's a specific market—fetish porn—where you'd fit right in—"

"But I'm not really an actor despite my desire to act."

"Pish. They're not actors either. They're more like circus performers—acrobats and sword swallowers, contortionists and freaks of every stripe, to be honest. But they get paid well, and there would be men who could take you on as if you were a hot dog."

Cazzo brightened. "Really? How do I find this...um... what is it?"

"It's a production company." He gave Cazzo a card with an address in a building in the lower thirties named after the scion of an industrial family who later went on to form a large studio dedicated exclusively to family entertainment.

"Do I just show up there?"

"Well, you'll have to audition, but I suspect you will pass that easily enough."

"Thank you," Cazzo said with uncharacteristic gratitude.

XV

I'M CANDLEWYCK NOW
(CAZZO MEETS AN OLD FRIEND)

CAZZO'S AUDITION CONSISTED of dropping his pants and getting an erection so he could be measured and tested for hardness. (Did you know that anal sex requires a penis that's thirty percent harder than for vaginal sex?) He also had to simulate sex noises and make an "I'm coming" face. This last part was the hardest, as he'd never come in front of a mirror with his eyes open.

The director, who looked rather like a hedgehog, brown and prickly, congratulated Cazzo on passing his audition, handed him a sheaf of forms to complete and directed him to wardrobe and the still photographer for his promotional photos. He would do his first scene later that day with Candlewyck, a studio veteran, the director explained, and one of its biggest stars.

. . . .

Candlewyck had presented at his first audition, some years earlier, introducing himself with his given name. His first name was innocuous enough, but paired with his last name, it became Christian and multisyllabic; it was fraught with Biblical meaning. On hearing it, the director had frowned and looked him up and down with the cold, appraising eye of a diamond merchant evaluating an uncut diamond. Noting he was long and thin and pale and blond and intense, the director had promptly renamed him Candlewyck.

"You're a porn actor," the director, himself a former porn actor, told him. "You are no longer a person. To be successful, you must wear the mask of a porn actor. Off camera, you can take it off, but you must always wear it on camera. It is your brand. It is what viewers want you to be, and they want you to always be that. Understand?"

Candlewyck became his porn name. And as the mask endured as the face itself, it became his chosen name as well.

The director introduced Candlewyck to Cazzo on the set where they would be filming. Candlewyck had been doing fisting porn for a while. Heck, he was known for "arm swallowing," but this was something altogether different. Candlewyck had never seen a dick quite like this one, though there was something vaguely familiar about it. The head was as big as any fist he'd ever gobbled up; it was as long as a man's leg, and thick as a hambone. Still, he was game. Especially since this shoot was paying twice as much as usual and promised to catapult him into the stratosphere of the porn industry.

. . . .

Cazzo watched his would be co-star approach. He was slender and rough-looking. His body was smooth and hairless and very, very white, without a freckle or the slightest blemish or hint of color that might have indicated he had once been kissed by the sun. He wore tiny shorts and what had started its life as a tank top but which was now, thanks to the clever intervention of a pair of scissors and a natural aversion to wearing clothes, a loincloth for his abs.

Cazzo smiled nervously under his co-star's scrutiny. When Candlewyck brushed his blond hair off his forehead and looked at him with his light eyes, Cazzo recognized him. "Gad? Gad is that you?"

Candlewyck nodded. "Cazzo?"

"Yes, it's me. Fancy meeting up again like this."

Candlewyck said nothing.

"Gad—"

"I'm Candlewyck now."

"Candlewyck—"

"You just left and never came back."

Cazzo shrugged, he hoped charmingly. "Were you in love with me?"

"I thought I was. You were everything I wanted and a person. You made me think—if only for a few hours—that I could be a hole *and* loved. But then you walked away and showed me that you only wanted what every other man I'd ever met wanted—an unresisting hole to shove his dick or his fist or his foot in. I became what I'd already feared I was—what I am today. A hole."

"Gad—Candlewyck—I'm sorry."

Candlewyck shrugged. "Don't be. You showed me that dreams were for other people. Not people like me."

"I dream, too. I dream of being a real man."

"Yeah, well, good luck with that. Listen, I have to get to the gym—gotta be pumped up for tomorrow. I'll see you in the morning." Candlewyck picked up his gym bag and walked away.

Candlewyck arrived bright and cheerful and wearing scarcely more clothes than before. If he recalled their conversation from the previous evening, he gave no indication of it when he arrived on set. He greeted Cazzo with warm professionalism.

As he moved about, being fussed over by the makeup artist, the wardrobe person and various assistants and flunkies of indeterminate role, Candlewyck burned with bright charisma, and like a moth, Cazzo found himself unable to resist the allure of the flaming pyre.

Candlewyck was polite and relaxed when the two assistants lifted him into the sling to film his scene with Cazzo. He smiled encouragingly.

Cazzo blinked in the bright lights, but he went to work diligently. It had been so long since a man had allowed his monstrous swollen member inside him. With Candlewyck, it was like being swallowed by a warm, wet, bottomless canyon; no matter how hard or far he pushed, he felt he could still go deeper, push harder. There was no resistance. He was warmed and welcomed. He was ecstatic.

Almost before he knew it, he was approaching climax, Candlewyck moaning and encouraging beneath his assault: *Harder. Deeper. Oh, oh, ohhh!*

"This is it," the director shouted. "The money shot! Pull out! Pull out so we can catch it on camera!"

Cazzo pulled back and back and back. When he was finally free from Candlewyck's swallowing, greedy hole, his orgasm shot onto the camera lens and drenched the cameraman with its slick bounty, making him gasp in horror and admiration.

After the fluffer had cleaned him and Candlewyck and the poor cameraman, and the cleaners had scrubbed every surface with disinfectant and changed the sheets and the lights were turned off, Cazzo asked Candlewyck, "Would you like to get some dinner?'

"What?" Candlewyck demanded. "No. Listen, this wasn't a date or even a hookup. It was a movie, a job. It was great and all—really, *truly*—but it was nothing more than a job well done. So, don't be getting all dewy-eyed and asking me out on a date.

I don't need drama or romance. You're just a dick—a big, fat, juicy, *amazing* dick. Usually, only getting fisted gets me off, but you—*that*—" He pointed at Cazzo's dick, and Cazzo's breath quickened. "You're way bigger than I remembered and even better than I remembered, and believe me, I've carried memories of our night together." Recovering himself, stepping back into character, Candlewyck shrugged. "But still just a dick."

Cazzo's cheeks flamed, and his great cat's eyes filled.

Seeing his unexpected hurt, Candlewyck softened. "Look, I'm sorry. That probably came off as harsh. I wasn't trying to insult you when I said you were just a dick. Hell, I'm just a hole. And that's OK. Besides," he continued touching Cazzo's face and smoothing away a tear, "I can't eat tonight. I have another scene to shoot, and I have two clients to service after that."

"You do this with clients?"

"Sure. I told you, I'm just a hole. The hottest hole and the best in the business, but still just a hole, and I need to make coin while I'm still hot."

Cazzo saw Candlewyck in a new light and cringed. He felt ashamed. He set about the difficult task of strapping his cock to his leg and then wrapping his kilt around his waist.

XVI

BEING A MAN MEANS DOING HARD,
UNCOMFORTABLE THINGS. IT MEANS DOING THINGS
YOU WANT MORE THAN ANYTHING NOT TO HAVE TO DO
(CAZZO PROMISES TO MAKE AMENDS)

B ACK AT HOME, Cazzo told the Magical of his adventure, his cheeks enflamed through the entire humiliating tale. "I miss my Daddy so much," he wailed.

The Magical went to make him a soothing cup of tea.

Recounting his tale, Cazzo had become helplessly excited at remembering what it had felt like to be buried in Candlewyck. The more he remembered, the thicker and longer he grew until his cock was like an elephant's trunk beneath his kilt.

"I miss my dear Daddy," Cazzo repeated when the Magical returned with his tea. "And then there's the burden of this." He gestured at the elephant's trunk beneath his kilt. "I'm so tired."

"That does seem rather burdensome," the Magical remarked.

"I can no longer wear pants," Cazzo complained. "I can only wear a kilt, and now, for the sake of decency, it must reach my ankles."

"I once told you to be careful you didn't grow too big for your britches. I also warned you your cock would grow each time you broke your promise of fidelity. Do you remember?"

"No."

"Well, I did, and you replied your dick could never be too big."

"I was wrong. No one wants me to fuck them anymore."

"Will you be true to Joseph?"

"Yes." Cazzo thought of his poor dear Daddy and then immediately thought of Candlewyck, of fucking him while simultaneously jerking himself off. He stood to shrug off his excitement and stumbled when his elephant's trunk, heavy as a cannon, didn't move with him.

The Magical laughed.

"How can you laugh at me?" Cazzo demanded, anxious at the increasing weight and immobility of his elephant's trunk. Embarrassed and mad, he tried to leave only to discover he was anchored in place.

He looked so unhappy, the Magical felt sorry for him. With a shrill whistle, they summoned a flock of micro dragons of the same size and mystery of hummingbirds. Opening their mouth and releasing a series of very unmusical blue notes, they set the dragons to work; the dragons' light fiery breath melted Cazzo's manhood and reshaped it until it was smaller but roughly the size of a very well-hung Brazilian porn star.

"Oh, thank you, Magical!" Cazzo cried with relief, easily tucking himself away. Still, not one to be satisfied, he added, "I wish I was a real man."

"Being a man," the Magical said, "means doing hard, uncomfortable things. It means doing things you want more than anything not to have to do."

"Like what?"

"Like learning from your mistakes. Like learning from those who are wiser than you. Like making amends."

Cazzo nodded enthusiastically. "I can make amends. I will go and find my Daddy and make amends. Oh, thank you, Magical, for your guidance."

The Magical, dubious and blue, smiled encouragingly. "Godspeed, Cazzo, Godspeed."

XVII

YOU WERE A TOY TO TAKE UP AND USE,
THEN ABANDON, WITHOUT THE ABILITY
TO OBJECT OR CONSENT TO YOUR USE OR ABUSE
(CAZZO MEETS GOOD OLD BOYS DRINKING
WHISKEY AND RYE AND SINGING)

CAZZO OPENED THE door to the apartment he'd shared with Joseph. As they did every night when he came home, the buds on the vines that crisscrossed the balcony wall stretched on their stems hoping to see Joseph. Not seeing him, disappointed, the buds once again burst in blooms of red, like burst blood vessels or welts raised on a saint's abused flesh. Seeing the blood burst, a silent, daily rebuke, Cazzo turned away and headed back out the door into the night.

Fleeing the apartment and the judgment of the flowering vines, Cazzo wandered aimlessly, as was his wont since he'd begun searching for Joseph. Cazzo passed a bar named Cranky Joe's. At the outside bar, four good old boys were drinking whiskey and rye and singing raucous songs. It was quite a sight to behold, and Cazzo paused in his perambulations to watch them.

The most belligerent of the four verbally accosted him, demanding, "Yo! Watcho lookin' at?"

The men were unremarkable; outside of their boisterousness, they had nothing to recommend them, but Cazzo was drawn to the leather bomber jacket one of them was wearing. Now, he answered, "Your jacket."

"Ah, you like it?" the man asked, turning up the collar and caressing the soft leather admiringly. "Wanna buy it?"

"I have no money," Cazzo answered truthfully, "but we can trade."

"Trade? Has that ever worked?"

"Yes. It's how I got this jacket," Cazzo replied, indicating the purple-and-aqua letterman's jacket he was wearing, which until he spotted the leather bomber jacket had been his favorite article of clothing ever.

"You traded for that? I'd have thought you got it for lettering in cocksucking." He poked the good old boy nearest him in the ribs and guffawed.

"No," Cazzo said earnestly. "I traded this for it." He grabbed his crotch.

The good old boys sobered. "Well, looka here, fellas, we got us a goddamned fairy!"

Cazzo frowned. "I'm not a Magical." Then more firmly, he added, "I'm a man."

"A man who wants to be a woman! Let's get 'im, boys, and make him the woman he wants to be." As a unit, they lurched toward Cazzo, who, startled, stepped back and, tripping on his untied shoelaces, tumbled to the ground. The good old boys fell on him. Cazzo, unaccustomed to violence, didn't know how to react and so didn't resist.

The four good old boys dragged him down a long, dark alley to a chain-link fence. Hoisting him upright, they stretched out his arms and, with cord they produced seemingly out of thin air, tied him to the fence so that he hung awkwardly.

The most timid good old boy, the one who seemed least sure of their enterprise, volunteered to act as lookout. Cazzo could see him at the mouth of the alley, his head swinging right then left, then right again, like the pendulum of a great, dysfunctional clock.

The one who'd first challenged Cazzo pulled a switchblade out of his pocket and slashed at Cazzo's pants, which fell to the ground in a khaki heap, revealing his cock, which was, even in its now-reduced state, stupendous. The men stared at him in surprise.

"Hollee crap, willya lookit that!"

Under their gazes, which were equal parts surprise, admiration, and envy, Cazzo started to get hard. As his cock rose and stretched, it began to throb; the vein that ran from its base to its head wiggled like a serpent. This seemed to infuriate the men, and they fell on him, punching, kicking.

"Let's make this fucker the woman he thinks he is," the one with the switchblade said before slashing at Cazzo's cock. The silicone gave way, then bounced back. Now he slashed at it madly. Each slice into the silicone healed almost as quickly as it formed. "What the hell?"

"Grab it and hold it, boys. I'll *saw* it off."

Two of the good old boys, first picking up handfuls of fallen leaves as kind of makeshift gloves, grabbed hold of Cazzo's cock and pulled it towards them, while the other sawed at it with his knife. Then, without warning, it began to rain—if you could call it that. A thick, blue moisture like motor oil fell from the sky. Everything became slippery, and the two good old boys lost their grip on Cazzo's cock. Suddenly released, it swung left and struck the man with the knife in the ribs, breaking several and knocking him to the ground. Terrified by the strange blue rain which clung to them and burned like acid, the two other good old boys grabbed their fallen comrade and, following the lookout who was already making haste down the street beyond the alley, half dragged and half carried him as they slipped and skidded along the alley.

Cazzo drooped insensate and barely conscious. Waking briefly, he cried out, "Help, help! Oh, poor pitiful me. Will no one come to help me?"

A quartet of pigeons, big as turkeys, flew into sight. They looked like garden-variety rock pigeons except for their size and their feathers, which were aquamarine rather than the usual sooty white and gray. Two of them set to work with their short beaks on the ties that bound Cazzo's wrists to the fence. Freed, Cazzo slid to the ground. Each bird grasped a wrist or an ankle in their talons and flew away with him, spreadeagled and drooping, a sagging Christ hanging from a cross made with his own hand, but safe in their grasp.

As they flew, the pigeons, urbane and quite learned, discussed the homophobia and culture of violence that accompanied it, and the role gays had played in their own oppression, and even the validity of gender-neutral pronouns which had co-opted the plural for use as the singular.

"You must take this medicine," the Magical said, this time appearing as a great snowy owl, white with knowledge, and flecks of blue, and crackling with parental concern.

"Is it quite bitter?"

"Quite."

"Then, I won't take it."

"Be aware, it's quite bitter, but not as bitter as your recent experience."

Cazzo made a face. "I won't take it."

"It will restore you."

"I won't take it."

"If you don't take it, you will become what you were before."

"What do you know of me before you met me?" Cazzo asked with not a little hostility, a hostility that was surprising in its passion given how weak he was.

"You were a toy to take up and use, then abandon, without the ability to object or consent to your use or abuse."

Cazzo opened his mouth and swallowed the bitter medicine.

XVIII

THE MAGICAL HAS PASSED
(CAZZO FINDS THE BEAUTIFUL APARTMENT EMPTY)

THE DOOR TO the Magical's apartment swung open when Cazzo knocked. Inside, the walls that had been painted shades of blue—the cobalt of an open field at dusk, the cerulean of a Caribbean sky after a hurricane, the Prussian blue of a sea at midnight—were bare and white; the magnificent Turkish carpets in indigo and azure and cornflower had been rolled up and taken away, leaving scuffed white ash floors.

Cazzo heard the soft swooshing of a broom going about its work and looked up just in time to catch the super secreting himself in a closet, lest he be discovered and asked to perform some task. Cazzo walked up to the closet door and knocked politely. His knock was met with silence, though he could hear the super's anxious breath. "Do come out, oh, Super. I won't ask you to do anything. I only ask if you know where my dear Magical has gone?"

The door swung open, and the super squinted at him suspiciously. "Indeed, I do," he said sadly. "She has passed on."

"They," Cazzo corrected him. "But where did they go?"

"You misunderstand me. The Magical has passed...*on*. They are no more."

"No. No, that cannot be."

"Indeed, it is," the super said, stepping out of the closet and resuming his sweeping of the scuffed, white ash floors. "They passed from a broken heart."

"A broken heart?"

"Yes. One can live with a broken arm or leg and even a broken brain—just look at the American president—but not with a broken heart."

Now, with the Magical gone and every man he met rejecting him, Cazzo began to miss his Daddy dear something fierce.

Daddy dear's absence began to tear at his heart, clawing tears from his eyes and ripping a piercing cry from his throat. Resolving to find him at last, Cazzo began walking across the city, peering into dumpsters and overturning trash cans and crawling through the collected leaves in curbside gutters. Tears streaming down his face, he staggered through the villages of the homeless beside highways and under railway bridges, lifting blankets of newspaper and peering into tents constructed from discarded trash bags. He crawled under rocks and clawed through weed-choked public gardens. And still, he could not find Joseph.

XIX

THAT'S LIFE, ALL IRONY AND INJUSTICE
(CAZZO REUNITES WITH AN OLD FRIEND
AND FINDS JOSEPH)

"OH, WHAT'S THE use—I will never find my poor Daddy,"
Cazzo wailed and sat on the edge of the pier overlooking
The Great River.

Cazzo was pulled out of his grief by the sound of another's
tears. He followed the sniffles to a bench, where he found a thin
man, pale as moonlight and barely clothed, stretched out.

"Candlewyck, is that you?" Cazzo asked.

"Yes, it is I, Candlewyck."

"Candlewyck, what happened?" Cazzo sat beside him and
took his pale, cold hand. He stared at Candlewyck's navel,
exposed by his midriff shirt; Candlewyck didn't so much wear
clothes as scraps of clothes.

"Candlewyck," Cazzo asked again, "what is it? What
is wrong?"

"Gad," Candlewyck said. "My name is Gad."

"Gad," Cazzo tried again. "Gad, what's wrong?"

"I fear I'm dying."

"How can you be dying? You're still young."

"But I'm tired. I am dying from overwork. You see, I worked
so hard. I wanted to be a star so badly, I didn't realize that all

stars—no matter how brightly they shine—die." He sniffled again. "Now that I am dying, I wish I had had dinner with you."

"Oh, Gad—"

"Thank you, Cazzo."

"For what?

"For *seeing me*. You saw me as a man when everybody else saw me—*and I saw myself*—as only a hole. But then again, I was a man and I wanted only to be a hole."

"Oh, the injustice. Oh, the terrible irony," Cazzo cried. "You are a man who wanted only to be a hole, and I am only a dick who wants more than anything to be a man."

"That's life," Gad said, "all irony and injustice." And then he died.

Cazzo sat for a long while, then dried his tears and, removing his purple-and-aqua letterman's jacket, laid it over the nearly naked Gad.

Continuing his quest, Cazzo asked every man who passed him in the falling night, "Have you seen my dear Daddy?"

"No," answered one man dressed in leather from head to foot, "But *I'll* be your Daddy."

"Oh, you don't understand," Cazzo said, beginning to cry again. "I've lost my one true Daddy."

"Oh, cry me a river," the leatherman said, adjusting his cap and walking on, making Cazzo cry harder. He cried until the pier beneath his feet became slippery with his grief; losing his footing, he tumbled into The Great River and was washed away.

The Great River, whose current only knew one route, carried him uptown and across Broadway, where it belched him into a sewer in the theatre district. Cazzo, made of silicone, floated in the stagnant water, eventually drifting into the broken plumbing lines of an abandoned, ramshackle theatre off Broadway.

Climbing out of the pipe into the damp gloom, Cazzo shook himself off and looked around. Seeing light at the end of a hall, he followed it until he came upon a small, bright, painted lamp on a small, painted bureau in a small, confined anteroom. Cazzo sat down to think at a little painted table which held a painted loaf of French bread and a painted jug of wine. Because they were both painted, he was able to eat and drink while avoiding both carbs and a hangover.

He'd been sitting and thinking for quite some time when he noticed age and damp were causing the painted sets to flake and peel; already, there were crumbs of bread falling from the table. Soon he'd have nothing to eat.

Cazzo cried out, "Help, help! Oh, poor pitiful me. Will no one come to help me?"

Joseph's ears pricked up at the sound of crying. He had been in this infernal place for more than two years and until now had not heard a sound. The current of his tears, combined with the relentless heavy rains, had washed him into the basement storeroom of an abandoned, ramshackle theatre off Broadway. The room contained the remains from the set of a revival of *Pinocchio*: a wooden fireplace containing a painted roaring fire which had kept him warm and dry, and a painted stove on top of which boiled a painted pot of sweet potatoes. The potatoes were bland but nutritious; a painted frying pan contained a frying fish, but since it was painted it released no odor, a very good thing, for Joseph couldn't abide the smell of frying fish. The pools of salt water, sourced from his tears, eddying about his bare feet, soothed his skin and kept him clean.

Hearing the crying again, he rose from his painted chair and made his way into the dark and damp hallway. He saw light. Now he could hear words: "Help! Help! Oh, poor pitiful me." He hurried towards the voice.

Joseph entered a small anteroom containing a painted bureau and lamp and a small, painted table with some breadcrumbs, a few drops of painted wine, and…Cazzo.

"Cazzo?"

"Daddy? Daddy! Is it really you?" Cazzo cried, throwing himself at Joseph's feet and hugging his knees. "Oh, Daddy, I've found you at last."

"Get up, dear boy. Come, stand, let me look at you," Joseph ordered.

Cazzo stood as Joseph inspected him.

"Yes, you are still good-looking, but then you were finely made. You've held up well."

"Daddy, have you come to save me?"

"I? Save you? Surely you have come to save *me*."

"I save you?" Cazzo said in astonishment. "But look at you—you are healthy and robust. I am in danger of wasting away for I have barely any bread or wine left."

Taking pity on his creation—for what else is a father to do?—Joseph said, "Come with me. I have fried fish and some boiled potatoes that are bland but nutritious."

. . . .

Now that he had eaten his fill of fried fish and boiled potatoes, Cazzo tried to think of a way out for him and Joseph. There *had* to be a way to escape this theatrical dungeon, this anteroom to doom. He wished for the first time that his head contained brains instead of two grades of silicone.

The stairs had long ago collapsed, and the disintegrating floorboards were unreliable. Plus, the building was boarded up. The slats between the boards covering the windows through which Joseph had passed when the river washed him into the basement had grown narrow, or perhaps Joseph had grown wide. In any case, they couldn't get out that way. The plumbing pipe out of which he himself had climbed was filled with water; Joseph would surely drown.

Just then, there came a great crash; the building shuddered, and a shaft of sunlight pierced the dark. It was then that Cazzo remembered watching a news story on one of the great billboards in Times Square: a row of abandoned theatres off Broadway were to be demolished. Surely this had to be one of those old theatres scheduled for demolition.

There was another tremendous crash, and the building shuddered again. A great black wrecking wall burst through a masonry wall, sending dust flying and splintering the ancient boards sealing the windows. Sunlight flooded the basement as the wrecking ball dangled inert from a heavy black chain not far above their heads.

"Come, Daddy," Cazzo called, "we must make our escape!"

Joseph stumbled into the light, squinting. "How?"

"We need to jump up there." Cazzo pointed to the ruined wall above their heads.

"Are you mad? I cannot jump up there."

"I know you can't, but I can. Quickly, get on my back and put your arms tight around my neck. I'll take care of the rest."

Joseph was dubious but did as he was told. Cazzo squatted and, bouncing on the silicone balls of his feet, launched them into the air. Opening his arms, he embraced the wrecking ball; his open palms, like suction cups, stuck to the ball as it dislodged itself from the theatre's dusty interior and swung into the street.

Once they were clear, Cazzo released his grip, and he and Joseph fell into a massive dumpster, which fortunately was filled with old playbills and mattresses and insulation.

Unfortunately, all of the soft materials on which they landed combined together created a kind of trampoline, and they no sooner landed than they were catapulted out of the dumpster and into The Great River.

"Acck," Joseph coughed as river water splashed over him. "What good was escaping only to drown in this filthy river?"

"Hang on, Daddy. I can swim," Cazzo called over his shoulder, and he began to swim with all his might.

Alas, they had a great distance to travel, and the river was hostile. Tiring, Cazzo's normally light-as-a-feather silicone limbs began to feel leaden, and more than once he sank, causing them both to splutter and spit out grimy water on breaking the surface again. "Oh, woe is me," Cazzo cried. "I have acted very stupidly again, and now my poor Daddy will drown in this filthy river."

As soon as these distressing words fell from his lips and he began to lose hope, a large blue cuttlefish swam up under them and called out, "Hang on." The cuttlefish wrapped four of his eight arms around them and took off like a speedboat gliding above the waves.

The cuttlefish swam along the pier until they came to a jetty that dipped down into the water. Here, it used its arms to set Joseph and Cazzo on dry ground. "Thank you, Cuttlefish," Cazzo called as the cuttlefish turned around and sank below the river's surface.

"Now what?" Joseph asked.

"Now we walk home."

"But it is so very far away."

"I know. We shall walk slowly and rest often, and when you are too tired even to sit and rest, I shall carry you, Daddy dear." And true to his words, he did.

When Cazzo opened the door to Joseph's apartment, Joseph gasped, for the linenfold paneling on the walls gleamed, the crystal chandeliers sparkled, and the vines on the terrace, stretching to see if Joseph had returned, birthed large yellow flowers.

"But how can this be?" Joseph wondered. "I thought surely the bank would have foreclosed by now."

"I paid them off."

"You? How?"

"I worked."

"Worked? What work are you fit for? I made you for one purpose."

"Yes, and it is a purpose I was well suited for—you said so yourself." Cazzo hung his head. "I worked as a prostitute."

"You what? Testa di Cazzo!"

"Judge me if you must, but I am not ashamed. Sex work *is* work. It can also be honorable work if you want it to be—"

"I cannot believe you sold yourself. You know how I felt about that."

"Yes. But being a man means doing hard uncomfortable things…"

Joseph was cranky and unforgiving, so Cazzo bid him goodnight and retired to the small study where he spread a blanket and lay down on the ancient chesterfield sofa. Exhausted, he soon fell asleep. And while he slept, he thought he saw the Magical, happily blue and smiling.

"Magical," Cazzo cried in joy. "You've been restored!"

"Yes. The tears of your genuine grief were as nourishing rains after a drought."

"Oh, Magical, I am so happy to see you alive. It has all been so very hard without you and my poor dear Daddy."

"You have done well, Cazzo. Blessed are the sons who minister tenderly to their parents and forgive them their judgments. You have proven yourself to be an excellent son. My gift for your good and caring ways is my forgiveness of all your wrongs."

"Might I have another present?"

The Magical was surprised by his impertinence. "Why, what greater gift could you ask for than forgiveness?"

"I want to be a real man."

"Ah! Be careful what you wish for Cazzo," the Magical warned.

"It's not a wish, it's my dream. And I deserve to have it come true."

"Sleep, Cazzo, sleep," the Magical said. "Do not agitate yourself further."

"Oh, go!" Cazzo shouted. "What good are you? Just go and leave me alone!"

With those words, the Magical slowly dissolved into a cloud of powder-blue dust and gently blew away like a cloud scudding across a stormy sky.

BE CAREFUL WHAT YOU WISH FOR
(CAZZO BECOMES A REAL MAN AT LAST)

IMAGINE HIS ASTONISHMENT when upon awakening, Cazzo felt quite made of flesh and blood instead of silicone. In fact, Cazzo was quite bewildered; he couldn't tell if he was fully awake and living or asleep and dreaming with his eyes wide open.

Collapsed in a heap in the corner, his former self was so muddled and weak it was impossible to imagine it had ever stood and walked and fucked like a man. On the floor beside it, a puddle of silicone congealed; at its center, his former magnificent cock lay, its large balls flattened, oozing like two soft-boiled eggs dashed against a wall.

Cazzo ran to the pier glass leaning against the wall in the living room. Before it, he saw what appeared to be his reflection: pale skin, bristly dark hair, and worse—worst of all—his magnificent cock, *his elephant's trunk*, was now a shriveled Vienna sausage!

"Magical! What have you *done*?"

He ran back into the bedroom on thin, spindly legs. "Daddy, Daddy dear! Wake up!"

Joseph snorted and rolled over. Cazzo drew back in horror, for in Joseph's place was a horrible old man with a scraggly white beard that scarcely covered a wrinkled turkey's neck.

"Who are you?" Joseph asked, alarmed. Even his voice was different, hoarse, his pronunciation coarse.

"Where's Joseph?"

Joseph squinted. "Why, I'm right here," he said. "But who is asking? Who are you?"

"Daddy, what happened?"

"I...don't know..." Joseph rasped, perplexed that he was being questioned so aggressively by this rude stranger.

Be careful what you wish for. The words floated on the air, each letter a dancing blue mockery. *Be careful what you wish for.* Cazzo covered his ears and closed his eyes. The words, dissolving into dust, blew against his closed eyes and over his stopped-up ears, tinting the air light blue, then cobalt, then black.

The End

Act 3:
Into the Unknown

Nothing makes you grow up faster than death and fame. Now, just a few years into my second decade, I found myself hurtling, headlong and unsure, into adulthood. Into the unknown.

Chapter 42

TRISTAN

M Y DAD IS *dying. I am twenty-three years old, and I am about to be orphaned.* I blinked and tried to focus on the doctor's words.

"How could I not have known he was this sick? You must think I'm a terrible son," I said. Since we'd returned from Paris, I'd noticed he'd seemed slower, quieter, but I'd assumed it was just age.

"No, no. We think no such thing."

Beside me, Javier was looking desperate and frantically rubbing my hands, which were cold.

"How—what happened?"

"Your father has a rare form of a very aggressive cancer of the lymph nodes. We didn't think this treatment option would help much, but he refused to go to one of the larger university hospitals that offer more options including some promising clinical trials of experimental treatments."

I knew without having to ask him that Dad had refused to go to a university hospital because they were farther away and would be harder for me to get to. He was an excellent son, and excellent sons are always considerate, placing the needs of others above their own. Perhaps that's where I had fallen down as an excellent son in service to my mother: I'd placed my need to love Max above my mother's need for me to be...*otherwise.*

"How…how long does he have?" Javier asked, pulling me out of my head and back into the conversation.

"It's hard to say really," Dad's doctor, a small-framed Asian woman, said. My dad, I knew, thought the world of her. "It could be a few months. It could be a few weeks."

"Though," the attending hospice doctor, a tall, ashen man with a face like sour milk and the demeanor of a pallbearer added, "I shouldn't be surprised if he only had a couple of weeks."

· · · · · · · · · · · · · · · · · · · ·

The chaplain, a mild-mannered, harried man, arranged for a CD player for Dad's room. I brought his favorite CDs from home: Placido Domingo and Harry Belafonte—Dad's taste was nothing if not eclectic. Sometimes we'd watch the daytime soap operas; he'd fill me in on all the characters and their history and past shenanigans; other times we'd sing along with his CDs, mostly Harry Belafonte's "Jump in the Line (Shake, Señora)." I read to him from the magazines Javier brought: *Hello*; *English Cottage Living*; *Italian Vogue*; *People*; *Martha Stewart*. One rainy Saturday, I read to him from the leather-bound edition of *Pinocchio* he'd gotten for me one Christmas.

Chapter 43

TRISTAN

"SO, YOU MET Dr. Gloom-and-Doom?" Dad asked.

"Yes."

"Did he say I'd be dead tomorrow?"

"No. Two weeks, actually."

Dad chuckled. "I hate him."

"I hate him, too." I watched Dad and envied his equanimity.

I hadn't brought my mother up in conversation since our flight to Korea six years earlier. Now, as Dad lay dying, I found I was finally ready to talk about her.

"Did you love her?" I asked him.

JOHN

HOW COULD I tell Tristan, yes, I loved her? How could I explain it had become increasingly clear to me that I could only love one of them, that I needed to choose? If I'd honored my vows and chosen her, I'd have had to stay, but she'd have destroyed him. And if I'd chosen him, I'd have had to leave and take him with me. What good would it do to admit to him now that I'd chosen him, but that I hadn't made the decision to leave soon enough?

"I did," I said.

"Do you think she loved you?"

I was surprised by the question. I couldn't tell him yes, I thought she loved me, but then he'd come along and she'd had no room left in her heart for anything or anyone *but* him? How could I tell him that I'd learned that some women are like that—the child matters most? That I supposed that's why black widow spiders kill their mates?

"I think so. I think she loved us both." Him more than me, to be sure, but there was no need to tell him that.

"Tristan, you've been an excellent son. I'm sorry I wasn't a better father."

"Are you kidding?" Tristan looked at me in that intense way of his. "You've been the best dad I could have asked for."

"I meant before your mother died. I must have seemed disinterested, removed…"

"Not always. Just sometimes."

"Honestly, I never meant to cede my role as a father, but your mother convinced me that everything I did was wrong. Mistakes I could have lived with, but she also convinced me that my every mistake was causing you actual harm—and that I couldn't bear the idea that I might hurt you so I…stepped back. Later, after you started walking and talking, I again held back because the two of you seemed to have an innate understanding of each other, despite your mother's failure with her spreadsheets. And you shared a language I didn't speak or understand—"

"But I don't speak Korean."

I laughed. "You did. Until you were about five. I'll never forget, we were having dinner, and you and your mother were having a conversation in Korean—I have no idea what it was about, but you looked so serious, and then you switched to English. When your mother asked why—*in Korean*—you answered in English that it wasn't fair to speak in a language I didn't understand in front of me."

"I did?"

"You did. Even then, you had this sense of fairness, this affinity for the excluded. You were like a juvenile Jesus—

you were forever bringing home stray cats and wounded birds. It's how you and Judy became friends. She was this overweight kid with pigtails that everyone teased and no one would talk to, so you befriended her... Anyway, that night at dinner, you refused to talk in Korean. Your mother was so frustrated, but you never spoke in Korean again. And if she spoke to you in Korean, you would only answer in English, and you would translate for me what she'd said before you would answer."

Chapter 44

JAVIER

I WAS STANDING IN Papa's hospital room with my back to the door, looking out the window at the churning brown river which seemed intent on capsizing the occasional speedboats and the barges that were being loaded and unloaded at intervals along its length.

The dementia patient down the hall was screaming. This time, she was accusing the nurses of stealing her shoes so she couldn't leave.

"Hello."

I turned around and found myself facing a nurse's aide carrying a tray.

"Hi."

"You must be Javier," she said, setting the tray down.

"I am. How did you know?"

"Your father talks about you all the time."

"He's not my father."

"But you call him 'Papa,' right? And he thinks of you as his son."

I blinked against what I would have sworn was a stray eyelash in my eye, making it tear in irritation.

She winked at me. "He worries you're too wild to ever settle down. Anyway," she continued, changing the subject, "your father should be back from radiation in about twenty minutes.

If his lunch is cold, just press that button beside his bed and someone will come and warm it up for you."

"Um, sure, thanks."

She left, and I returned to studying the river, grief boring a fresh hole in my soul.

Chapter 45

TRISTAN

"CAN I GET you anything, Dad?"

"No. But what about you?"

"What about me?"

"Do *you* need anything?"

Yes. I need you to live, I wanted to say but could not.

"You've been here all day. Have you even eaten anything?"

"I'm not hungry."

"You're an excellent son, Tristan," my father said, "but you need to start thinking of yourself—"

"Dad—"

"No, let me finish. Son, I want you to be happy. You *deserve* to be happy—after...everything. Anyone who knows you will tell you that. You deserve to be happy, but only you can decide what will make you happy."

"Dad—you make it sound like I've been unhappy. I haven't been. Truly, I haven't."

"Not being unhappy isn't the same as being happy, though, is it?"

"Dad. I—"

He held up his hand, again. "All I'm saying, Tristan, is all these years you've put me and my needs before yourself and your own. And before that, you put your mother before everything. And after she died, you took on the guilt for her crime. It's time to let that go."

How could I tell him that I didn't know how to let go of my guilt, of him, of my love for Max?

My phone buzzed with an incoming text message. "That's Javier," I said. "He's at the airport. He'll be here in about a half hour. He wants to know if you want him to pick up anything for you. Magazines? Ice cream?"

"No, I'm good, thanks."

I texted Javier back.

"Javier is so kind," my father said, "spending time here with me when you can't be here. Taking time out of his life to check in on us."

"He's a good guy," I agreed easily.

"He's been a good friend, and he's a good-looking young man."

I looked at Dad in surprise. "Yeah, I suppose he is."

"Is there anything between the two of you?"

I wanted to laugh. The idea. Javier! Javier was a good friend, and I loved him dearly, but he was so cheerfully promiscuous that I had placed the men in the world into two categories: the Haves and the Have Nots. I was definitely in the Have Not camp.

"No, we're just good friends."

JOHN

"DON'T WAIT TOO long to find someone to settle down with," I said. "I was sixty before I allowed myself to fall in love."

"Why *did* you wait so long?"

"I devoted my youth and middle age to being an excellent son. One day, I woke up and both my parents were gone, and I was…alone. I didn't even have a single person I could call friend."

I fell silent, and Tristan instinctively remained still, letting me find my words in my own time.

"I don't regret taking care of them, but I do wish I'd had the fortitude to carve out a space for myself, for my own life. It wasn't until after they died, and I started to look at the world around me, that I realized I could have been an excellent son *and* a good husband and father."

I turned to look out the window, beyond which the sun bounced off the smooth surface of the river. A motorboat passed with two water-skiers trailing behind it. Suddenly, one slipped under the water. Seconds later, he emerged, struggling to stand up. I imagined I could hear him laughing with childish happiness.

"You know, every morning when I wake up, I turn and look out this window, and I think to myself, well, John, you lived to see another day."

"Are you scared?" Tristan asked. "I mean of dying."

I rolled onto my back and stared at the ceiling. "No. No, I'm not. I just wish I could live long enough to see you settled down with someone kind."

Chapter 46

TRISTAN

"Miss Dorothy! What are you doing here?"

"Hello, Tristan." She stood, and we hugged awkwardly.

"How did you—"

"Javier stopped by the shop to pick up a hat he ordered. He told me. I hope you don't mind."

"No, no, of course not. I should have thought to stop by and tell you. I know how much you always liked Dad."

"I liked your mother, too."

I nodded. "Has he been awake?"

"No."

"Dad," I said, "I'm here, and look. You have a visitor."

He opened his eyes and smiled. "Hi, son." He saw Miss Dorothy. "Salt?"

"Hello, John."

"I'm going to run downstairs to the snack machine. Anyone want anything?" Neither of them appeared to hear me, so I backed out the room and closed the door.

Miss Dorothy became a regular visitor, keeping Dad company when Javier and I could not. Dad granted her certain privileges he did not accord us; she cut up his food and fed him, she called the nurse when he was in pain.

Chapter 47

"D AD, ARE YOU in pain? I can call the nurse."

"No. Maybe in a few minutes. The pain meds will just make me sleep."

"That's not such a bad thing."

"Yes, it is. It means I have less time to spend with you boys."

Javier excused himself and went to the bathroom in Dad's room. It was the first time I had heard him cry. Dad turned his head at the sound. Turning back, he stared at the ceiling and said, "You can call the nurse now."

....

Javier and I were waiting in the visitors' room across the hall—the same room where I first learned my father was dying—for the nurse to finish cleaning up Dad. Javier looked pensive.

"What's wrong?" I asked.

"You're so strong," Javier said.

"No, I'm not."

"Tristan, yes you are. I don't know how you've gone through everything before and now this."

I shrugged. "You do what you have to do to get through. You'd do the same."

"No, I wouldn't. I would fall the fuck apart, but not you. You're like Teflon—whatever life throws at you, you manage to

228

scrape off. Me? I get stuck and burned. Then, when I finally tear free of the calamity, I leave chunks of myself behind, dragging away only the burnt, crusty edges." He shook his head as if to clear it. "I guess I'm trying to say I admire your strength."

"Thanks, but I'm not strong. My dad is—"

"You get your strength from him—"

"I wish. You know, the other day I was in his room, and he was quiet—"

"When isn't Papa quiet?"

I laughed. "His silence has texture. And this quietness seemed different. I asked him if he was in pain, and he admitted he was. I went to fetch the nurse because at this point, he can have pain meds whenever he wants. When she came in, he chatted with her, asking her how she was. She finally said, 'Your son says you have some pain…'

"He nodded. 'On a scale of one to ten,' she asked him, 'how bad is it?' 'Seven,' he said. Seven! And he didn't say anything. And when she asked him how he was initially, he answered, 'Fine.'"

I started to cry, and Javier wrapped me in his arms, holding me until my tears escalated into full-blown sobs and then faded away.

"I'm sorry," I said.

"Don't be. It's what I'm here for. I'd rather you cry with me than Papa."

I dug at my eyes with my knuckles. "You know, Javier, as hard as this is…I think it would be even harder without you. Thank you for being here."

"I wouldn't be anywhere else, Tristan," Javier said quietly. "You know that."

Chapter 48

JAVIER

PAPA HAD BEEN looking out the window at the silver and brown river, which was full of activity that morning: barges being loaded; water-skiers being pulled behind sleek white towboats; a police boat dragging the edges of the river looking for who knows what. Staring out the window, without looking at me, he said, "You'll have to help Tristan get rid of my things."

"Yes, Papa," I replied, startled. "I will."

He turned to look at me. I noticed for the first time the difficulty in his movement. Shit. The doctors had told us this would happen; he'd stiffen, stop swallowing, fall silent. I wondered if Tristan had noticed the deterioration and hoped he hadn't.

"Look out for Tristan. After I'm gone, you're all he has left."

TRISTAN

DAD WOKE UP abruptly. "I'll be dead soon."

"Don't say that, Dad."

"It needs saying. Listen to me, Tristan. You've always been afraid of the unknown. I worry that you never stopped loving Max because he was known, and you know how the story ends—"

"Dad—"

"Wait, son. Hear me out. I'm going to die, and everything will change. Everything will be new and unfamiliar. I need you to embrace the unknown."

"I'll miss you, Dad. Always."

"I know. Don't mourn me too long. Fall in love. Make a life. If you're sure Max is the one, find him, and rewrite your story."

"OK."

"You know that phrase that there are no second acts in American lives?" Dad asked.

"Yes. It's a quote from F. Scott Fitzgerald."

He nodded and smiled to himself; I knew he was thinking, *Of course you would know that.*

"Well, don't believe it. It's not true."

"What do you mean?"

"I mean, you can have as many acts in your life as you want. And if you're in the middle of an act and it's not working for you, you can end it and start over. Write a new script. Or improvise—that's probably even better. But whatever you do, don't bring down the curtain. Just stay on that stage until you end up living the story you want to live no matter how many acts you need."

"Don't spend a whole lot of money on my funeral," my father said out of the blue, turning his attention away from *The Bold and the Beautiful.*

"OK... What kind of casket do you want? Do you want it open or closed?"

"I don't care—something simple. You can decide whether it's open or closed. I want a flag, though. I'm entitled to a flag."

"OK, Dad."

"There are papers in the file cabinet in my den. The deed to my burial plot is in there. You'll need to retrieve it and give it to the funeral home."

I nodded silently, not trusting myself to speak.

"There are four plots—"

"Four plots?"

"Yes. One was for your mother, and one is for me."

"What are the other two for?"

My father exhaled, and his eyes twinkled just a bit as he stifled a chuckle. "Your mother insisted we buy the plots on either side of us—she didn't like the idea of spending eternity buried next to a stranger."

I laughed. I couldn't help it.

"I can't remember the last time I heard you laugh," Dad said.

"Dad?"

"Yes?"

"If you already had a funeral plot, why did you bury Omma in Korea?"

JOHN

How COULD I tell Tristan the truth—that I didn't want to be buried next to Grace when I died? Before you judge me, think about this. My *wife*—a woman I had loved for more than twenty years, the mother of my child, a woman I thought I knew as well as one person could know another—willfully shot a seventeen-year-old. A child, really, but worse, a child *her* child had loved. Whatever love I had for her—whatever forgiveness I might have mustered—died when I read the police report, when I read that she had bought a gun and went to target practice daily for a month.

"Burying your mother anywhere near us would have resulted in her grave being desecrated. You have no idea about the hate mail and calls we received because of what she did. The hate, the death threats. It came from all sides—those who hated her violence and homophobia and those who hated you and Max for who you were, who thought the two of you should have died while she lived a hero. You didn't need to deal with that on top of losing—on top of everything else."

"That's why you had my phone disconnected."

"Yes. I never wanted you to see what people wrote, the messages they left. Max's father did the same thing for the same reason."

"But you saw them?"

I nodded.

"Oh, Dad. I never thought about how hard this must have been on you."

"I know. I never wanted you to. You were still a child. You had your own grief to deal with, and I thought you deserved to hold on to whatever childhood, whatever innocence you still had. Taking her back to Korea, taking you away was the best thing I could do to protect you."

Chapter 49

TRISTAN

I ARRIVED AT THE hospital to find Miss Dorothy asleep in the chair beside Dad's bed, her head thrown back, the tracks of her earlier tears like a salt run on her aging face. Her hand lay on top of his. She opened her eyes.

"Hi," she said, sitting up.

"Hi. How is he?"

She shrugged. "He's not said anything, and he hasn't opened his eyes."

Dad had lost the ability to swallow a week or two before and the ability to talk shortly after that. At some point—I couldn't remember when exactly—he'd stopped opening his eyes.

"Have you said anything to him?"

"No."

"He can still hear," I said. I kissed Dad on the top of his head. "Dad, I'm here, and so is Miss Dorothy." He smiled. My father was still there, entombed in a body that had betrayed him.

I opened the package containing swabs and, dipping one in thickened water, swabbed his cracked lips and the inside of his mouth; he sucked on the swab for a moment or two.

Chapter 50

MAX

"Hello?"

"Max! Hello! Happy birthday, son!"

"Dad, you know—"

"I know you don't celebrate your birthday anymore. But you're still my son, and the day of your birth is special, at least to me, because it was the day that brought you into my life and changed everything for the better."

"Give me the phone," my stepmother said in the background. As soon as he handed her the receiver, she began to sing "Happy Birthday" loudly and off-key. I couldn't help but laugh. I thanked my parents and hung up. I thought of Tristan, wondered how he was celebrating *his* birthday. I turned off the ringer on my phone and, pulling the covers over my head, went back to sleep.

TRISTAN

"Hello?"

"Tristan." It was Javier. He'd only spoken my name, but his voice was quavering.

"What's wrong Javier?"

"You need to come—"

"I will. I told you I'd be there—"

"No, you need to come now. The doctor says Papa is actively dying."

When I got to Dad's room, Javier all but collapsed in my arms. "I'm so sorry," he said. "I have been praying for Papa to die and for his suffering to end. But now I find I'm not ready to let him go. I'm not ready."

"It's OK," I said. "He's not going to die. Not today anyway."

"What do you mean?" Javier wiped his eyes. I looked at the bed where Dad lay, not breathing.

"It's my birthday. Dad won't die on my birthday because it would cease to be my birthday and forever be the day he died." Dad was an excellent son, and excellent sons don't steal others' thunder. Dad frowned as if he were climbing a great hill and started to breathe again.

"Happy birthday," Javier said, handing me a small box.

"What this?"

"It's from Papa. He asked me to get it from the house and wrap it for him for your birthday. Go ahead, open it."

I opened it. Inside was a fountain pen. At first, I thought it was one of Dad's—he collected fountain pens—but then I realized it was new and I'd never seen it before. It was Montegrappa's Salvador Dali Surrealista "Geopoliticus Child" limited edition fountain pen in 18k gold. The design was based on Dali's masterpiece, *Geopoliticus Child Watching the Birth of the New Man*, which shows a man breaking from an egg.

I remembered my conversation with Dad in which he'd told me to step, unafraid, into the unknown. I wanted to cry: mute and sightless, he was still guiding me.

．．．．．．．．．．．．．．．．．．．．．．．．．

"Dad," I whispered, "it's midnight. It's no longer my birthday. You can let go now."

Chapter 51

JAVIER

Papa. I'm going to run out and get some breakfast. I'll be back in twenty minutes." I kissed him on the top of his head as I'd seen Tristan do. I'd sent Tristan home the night before to shower and change and sleep in his own bed instead of the couch in Papa's room. The breakfast the nurse had offered— oatmeal and a fruit cup—hadn't appealed to me, so I headed to McDonald's for a rare treat: a sausage McMuffin with egg. My trainer would have my head if he found out.

I knew as soon as I stepped into the room. I dropped the McDonald's bag containing my breakfast, my hunger gone. It was so still in the room. Papa lay motionless, breathless. I stood quietly beside his bed without moving, as if any movement might wake Papa from his eternal slumber. I was still standing there motionless, nearly breathless, when one of the nurses came upon me.

"He's dead," I said.

A few minutes later, the attending physician confirmed what I already knew to be true. "I'm sorry for your loss. He fought a good battle. But he suffered. His passing is a blessing."

I nodded without speaking.

"Would you like me to call his son, or would you like to tell him?"

"I'll tell him," I said, rousing myself as if from a stupor.

"Tristan..."

"He's gone, isn't he?"

"Yes."

"I'm glad. Does that sound awful? I'm so torn. I loved him so much, yet all I did these last weeks was pray for his death." He started to cry.

"It's not awful—I was praying, too." Now we were both crying. "I just stepped out to get some breakfast. When I came back, he was gone. I'm so sorry."

"Don't be. Dad was so private. I'm sure he didn't want either of us to see him die. That's why I went home last night."

"Why didn't you tell me?"

"I didn't have the heart to. I know you wanted to be with him."

I sniffled and wiped my nose. "Do you want to see him? They can leave him in his room for up to two hours. After that, they'll take him to the mortuary. They have a little ceremony. The chaplain will bless him, and they will drape him with a flag, and they play 'Taps' as they take him away. Would you like to be here for that?"

"No. But you stay and take my place—you were like another son to him."

"Tristan, I'm so sorry. I loved him, too."

"I know you did."

TRISTAN

I HUNG UP the phone, feeling I don't know what. Dad was gone. I was relieved and devastated. Dr. Gloom-and-Doom had given him two weeks to live, yet Dad had lived four—mostly out of spite, I was sure.

JAVIER

As I FOLLOWED our solemn procession, every veteran on that floor came to the door and silently saluted him as we passed. Even the dementia patient who'd screamed all night and accused the nurses of hiding her shoes so she couldn't leave fell silent as we passed. In their worn faces, etched with the heaviness of their sacrifices for their country, I could see the military might.

A simple melody, eloquent and haunting, just twenty-four notes and one-hundred and fifty years of history, "Taps" said more about Papa, about the country he'd fought for, about the respect he'd earned, than any words ever could.

Until Papa died, I hadn't believed in death. That is, I hadn't believed in the finality of it. I had always insisted to myself that life is energy. The Law of Conservation of Energy maintains that energy can neither be created nor destroyed; it can only be transferred or changed from one form to another. So, if life is energy, it follows that life can only be changed, not destroyed. What most people think of as death is actually a transfer of energy, the thinking goes. With death, that energy transitions to a different place; maybe that place is heaven, or hell, or someplace in between. I don't know. At least, that's what I believed until Papa died. Now, I knew he was simply gone and I'd never see him again.

As I watched the orderlies disappear into the elevator with Papa, I admitted to myself at last that my parents hadn't—would *never*—love me. Watching Papa, who *did* love me, suffer and die was one of the hardest things I've ever done. Those four weeks he lingered was too long a time for him to suffer—he deserved better—yet it hadn't been long enough to love him in return for all the love he'd given me—a boy who'd never been loved before.

Chapter 52

JAVIER

"JAVIER," TRISTAN EXCLAIMED, "you're wearing a hat."

I was wearing Papa's fur felt Stetson Stratoliner Fedora, with the grosgrain hat band accented with a special edition stratoliner airplane pin. I had admired it when we were all in Paris.

"Yes," I said. "It's Papa's. He gave it to me."

"You said you wouldn't wear a hat until you were old and bald."

"I *am* old, Tristan. I have never felt so old."

I led Tristan outside, where his father's Lincoln waited in the driveway. I opened the back door and helped him inside, then climbed into the back seat after him. The original plan had called for me to drive us in Papa's Lincoln—it was warm enough to drive it with the top down—but I'd backed out at the last minute, realizing that in losing the man who had been for years a stand-in for my own absent father, my grief was almost as great as Tristan's, and I was no more capable of driving than he was.

An elderly neighbor, one of Papa's few friends—one of the few who had stuck with him after Tristan's mother tried to kill Max and been killed herself—had volunteered to drive, thinking, as Tristan and I agreed, Papa would have gotten a kick out of his beloved Lincoln being a part of the funeral cortège.

TRISTAN

Miss Dorothy came up to me as Javier and I stood like sentries carved from the gray fabric of grief beside Dad's casket. She kissed me on the cheek. "I'm so very sorry."

"I know. Thank you."

She looked different. I wondered when she had let her hair go gray. And in this age of relaxers and weaves, I was surprised to see her otherwise straight hair was kinky at the roots. Her dress, as it always had been, was impeccable, and her carriage erect, proud. She had descended into the handsomeness some women attain when they give up the fight against the years assaulting the citadel of their youthful beauty. Despite all of this, she seemed...*broken*. I wondered if she had always been so and if the death of my father had stripped away its cover.

JAVIER

The recessional hymn was "Soon and Very Soon." Tristan had chosen the music but hadn't played, unable to mourn and play at the same time. He followed his father's coffin outside and stood aside as two men, dressed in black, their faces serious and etched with permanent sorrow, carefully loaded the casket into the hearse. I went to his side and took his arm and steered him to Papa's car.

・・・・・・・・・・・・・・・・・・・・

We stood silent graveside as the honor guard played "Taps." After they carefully folded the flag that had draped Papa's casket into a triangle, they gave it to Tristan. Then attendants from the funeral home gave everyone a rose to either keep in memory or lay on Papa's casket as they said their final goodbye. Tristan instead gave his to me and walked to where Papa's casket hovered over the open grave ready to welcome him into its gaping jaw. He knelt and pressed his lips against the cool polished wood of the casket. The gesture almost broke my heart.

TRISTAN

I GAVE MY rose to Javier and almost without thinking walked to the edge of Dad's grave. I knelt and pressed my lips against the cool polished wood of the casket. "Bye, Dad. I did my best," I said, and in the way of all excellent sons, added, "I hope it was enough."

And just like that it was over.

JAVIER

IT's OVER. PAPA is buried. And now we have to go on living. How?

We were once again sitting in the wide back seat of Papa's Lincoln. Tristan put his arm around me and leaned his head against my shoulder. I stroked his hair and tried not to look at his grief-stricken face. I handed him the single rose I still held, feeling like Jackie Kennedy offering a fistful of brains and bone to an EMT hoping to restore what had been.

Chapter 53

JANE BENTHAM

JAVIER

I WATCHED TRISTAN AS he sorted through Papa's things. Now and then, he'd hold a shirt or a jacket up to his chest and, smiling, fold it neatly and say, "I can wear this. I think I'll keep it," even though every item was at least two sizes too big for him.

I pulled a shirt out of the pile and said, "I'll keep this one," even though it was no more likely to fit me than Tristan.

Later, we found an old wallet of Papa's. In it was every class picture Tristan had ever taken. Flipping through them was like watching time-lapse photography: a boy growing into reluctant manhood, too much heaped on his narrow shoulders.

I looked from the pictures to Tristan. "Your father asked me to take care of you. It occurs to me I have absolutely no idea how to."

"You don't have to take care of me. Just being here—your presence in my life—is enough. I don't know how I would have made it through losing Dad without you."

"You've been through so much..."

"Losing my mother was easier in a way. I was so angry at her. And terrified that I'd lost Max. Now...now I *know* I've lost everything."

"Tristan—that's just grief talking. You'll get over it."

"No. See, Javier, that's just it. I won't get over it. Grief isn't a phase to be passed through, or some hurdle you must do your best to jump over, or a sheer cliff you must rappel down the face of—no, it's an acid-etched stain. It carves something out of you. Over time, you learn to live without that piece of yourself, but you never stop missing it. When people think grief has passed, they are mistaking endurance for growth. The loss of my mother, Max, and now my father has changed me, given me a new way of seeing, of feeling. I'll go on because I have to—I mean, what can one do *but* go on? —but I'll never be the same."

Chapter 54

JAVIER

"Tristan? Tristan, why are you crying?" I sat on the floor next to him and pulled him to me.

He shrugged. "Nothing—it's stupid really." He sniffled and made what I imagine he thought was a brave face.

"Tell me."

He sniffled again. "This morning, I got up, and I decided it was time to stop feeling sorry for myself and get out. So, I took a shower and shaved. And then I decided I wanted to look nice, so I put on that shirt you brought me from your last trip to Italy. It has French cuffs," he said, as if I couldn't see that. They were uncuffed and covered his hands. "I used Dad's cufflinks."

"The ones you wore to his funeral?"

"Yeah, and I went out."

I exhaled. This was good. "Where'd you go?"

"To the park."

"The park?"

"Yeah. I couldn't think where else to go."

I tried for a moment to imagine him in the park in a yellow French cuff shirt of Italian linen. "What did you do?"

He shrugged. "I bought hot pretzels from a vendor until I ran out of money."

"What did you do with the pretzels?"

He looked at me through red-rimmed eyes. "I fed them to the birds."

I threw back my head and laughed. "All over the city, pigeons are dropping dead from hypertension. Film at 11."

He smiled weakly.

"OK, so tell me why you were crying."

"I put in Dad's cufflinks without thinking about it." He opened his hand. In his hand were the cufflinks: lapis blue porcelain sitting in crowns of silver. "I went to toss a piece of pretzel and I caught a glimpse of his cufflinks. I started to cry—I mean, I was *bawling my eyes out*. It's so ridiculous."

"It's not ridiculous," I said, pulling him closer and fighting my own tears.

"Javier, I miss him so much."

"I know you do, baby. I know you do. I miss him, too."

TRISTAN

JAVIER GLANCED AT his watch. "Do you have somewhere to be?" I asked.

He smiled sheepishly. "I have a date."

"Oh!"

"I can cancel it and stay here with you."

"No—no. Go, have a good time."

Javier stood and smoothed out his trousers. "You should do something fun."

"Like what?" I was genuinely perplexed by the notion.

"I don't know. See a movie. Go out to dinner. Go for a walk in the park—well, maybe not that last one."

I laughed. "I'm fine here."

"Tristan, you have to get out of this house. Do something. You have to get on with your life." He said that last part with such tenderness, I almost started to cry again.

"I know. I will. I'm just not ready yet."

Javier held up his hands in surrender and backed away. He reached for his shoulder bag and a book slipped out of it. He tossed the book, which had a plastic-looking marionette on the cover, to me. I caught it awkwardly, read the title: *The Adventures of Testa di Cazzo.*

"What's this?"

"A book."

"Ha-ha. I can see that. What's it about?"

"Are you kidding? It's an international sensation. Everyone's talking about it." I looked at him blankly, and he sighed. "It's an erotic retelling of *Pinocchio—*"

"Ugh." I dropped the book.

"No, really. Read it. It's amazing—funny and different. Everyone is reading it."

He kissed me on the top of my head and practically ran out the door. *Another conquest to be made, another heart to be broken*, I thought, picking up the book and opening the cover.

. . . .

The sun was just starting to rise, the sky blushing with the new day when I closed the book, finished. I leaned back against the sofa, exhausted as I hadn't been in years but too keyed up to sleep. Who had written this? It was at once new and familiar. I picked up the book again and read the author's name for the first time. I blinked, opened the book and scanned the author's meager bio. I recognized his name. We shared a hometown. Disbelieving, I thumbed to the dedication and read it.

Like my heart, this book belongs to TJ.

No! It couldn't be. *Could it?* I picked up my phone and googled the author's name: Max Wong. I clicked through the images, and there was...*Max*...looking older, more confident but unmistakably Max. I leaned back against the sofa, closed my eyes, and cried.

I was still stunned and disbelieving when I heard Javier's key in the door. My back ached and my eyes were burning. "Hey," I called, "I'm in here."

He appeared in the living room doorway looking flawless and rested as always, though I noticed he was wearing the same clothes from yesterday. "Hey," he said cheerfully.

"Hey. How was your date?"

"Another loser."

"I'm sorry."

"Don't be. I got laid and he picked up the tab for dinner."

That was Javier making lemonade out of lemons. Again.

"How was *your* evening, my reclusive friend?"

"Fine. I read that book you gave me."

"The whole thing?"

"Yeah. I've been up all night."

"What did you think? Didn't I tell you—"

"I know the author," I interrupted.

"Max Wong. Of course you do. Everyone does. He's everywhere."

"No, I know him *personally*. It's *Max—my* Max."

"*Your* Max? You mean Max, your high school boyfriend? The one your mother..." His voice trailed off.

"Yes. *That* Max."

"Are you sure?"

"I'm sure. I looked him up. It's Max."

"Wow."

"I think he dedicated the book to me. Listen." I read him the dedication.

He let out a low whistle. "Now what?"

"I don't know," I admitted.

"Wait! He's here."

"Here?"

"Yes. In town. Or he will be. He's doing a series of book signings." Javier pulled out his phone. "I was right!" he shouted triumphantly. "You have to go see him."

"What?"

"You should go to his book signing."

"I can't just waltz into his book signing and say, 'Hi, Max. How have you been?'"

"That's exactly what you should do."

"Javier, it's been six years."

"Look, Tristan, you dropped out of his life pretty abruptly. It seems to me dropping back into it abruptly creates a kind of... *romantic symmetry.*"

Javier must have noticed my silence because he stopped talking and asked, "What's wrong?"

"I think I'm still in love with him," I blurted.

"All the more reason to go."

"What if he's not still in love with me? What if the TJ in his dedication isn't me?"

"Well, there's only one way to find out."

"What if he doesn't remember me? Or doesn't want to see me? My mother did try to kill him, you know."

"He dedicated his book to you."

"We don't know that."

Javier lifted an eyebrow in the way that always annoyed and disarmed me.

"OK, let's say I do go—what—what would I say?"

"'Hi, Max. How have you been?'"

"Ha-ha. What would I even wear?"

"Let's go check out your closet."

I turned around to face Javier. "Well? What do you think?"

"I think that's it. That's the outfit. It's casual but not too casual. It looks like you put in some effort because seeing him is special but not so much that you look...desperate."

"Gee, thanks."

He continued scrutinizing me.

"What?" I asked, turning around to examine myself in the mirror. Our eyes met.

"I always forget how handsome you are," he said.

JAVIER

"Do you think I'm crazy?" Tristan asked as he slipped out of his suit.

"Why would I think you're crazy?"

"For thinking I'm still in love with Max."

I thought for a few minutes, uncharacteristically not just shooting off my mouth with whatever came into my head. "I think only you can answer that question. But I will tell you, I've never seen you so happy. When you mention his name, you smile. After Papa died, I was afraid I'd never see you smile again."

"I've only ever been with one person—Max."

"Sometimes one is all you need."

"So, you think I can still be in love with him, even though I've never loved anyone else and haven't seen or spoken to him in six years?"

"Yes, yes, I do. Though I would say be sure you're in love with this Max and not the Max you knew in high school."

"What do you mean?"

"I'm not sure, but people change. Look, all I can tell you is I fell in love with this guy—Eric—freshman year. We were secret boyfriends on and off for seven years."

"Wait. He was at school with us?"

"Yes."

"And I didn't know? You didn't tell me?"

"I didn't tell you. I didn't tell anyone. He wasn't out, and he didn't want anyone to know he was gay. Still, he was the one."

"What happened?"

"He started dating a girl—a lower classman. He changed. Not just his apparent orientation. He worked to lose his accent. He cut off all his beautiful, long, dark hair. He got circumcised. He started working out and lost the chubbiness I found so sexy. He got tattoos and spoiled his beautiful brown skin."

"I'm afraid to ask how that turned out."

"They broke up because, you know...*gay*. I hoped he'd come back to me, but instead, he started sleeping with all these guys. To make up for lost time, I suppose."

I looked at him in surprise.

"I know. I know I sound like a hypocrite. It sounds like I'm judging him when God knows I slept around enough, but for me, it was different. I was trying to forget him while remaining free for him. Anyway, we hooked up a few times after we graduated from American. I finally realized that I wasn't in love with him. Hell, I couldn't even say I liked him at that point. You see, I loved who he was when I met him, but he wanted to be someone else, and I didn't notice because I kept seeing who he had been. I was still in love with the boy he had been, when he had in fact become someone else."

Chapter 55

MAX

I SCANNED THE CROWD for him. The crowd was always the same: awed English majors, devotees of popular culture and bored housewives with too much time on their hands. Their faces were always the same: bland and earnest faces, and his was never among them. I stifled a sigh and went back to mingling and gracefully accepting the praise of adoring strangers, all the while listening for his voice, his presence, sure I could pick out the rhythms of his heart, which would beat in synch with mine.

TRISTAN

JAVIER NODDED TOWARDS the front of the bookstore where a man stood at a modest podium, reading, while a crowd of people, their faces worshipful, sat in rapt attention.

"That him?" he asked.

I followed his gaze. It was him. Even at this distance, after all these years, I recognized him. Just then, he looked up, and even though I was sure he couldn't see me, I felt as if he'd wrapped his arms around me. I fell into his imagined embrace. My knees felt weak. Blood pounded in my ears. Tears blurred my vision.

Javier touched my arm, concern causing his brow to furrow. "You OK?"

"Yeah, fine," I said. "That's him."

"You gonna be OK if I leave?"

"Yeah."

"OK. Text me later." He leaned in and kissed my cheek.

I stepped up to the counter and purchased Max's book. The clerk thanked me for my purchase and said, "Mr. Wong is just finishing up his reading now. Then he'll begin signing books if you'd like to wait."

MAX

I HATED READINGS and even more book signings. I promised myself after each one that once I found Tristan, I'd never agree to another one. I waved the next person in line forward and plastered a pleasant smile on my face. Taking his book, I asked, "Who should I make it out to?"

"Kyle."

As I started to write, he said, "You're so exotic looking. Where are you from?"

I looked up at him wearily. "My mother's womb," I said.

"Hey! You'd be much more attractive without the smart mouth."

When I said nothing, he continued, "You know, it's not like you're hot or anything. I mean, I don't usually find Asian guys attractive, but I'm attracted to talent, and you are *very* talented."

"Thanks." I nodded curtly, finished signing his book and handed it back to him, not even bothering to smile. He snatched the book from my hand and stomped off. If he was angry now, just wait until he read what I'd written.

As a writer,

I appreciate everyone who supports me by buying a book,

even if they're ASSHOLES.

Best,

Max Wong

TRISTAN

I was close enough now to get a good look at Max. He had let his hair grow long. Freed from its habitual scrunchy, it cascaded to his shoulders like black silk unfolding in a breeze. Occasionally, he would toss his head to move his hair out of his face; other times, he would rake it back with impatient fingers. I couldn't stop looking at him.

When I'd known him, he'd declared himself ugly; his face had been undecided, caught between boyhood and manhood, between handsome and ugly. Evidently, his face had decided to become extremely handsome. I'd always found him attractive; now he took my breath away.

Looking at Max's hands with their long, tapered fingers flying over pages, grasping a vintage Cross pen firmly as he signed his name and the occasional kind phrase over and over, after all these years, I could still feel his hands like an open flame skipping over my burning teenager's skin, a pinch here, a lingering caress there.

The next person in line stepped up to Max and surrendered his book. He was dressed in hipster black and seemed to take up more space than everyone else. He said something to Max, and Max responded, looking cross. Their tense exchange ended with the hipster snatching his book from Max. As he stepped out of line, he opened the book and read. He seemed furious. He snapped the book shut and stepped towards Max, pushing the next person waiting for Max's autograph out of the way.

Someone I can only describe as a human fireplug—solid, squat, with short arms, severely cropped hair and a firm, no-nonsense, take-no-prisoners stare—stepped from behind Max. The fireplug barked a short command as if calling a dog to heel. The hipster gave them a measuring look, then, with a contemptuous curl to his thin lips, made a show of depositing the book Max had just signed into a trashcan. Max watched him bemused, then returned to signing the book in his hand.

Finally, it was my turn. The terrifying fireplug beckoned me forward impatiently. Max looked up.

"Hello, Max," I said. I was surprised by how steady and normal my voice sounded. "It's been a long time. How have you been?"

"Tristan!"

"Yes," I said, nodding, though Max hadn't asked a question, had recognized me instantly. He stood and stepped from behind the table. The fireplug stepped forward. Max waved them back.

He wrapped his arms around me, and I fell into his embrace, for real this time. The room began to spin. Blood pounded in my ears. Then the room flipped top to bottom so that I couldn't tell up from down or differentiate where I began and where Max ended. I assumed this is what it felt like to be falling down drunk.

There was much throat-clearing from the fireplug.

"Um, listen," Max said releasing me, "I have to finish this book signing. Can you stay? Are you free? Can we, maybe, grab a drink and go out to talk?"

I nodded. "I'll wait. Take your time."

I turned to leave.

"Tristan…"

"I know, Max, I know."

MAX

"TRISTAN," I SAID. I'm sure I spoke other words, but none of them mattered, only his name. I'd said it a hundred times—a thousand times—over the last six years, silently, sadly, till it became a static ritual. But now, saying his name out loud, in his presence, everything changed and moved again.

The woman standing in front of me coughed conspicuously. I smiled and, taking the proffered book, asked, "Who should I make it out to?"

"Thelma," she said, or Jessica, or Clare; her name didn't register. Her name didn't matter. The only name I could hear, the only name I cared about was Tristan.

After I'd signed each book—and it seemed to me I'd signed *hundreds*—I'd look over to where he stood. Don't judge me; I'd lost sight of him once; I wasn't about to lose sight of him again.

Over the years, I'd occasionally tried to convince myself that ours was a teenage love running like a mysterious fever through every inch of our hormonal bodies and destined, one day, to disappear as mysteriously as it had appeared. But here he was. And here I was, faced with one inviolable truth: he is *The One*. Enabled by drought—no one had loved me before or since— the embers of our teenage love affair burst into flame anew, consuming the last six years, the crowd of readers in front of me, the seventy thousand painstaking words in the books they offered for my signature. *Tristan!*

TRISTAN

THE ENTIRE TIME I was waiting, Max would look up from signing autographs as if to make sure I was still there. Once catching my eye, he smiled, and I knew that what I'd suspected over the last six years was true: I loved him still.

MAX

AT LAST, I'D signed the last book. I made small, polite talk with the bookstore manager while others moved chairs and readied the store for its usual business. I could see Tristan standing by the front door. Finally, I was free. I started walking towards him.

Free to think of him at last, I wondered why he had come. Had he come to apologize and explain? Had he come to blame me for ruining his life and destroying his family? Or had he come because he, too, was still in love?

My heart raced and the blood rushing between my ears was so loud I was sure he could hear it.

TRISTAN

AT LAST, HE was finished, the last book signed, and the crowd of fans dispersed, melting into the late afternoon. The store manager went over to Max and made a fuss. A salesperson rushed over with a stack of books, and Max graciously but impatiently signed them. Finished, he pushed the stack to the clerk and stood. Max waved, and then he was walking towards me. I noticed he had a slight limp. The fireplug watched him walk away, casting a baleful glance in my direction.

"You ready?" he asked quite as if *I'd* been the one keeping *him* waiting. I nodded. He guided me to the door and held it open. Once we stepped into the cool air, he tucked my arm in his as if he were afraid I would run away.

"Who," I asked, "was that terrifying person standing behind you?"

Max laughed. "Oh, that's V—the assistant assigned to me by my publisher."

"Vee?"

"Yeah, just the initial 'V.' I don't know what the V stands for, though I often imagine it's short for the violence they would like to do to me."

"Who's they?"

"V—V is nonbinary, so they use they/them pronouns."

"Ah."

"Max!" someone called.

We stopped, turned around. The terrifying fireplug, carrying a black leather book, was huffing and puffing after us. Reaching us, they said, "Max, where are you going? We need to debrief."

"Can we do that tomorrow? I have a date with Tristan."

V gave me an even darker looker than they had before.

"Oh, excuse my bad manners," Max said. "Tristan this is V. V, Tristan."

V offered what for someone else might have been a smile, but from them it seemed more a baring of the teeth, a warning: *mess with me and I'll bite your head off and shit down your neck.*

"My pronouns are they and them," V said. "What are yours?"

I looked at them in confusion. Max came to my rescue. "Tristan's pronouns are he and him."

"Um, right," I said, resenting that something as innocuous as an introduction had turned into a battlefield.

"OK, V, we'll catch up tomorrow. Bye, now." Max took my arm again, and V shot me a look that hit me like a blast of cold water.

"What do you want to do?" Max asked. "We could go for coffee or a drink, or we could go somewhere for dinner."

"Can we just walk for a bit?"

"Sure."

MAX

THE BABY FAT that had plumped Tristan's cheeks and softened his face had melted away, revealing prominent cheekbones and a strong brow line; the boy's face had been supplanted by a man's. He was still very handsome, though, and he still had the most kissable mouth I had ever seen.

Walking beside me, Tristan, dressed in a slim-cut pink seersucker suit that accentuated his slenderness and youth, was as immaculate as I remembered. I found myself wishing my own grooming was as impeccable and surreptitiously inspected my nails. I ran my fingers through my hair, which I knew was too long and in need of cutting. I checked my appearance in every shop window we passed. I tried to remember the state of my toenails. When had I trimmed them last? I tried in vain to remember. I was suddenly grateful that my own home was several states away, that the best I could offer Tristan was an impeccable, if sterile, suite in a hotel, paid for by my publisher.

TRISTAN

LOOKING FOR A connection between the handsome, self-possessed man whose arm was tucked in mine and the remote, self-conscious boy I'd fallen in love with, I examined Max's clothing. He was wearing a well-tailored black suit over a cobalt-blue silk T-shirt. "I see you're still wearing black."

"Hey," he said, "I wear navy blue now, too."

"What else has changed about you, Max?"

"Everything. Nothing."

"I want to know everything."

MAX

"I DO, TOO," I said. "What happened to you? I got out of the hospital, and you were just…gone."

"My father took me to Korea—I think he wanted me to see where my roots were. And he wanted my mother buried there."

"Korea? What was that like?"

He shrugged. "It was Korea, my mother's homeland. Everyone looked like me, but they spoke a language I didn't understand. Everything was familiar but different. Everything reminded me of my mother. After a few weeks, we left. Dad took me to Paris and enrolled me in The American School."

"You lived in Paris?"

"For a year, yes."

"I always wanted to go to Paris."

"I know. We were planning that trip to Paris for the summer after we graduated, remember?"

He snapped his fingers. "Did you see the Eiffel Tower? Did you go to the Louvre? What was seeing the *Mona Lisa* in person like?"

"I don't know. I didn't see any of that."

"You didn't see *any* of it? You were in Paris for a year! How is it possible that you didn't see any of—"

"I avoided all the landmarks—the Eiffel Tower, the Louvre, Versailles—all the places you and I talked about seeing together. Seeing them alone, without you, was impossible."

I nodded, lost in thought.

"What about you?" Tristan asked. "I heard you left school, but no one seemed to know where you went."

"I did. Once I lost the ability to run, I figured I'd lose my scholarship, but no doubt because it would have seemed intolerably cruel given all I had lost, the school board didn't revoke my scholarship or even kick me off the track team. In theory, I could simply have gone to practice every day waiting for a recovery we all knew would never come."

"Then there was the matter of my teammates—the ones who didn't know and were shocked when they found out about you and me, and the ones who'd pretended not to know, who liked to behave like you and I were just friends. I would have been forced to choose either those who stood with me, *us*, or those who stood against us. I didn't want anyone's pity or their charity, so I transferred back to public school.

"Back in public school, where I didn't know anyone but everyone knew me—or *thought* they knew me from all the media coverage—I kept to myself. I felt myself turning back into who I'd been before I met you. I hated that. Every day, the more I became my old self, the farther away you seemed."

We walked in silence for a few minutes.

"Why didn't you come to see me...after?"

"I did," Tristan said. "They wouldn't let me in the hospital. Security said you weren't allowed visitors outside of family. Before we left, I went by your house. Your aunts met me outside on the lawn and told me you didn't want to see me—ever again. They said you blamed me for what happened and that I had ruined your reputation with my 'sickness' and probably your life as well because you wouldn't qualify for the track scholarship you had been working your whole life for."

Tristan started to cry. I wrapped him in my arms. "That's not true. None of it—I swear. They told me you hated me and never wanted to see me again."

"That's not true, either. I wanted more than anything to see you. Dad cancelled my phone because the number had gotten out, and he said the messages people sent were too hateful for me to see. I wrote you every week though. The letters never came back, and you never answered."

"You wrote me?" I said, incredulous.

He lifted his tear-stained face off my chest. "Yes. Every week for the entire year I was away."

"I never got them. I swear."

"I suppose they all thought they were doing the right thing. I know my father did when he took me away."

"So many people, all trying to do the right thing for the wrong reasons. I wonder—if you are coming from a good place but make bad decisions, does it still count against you? Making a bad decision for the right reason?"

"I don't know."

We fell silent again.

"As soon as we came back from Paris," he said, "I went to your house, but no one would tell me where you were—not even your father. I suppose I can't blame them. I'd nearly gotten you killed."

"They didn't tell you where I was because they didn't *know* where I was."

"How's your dad?"

"He's good. He got remarried and moved to Florida. He and my stepmother run a cleaning business now."

"And how are *The Aunts*?" Tristan asked. I imagined I heard bitterness in his voice. Or maybe it was my own.

The Aunts! Those battle-axes. Why did he have to ask me about them? I had first cut them from my life, then carved them from my heart, then relegated their memory, antique reliquaries, to the farthest corner of my mind.

"You may remember Tashelle—my favorite aunt—she actually died while I was in the hospital. A car accident. The other two moved back to Toronto after I left and my father remarried. I don't keep in touch with them. I haven't seen them in years."

"I'm sorry to hear that. I know they were a big part of your growing up. Do you miss them?"

TRISTAN

MAX SHRUGGED. "NOT really. No. Some people don't deserve a place in our lives."

I thought of my mother and of Judy Iscariot. "Yes, you're right," I said.

"How's *your* dad?"

"He died earlier this year."

"Oh, Tristan. I'm so sorry."

"Thanks. He was eighty-three. Cancer. He fought a good battle, but it was time to let him go."

By now, we had reached the river. A muddy, slow-moving morass of pollution, it was named after some long-lost Native American tribe but was casually referred to as the Surekill River, a play on its actual name and a reference to the commonly held idea that swimming in it, or drinking its water, would surely kill one.

"What should we do now?" Max asked.

I held the railing in front of me tightly and stared at the river below, tumbling gently like a fat, brown cat grooming itself. In the distance, a sharp condo building, shaped like a yacht, all angles and aerodynamics, was anchored at the river's edge. The sun exploded a thousand times in each of its flat glass windows.

"Can we go to your hotel?" I asked, suddenly self-conscious and unwilling to take him back to my parents' house where I still lived and my childhood bedroom where there was still the same furniture and I still slept in one of the two twin beds my parents had bought when I was a teenager. Because excellent sons never quite grow up…

"Sure."

Max took my hand, and we started walking again. I felt the weight of his hand in mine, the strength of his grip. I tried to remember the last time I'd held someone's hand. It had been my father's, I was sure, though I couldn't remember when or why. And before that, Max's. And before that, my mother's.

Chapter 56

TRISTAN

MAX LED ME into his suite's lavish living room. I tried not to be overcome by its gilt-edged opulence. In front of a bay window that was swaddled in swags and jabots, a black lacquered piano stretched, inviting as a naked lover on a deserted beach. I turned my back to it.

"Can I get you a drink?" Max asked.

"I don't really drink, but I'll take a beer if you have it."

"I'm sure I do." Max, crackling with nervous energy, busied himself at the bar while I looked around the room. I inspected my reflection in the mirror over the mantel. To my delight, I found that I liked what I saw. Max walked up behind me, carrying an open beer bottle and a tumbler of bourbon. "You look good," he said. I turned to take the bottle from him. He nodded to the couch and said, "Shall we sit?"

I looked at the bottle in my hand. "Um…can I have a glass?"

Max chuckled and crossed the room to the bar. Returning with a glass, he carefully poured the beer into it and handed it to me. I admired the perfect head on it.

"I worked as a bartender for a while," he said, picking up his glass and tipping it to his lips.

I took a nervous sip from my beer. I must have grimaced at the taste because Max said, "Beer seems the unlikeliest thing for you to be drinking."

"I told you—I don't drink much. What about you? Do you always drink bourbon in the afternoon?"

Max looked at the glass in his hand as if he was surprised to find it there. "I find it helps. Especially at night. I find it helps to have a couple of drinks before bed. It takes away the pain, or at least, it *eases* the pain of missing you."

"I've missed you, too," I said, the slightest quiver in my voice. We looked at each other with a longing I think we both recognized, but neither of us moved. It was as if, having grown accustomed to looking at each other across the distance of years, we were now unsure how to view each other when separated by a physical distance of scarcely three feet.

Max moved to the piano and, setting down his bourbon, opened the piano's lid. He sat and began playing the theme song from *Mission Impossible* from memory. Its distinctive 5/4 signature filled the room.

"You remember how to play that?" I asked in surprise.

"Yes. It's still the only thing I know how to play, though." He moved into the second part of the melody, and I found myself humming along, almost able to feel the keys under my fingers. I missed the feeling for the first time.

"Did you know Lalo Schrifin based that rhythm on the Morse code for the letters M and I, which is dash, dash, dot, dot? If a dash is one and a half beats, and a dot is one beat, you get a bar of five beats."

Max stopped playing abruptly and stood, picking up his drink. "I did not know that." After a moment he asked, "Do you still play?"

"No."

Max took another sip of his bourbon. "Really? That surprises me. You loved playing. *I* loved that you played the piano."

"My mother encouraged me to take up the piano. Well, forced me, actually. She loved that I began playing because she wanted me to. She said it meant I'd always be her little boy, her excellent son."

"When did you stop playing?"

"Right after my mother's funeral. I figured I'd play for her funeral—I'd played at dozens before that. When I was up in the loft preparing, I heard my father arguing with The Church Saints—you remember them, they were always whispering and twittering with outrage that you were often in the choir loft with me on Sundays? Anyway, they told my father they didn't think it was suitable that I play for my mother's funeral given the scandal. I was determined to play, though, and my dad knew that. Music was always the way I expressed myself best. At her funeral, I said everything I had left to say, so there was really no reason for me ever to play again."

"I always imagined you'd go into music as a career. At the very least, I figured you'd be a music teacher. But I usually fantasized that you were writing rock operas somewhere."

"Nope." I took a swig of my beer.

"So, what do you do?"

"I'm an accountant. I take care of other people's money like nannies take care of other people's children."

"You're an *accountant*?"

Yeah, I was surprised too, but I chose accounting deliberately because it wasn't music. Music is romance and love and passion and endless possibility; I'd had enough of all four. Math is fixed, predictable; there can only be one answer to every problem. I shrugged.

"Can I get you another beer?" Max asked.

"No. I haven't finished this one."

MAX

I WENT TO the bar and poured myself another bourbon. I returned to the couch and sat down again, this time closer to Tristan.

"You mentioned you were a bartender. And now you write," Tristan said.

"Yup."

"How'd you get started writing?"

"I went to community college. I had no idea what I wanted to study. My last year, I took this crazy literature course. We read classics—*Alice in Wonderland, Pinocchio, Tristram Shandy, Diary of a Nobody*. Oh man, I fell in love with all those words and stories. The next semester, I took a creative writing class. I wrote mostly love stories. They were terrible." I laughed.

"So, what made you write a novel?"

"You."

"Me?"

"Yeah, you. I wrote it for you."

"I don't understand."

"I couldn't find you—and I'd looked for you for years. The September after graduation, I went to New York, to Juilliard, to see if you were there. I went to The Curtiss Institute in Philadelphia. If there was a music school you had mentioned, I went there looking for you. After a while, it occurred to me that if I couldn't find you, *you* had to find *me*. I needed a way to be famous—famous enough that you'd see me. So, I sat down and wrote that book. I knew my chances of writing a best seller were one in a million, but I was determined to be that one in a million. I also realized that I'd already been one in a million. At seventeen, I had found the man I wanted to spend the rest of my life with. He was beautiful and smart and kind and magical, and he loved me, too. But I was going to be that one in a million again."

"Max—"

"I chose *Pinocchio* as the basis of the story because it was your favorite book. I figured if I could make something of the story, it would surely catch your attention. Every writer I know dreams of landing a contract with a big traditional publisher and doing a book tour and winning awards and being celebrated. All I wanted was to find you.

"I had to be very intentional, though. I needed to reach you to speak to you. You know, at my readings I talk a lot about how my work uses words to create art, but that that art is created from found objects—people and things I've seen, snatches of conversations I've heard. But I was also leaving a trail of breadcrumbs in that book that would lead you back to me."

TRISTAN

MAX STOOD AND returned to the bar where he poured a third bourbon. When he returned to the couch this time, he brought the bottle with him.

"That young couple Joseph sees on the trolley and in Chinatown—that was us?"

"Yes."

"And Candlewyck's letterman's jacket—that was yours?"

"Yes."

So much in his book had seemed familiar; now I knew why. But I had one more question. "The TJ in your dedication—is that me?"

"It is."

"Why did you use my initials instead of my name?"

"I didn't know what your life was like. I didn't know if you went back into the closet...after. Or if I was only a phase or if you had gotten married. I didn't want to do anything to ruin your life if it was different and you were happy and not thinking about me."

"I didn't. It wasn't. You weren't. I'm not. And I've never stopped thinking about you."

MAX

"I'VE NEVER STOPPED thinking about you," he said.

"Are you hungry?" I asked.

"No. I feel like I should be, but I'm not."

I knew what he meant. Being in his presence, in the company of his words, as we erased the past and the distance between us, felt as if I were gorging myself at a gourmand's five-course meal. My soul was nourished; my flesh, which hungered for something else, would have to wait.

"Are *you* hungry?" Tristan asked.

"No. Just for your words, the sound of your voice."

He smiled and took a sip of his beer.

"Did the book shock you?" I asked.

"You mean the sex?"

"Yes."

"No. Well, maybe a little. When Cazzo started hustling, it seemed so...I don't know...*real*..."

"Remember when I said my writing was all found objects?"

"Yes."

"Well, that was another found object. I was a sex worker for a little bit."

"You were?"

"Yes. I'd spent a year traveling around the country visiting music schools hoping to find you. I'd sold my bike to eat and keep a roof over my head. I was broke, but I wasn't ready to give up looking for you or to move to Florida. I was a nineteen-year-old chimney sweep in a city without chimneys. I had nothing else to sell. Do you hate me?"

"For what? Doing what you needed to do to survive?"

I nodded, feeling miserable. I'd always known I'd have to tell him about that part of my life if I ever found him again, but I'd also been dreading it.

"Being a man means doing hard, uncomfortable things. It means doing things you want more than anything not to have to do."

"How did you—"

"It's in your book."

"Oh, right. My father told me that years ago."

"And you repeated it to my mother when she confronted you about us."

"You knew that?"

"Not till much later. My mother told my father, and he told me. He said hearing what you said made him rethink his entire opinion about what was happening between you and me. He said it made him realize we weren't kids messing around but two young *men* following their hearts and finding their way."

"I'm sorry about your dad. I don't know what I would do without mine—especially growing up without a mother." I leaned in closer and rubbed his shoulder.

"Thanks. I miss him so much. But every day despite myself, it gets a little easier."

We fell silent again until he said, "And for the record, you're not a sex worker. You weren't a chimney sweep. You are you. Why do people conflate what they do with who they are?"

"I don't know."

"What surprised you about sex work?"

"The discovery that a great many men wanted my...*company*. More surprising, that they were willing to pay for it—even the ones who wouldn't take me home at Thanksgiving or seat me at brunch with their friends." I thought of the asshole hipster and hoped I didn't sound bitter.

Perhaps Tristan picked up on my mood because smiling wickedly, he asked, "Did you do a great many unspeakable things with unspeakable men in unspeakable rooms?"

"No. You'd be surprised how tame most encounters were. Most just wanted to talk. I had this one guy who just wanted to cuddle. We'd get naked and crawl under this great big comforter—I swear it weighed like a hundred pounds—and we'd just hold each other for an hour. It was the only time all week anyone would touch me. I would have thought I was in love with him if I hadn't already met you and learned what it felt like to be loved, to be touched when the touch itself was the point."

Tristan touched my leg. I smiled and reached for the bourbon. "I don't know why I'm telling you all this," I said as I poured what even I had to admit was a generous amount of bourbon.

"Perhaps you just need someone to talk to."

"Oh, I need more than that." I took a long swallow from my glass. "Who do you talk to?"

Tristan shrugged. "Javier, I guess."

TRISTAN

Max took a swallow of his drink and sat back against the sofa's cushions while also moving a little farther away.

"Who's Javier?" he asked, trying to sound casually interested. "Your boyfriend?"

"No, just a friend. I met him when Dad and I moved to Paris—he's the one who gave me your book."

"I must meet him and thank him."

"I must, too. I mean, thank him for leading me back to you."

Max held my gaze a long moment, then sipped from his glass. Instead of breaking the spell, he only cast it deeper. His soft voice beckoned me into the unknown. Would I follow him? *Could* I follow him?

"I should go," I said. "It's late—"

"No. Don't go."

"You're falling asleep."

"I don't want you to go. I'm afraid I'm dreaming. If I am, I don't want to wake up."

"Me, either," I agreed, looking at him. We were silent for a few minutes.

"Don't go," he repeated. "Tell me one of your stories."

"One of my stories?"

He took another swallow of his drink and stretched his legs out so they lay in my lap. "Yeah. You used to always make up stories about people on the street. Tell me one now."

I looked at him in surprise. "You remember that?"

He nodded.

Chapter 57

TRISTAN

I WAS DREAMING. MAX was lying on the ground in a rocky, dirt-strewn landscape. Dark-green and navy-blue mist swirled around him. Somewhere behind him a volcano was erupting, belching ash and coal dust. He held out his hand and beckoned me. As I stepped closer on the quaking ground, I saw his other hand held his own beating heart; its veins and arteries disappeared into the black hole in his chest. He murmured softly, like snow falling on the creek behind my parents' house, so softly I couldn't make out his words, could only hear the beating of his heart.

The dream ended, and I woke abruptly. I was lying with my head on Max's chest, his arms tight around me. His heart beat steadily, rhythmically against my ear. I tried not to move, content to watch him sleep. Eventually, he stirred.

"Hey, you," he said, ruffling my hair. "You're still here," he murmured sleepily. "You weren't a dream." He smiled, stretched, ruffled my hair again. "I'm hungry."

"Me, too," I said.

"Let's order room service."

"What do you want?"

"A pitcher of mimosas."

"That's not food," I said, picking up the multipage room service menu we'd only glanced at last night. "What do you want to *eat*?" I reached for the house phone.

"I don't care. Order the whole menu—there's bound to be something we like."

"I can't do that. I'll order omelets."

"You like omelets?"

I shrugged. "Javier says you should always order an omelet on a first date."

"Why?"

"Because you don't have to chew it. You can sort of slide it around in your mouth and swallow it discreetly. No one looks good chewing."

He shook his head. "Wait—is this a first date?"

"Isn't it?" I held his gaze. Brazenly, I thought.

"I'm going to take a shower," he said. "Care to join me?"

"I can't."

"OK. Suit yourself. There's another bathroom in here somewhere." He turned away and slowly stepped out of his clothes. Without looking back, he strolled into the nether regions of the suite. I couldn't take my eyes off him.

"Hello? Room service. Hello?"

"Uh, yeah. Hi. I'd like to order breakfast."

"What would you like?"

"Omelets—two."

"What kind?"

"I don't care!"

"Sir?"

"Meat—I want meat. And vegetables. Spinach."

"Cheese?"

"Yes?"

"What kind?"

"Surprise me."

"Sir?"

"Cheddar."

"Yes, sir. Will there be anything else?"

"A pitcher of mimosas."

"Yes, sir. Will there be anything else?"

"Yes. Don't hurry."

I hung up the phone and shrugged out of my clothes like they were on fire.

I hesitated at the bathroom door. I could barely make him out in the clouds of steam. Now that the moment was here, the moment I'd longed for, dreamed of, I froze, my desire locked. You see, I'd read Max's book, in which he had written familiarly about things I had never imagined, incredible things that had seemed impossible until I'd googled them, found them to be real, possible, practiced. Had Max experienced those things personally? I couldn't help but wonder. And if he had, could he be satisfied with me? I, who'd only ever dreamed of holding his hand, of kissing him at midnight and noon, of guiding him gently inside me in the quiet of the night in my childhood bedroom in my parents' house on the bank of a creek, or under a blanket beneath the stars on a dune by the sea.

His back was to me, and his head was bowed as the water cascaded over him. When I stepped in shyly behind him, he turned and lifted his head. He smiled and opened his arms.

Max carried me into the bedroom. His lips never left mine and he never closed his eyes. We fell onto the bed with its dust ruffles and eight-hundred-thread-count sheets. And then we were moving together to an old, half-forgotten rhythm, like adults suddenly remembering a childhood dance, a dance unexpectedly recalled and joyfully enacted. He was leading. He was definitely leading. But if he was Fred Astaire, I was Ginger Rogers, matching him step for step, pleasure given for pleasure extracted, but doing it backwards and in heels.

And then it was over. Or maybe it was just beginning.

MAX

ONE MINUTE, I was in the shower, unsure he'd follow me. The next, he was standing behind me, gloriously naked. I carried him wet and slippery to the bed. I don't know who asked and who consented, but we were naked and kissing. Then it was over; we lay spent in each other's arms in the stickiness of satisfied desire, tangled in a thicket of love and damp sheets.

All the gaps in our history had been filled, the mystery of our separation solved. Now we just had to figure out where we were and where we went from here.

There was a knock on the door. Tristan groaned and whispered, "Room service."

"Come in," I yelled. When I heard the cart, I called out, "Just set it on the table."

There was a clatter of china and the tinkle of silverware. "Sir, I'll need you to sign for this."

"Just put my initials—MW—on it, and give yourself a generous tip."

"Sir, I can't do that. It wouldn't be right. I might get in trouble."

"Well, we don't want that. Come here then."

"Come here?" Tristan whispered furiously. "Are you mad? He'll see us."

"So?"

He started to beat me with his fists. I held him off. Laughing. Like every B-movie actress since time immemorial, caught in bed with a man by a bellhop, Tristan clutched the sheet desperately and pulled it up to his chin.

The bellhop, or whatever he was, appeared in the doorway and stopped, unsure. His mouth hung open. He was dressed like the queen's palace guards, minus the tall furry hat and solemn expression.

"Come in, come in," I said. "Don't mind Sister Mary Catherine here. Her first time out of the convent and *this* happens." I gestured at the bed and us. The young man twittered.

"C'mon, give me the bill."

He extended an electronic tablet. He was tall and awkward-looking with fingers that were long and bony with big knuckles. He reminded me of a bird on a wire. He bristled with potential as if he were newly hatched. He glanced at the tablet when I handed it to him. "Oh! Thank you, sir."

I waved him out.

"You're such an asshole," Tristan said when the front door closed.

"Yep. I'm the asshole you love. Now put on some clothes and let's go eat."

"In a second. I have to text Javier."

"Why? Was he worried that I'd dismember and eat you?"

"Ha-ha. No. We check in with each other every morning."

TRISTAN

"I'm glad you've had someone to look after you," Max said, pulling on a pair of black shorts. He sat on the edge of the bed next to me. I kissed his neck and breathed in the scent of him. He smelled different. Still clean, but not antiseptic; instead, he smelled expensive, of sandalwood and vetiver, like he'd been shopping at Albrecht's.

"What will you tell him about me?"

"The truth."

He sighed and stood. "I'm gonna start on breakfast. Don't be long, OK?"

I texted Javier: *He's still the same boy he used to be.*

Chapter 58

MAX

I WOKE TO THE sound of music. Finding myself alone in bed, I got up and wandered naked into the living room where I discovered Tristan, also naked, at the piano, playing like a man possessed.

"Morning," I rasped. I frowned. Then, clearing my throat, tried again. "Good morning," I repeated in a voice that sounded closer to my own.

Tristan pulled his hands from the keys as if they'd been burned and settled them in his lap. Echoes of the music he'd been playing—joyous, sensual, romantic all at once, rushed into the sudden silence.

I sat on the needlepoint bench next to him and kissed his mouth, still crushed and rank with sleep. "What was that you were playing?"

"Just something I composed to express how you make me feel."

"You composed that? Just now?"

"No, back in high school. I planned to play it for you at prom. My music teacher, Mr. Volkman, was helping me. You remember he was in charge of entertainment? I'd been rehearsing in secret with the band for weeks. That's why I was late for your practice the day—the day..."

"The day your mother shot me?"

"Yeah." Tristan hung his head.

"We haven't talked about this yet, but I get the feeling you blame yourself for what happened."

"I do. I pushed her too far. And look what happened. I—I—ruined your life."

"Tristan, listen to me. You didn't ruin anything."

"You almost got *killed* because of me. And as a result, you lost your chance at a scholarship."

"Please stop beating yourself up. You didn't pull that trigger."

"No. But maybe if I'd stopped seeing you—"

"Neither of us wanted that."

"She tried to kill you."

"No, she didn't."

"What do you mean?"

"I don't think your mother wanted to kill me."

"Max, she *shot* you—"

"In the *leg*. I was coming around the track. She had a clear shot at me. If she'd wanted to kill me, she could have shot me anywhere else—my heart, my head—but no. She shot me in the leg. Look, even my surgeon agreed. And he'd treated hundreds of gunshot wounds, so he would know. She only wanted to wound me to keep us from going to prom together."

"But even if we didn't go to prom, we'd have still been together. I don't get it."

"Don't you see? For her, your going to prom with me was being gay. If she could stop us going, you wouldn't be gay anymore."

"That doesn't make any sense."

"I didn't say it did. You just need to stop believing she tried to kill me, and you need to stop blaming yourself for a crime she didn't actually commit."

"What are you talking about? She *shot* you."

"OK, so *that* was a crime, but she didn't try to *murder* me."

Tristan, who had leaned forward when I began speaking, now sat back and closed his eyes. "Jesus. All these years I thought—"

"Even if she *had* tried to kill me, I would gladly take that bullet again if it would bring me to this moment here with you."

"I still feel so guilty."

"Don't. I feel guilty, too. You lost your mother. I grew up without a mother. I wouldn't wish that anyone lose theirs. I've spent so much time feeling I was responsible—if I had only left you alone like she asked me to. But I couldn't. I loved you too much. The worst part is if I had it to do over again, I still wouldn't give you up, even knowing how much you would lose. I love you so much, Tristan. I do."

"I love you, Max. Even after everything that happened—even with all my guilt—I never stopped loving you."

"Ditto, baby. Now, tell me about this song. You composed it in high school. Have you been practicing it all these years?"

"No, I told you. I stopped playing after my mother died. I swear this is the first piano I have sat in front of since my mother's funeral. But this morning, I woke up and I couldn't stop thinking about how it felt to make love to you again and wake up in your arms. Then I remembered this song."

I kissed him on the top of his head. "Play it again."

"I don't know," Tristan said, wiggling his fingers. "I'm a bit rusty."

"Stop making excuses and play. I want to hear again how I make you feel."

"OK." He placed his hands on the piano's keys.

"Wait. I want to record it." I ran into the bedroom and returned with my phone. Setting it on top of the piano, I said, "OK, now play."

Chapter 59

TRISTAN

W E WERE LYING in bed, limbs entangled. I felt we were
becoming less shy with each other, more certain that
we'd found each other again and that nothing between us
had been lost. The house phone rang, startling us both. Max
answered. After a minute, he sat up, disentangling himself
from me. Placing his hand over the mouthpiece, he mouthed,
"V. I'm in trouble. Again."

MAX

"I TURNED OFF my phone."

"Why? Why would you do that?" V demanded.

"I just wanted some alone time." I glanced at Tristan, who
was trying to look as if he wasn't listening.

"Tristan is still with you, isn't he?"

"Yes, of course he is."

"Dammit, Max, you had an interview this morning. I've been
calling and calling."

"Sorry. Just reschedule it. I promise I won't—"

"It doesn't work that way. The reporter was on deadline."

"OK. So, no big deal, right?"

"Wrong. I don't know what's gotten into you, Max. We need
to talk. I'm in the lobby. I'm coming up!"

I hung up the phone. "V is on their way up here. They want to
talk. You mind staying in here?"

"Nah, I'll be fine. Something wrong?"

"No. Yes. I missed an interview. V's mad."

. . . .

"What are you doing?" V asked. "You're fucking everything up."

"Will you calm down?"

"No. I will not calm down. We've worked too hard to make this book a success to throw it all away."

"Christ, V, it was one interview!"

"It was exposure. How do you think you sell books? Through exposure. Vince has a national audience—"

"I don't care if I never sell another book."

"What are you talking about? Every writer I know would kill to be you, to sell the books you do."

"Book, V, book. I only have the one, remember? I'm not even a real writer."

"Yes, you are. Everyone who has read *Cazzo* knows you're a writer."

"No, I am a man desperately in love."

"Look, I know the whole star-crossed lovers thing with you and Tristan—who doesn't?—but the world, your *life*, and certainly your talent don't begin and end with Tristan."

"That's where you're wrong, V. *Everything* begins and ends with Tristan."

"So, you're telling me Tristan is more important than I... I mean, than your career?"

"Do you?"

"I can't talk to you when you're like this." V picked up their black organizer and said, "Call me when you're ready to think with your head instead of your dick."

I think we were both stunned by their words, for they stopped at the door and without turning around said, "You have a reading at the mall at four. A town car will be downstairs at two forty-five. I'll be waiting as usual." Then they opened the door and slammed it with all the force I would have expected given their mood.

TRISTAN

MAX WALKED BACK into the bedroom looking like a chastened child, chagrined and pissed off.

"I have to go, apparently," he said, getting back in bed and propping himself against the pillows.

"Of course you do," I said. Suddenly self-conscious, I sat up and began scanning the floor for my discarded clothing.

Max pulled me against his chest. "I didn't mean now, this very second. We can shower and get lunch. My reading isn't till four. Car will pick me up at two forty-five."

I relaxed against him, listening to his heartbeat. Max stroked my hair and said quietly, seriously, "Why don't you come with me?"

"Yeah, I'm sure V would love that."

"Why would they care?"

"Because they hate me."

"V doesn't hate—oh, you heard our conversation, didn't you?"

"Yes. You were both pretty loud."

"I know you don't like V."

"V doesn't like *me*. Seriously, they're always looking up from that Bible or whatever the hell that black leather book they're always carrying around is and giving me dirty looks. It's like they're some sort of literary missionary, you're their religion, and I'm Original Sin."

"I'll talk to them."

"You don't have to."

MAX

V WAS THUMBING through their black leather appointment book. They had to know I'd gotten into the backseat beside them, but they appeared determined to pretend I wasn't sitting there. I cleared my throat. They looked at me warily.

"Yes?"

"I gather you don't like Tristan. Why?"

"I fear he will distract you from your work."

"My work—which you seem to revere—is simply populist trash. But even if it was as good as you seem to think it is, it only exists *because of* Tristan. Without him, there is no work. Without him, there is no *me*."

"Do you know what you'll be reading?" V asked, all business.

"Yes."

"Good. I brought your favorite pen for you to use." They handed me the antique sterling Cross pen.

"Thanks."

They grunted and went back to staring at their black book.

Chapter 60

TRISTAN

"COME WITH ME." Max said.

"Where?"

"On the rest of the book tour."

"Where are you going and how long will you be gone?"

"I don't know. V takes care of all of that. And honestly, I don't pay that much attention. As soon as I got to one city and found you weren't there, I was ready to move on to the next one, hoping you'd be *there*."

The waiter silently glided up to us and poured more wine. When he left, Max said, "Come with me. You have no reason not to."

"I can't."

"You can't or you don't want to?" Max pushed his food around on his plate.

"I can't."

He dropped his fork and looked at me. "Is there someone... keeping you from going with me?" he asked warily.

"No, Max, there isn't.

"Then why can't you come?"

"Look, I can't just go traipsing around after you!"

"Why not?"

"I just can't. That's all. I have a job—"

"Quit. You hate it anyway. I know you do. Accounting!" He made a terrible sound.

When I didn't say anything, he picked up his fork and savagely attacked his stuffed pork chop. "Fine. If you won't go with me, I'll cancel the rest of the tour."

"Can you do that?"

He shrugged. "I've no idea. They'll probably sue me and seize my royalties. I don't care. I've lived most of my life with very little money. I can certainly do that again."

"But you have a contract. You promised you'd do a book tour."

"So? I promised myself if I ever found you, I'd never lose sight of you again."

Max," I said. "You're not losing sight of me. You're going on a book tour. You'll be back."

"Will you be here?"

"Yes, always. Nothing and no one will ever separate us again. I promise you that."

"What will you do while I'm gone?"

"Think. Probably quit my job. Miss you."

He took my hand across the table. "Promise you'll miss me?"

"Promise."

Our waiter reappeared. "Can I get you gentlemen anything?"

"No," Max said. "I have everything I need right here."

MAX

"Listen to me, Tristan," I said when he got in bed next to me. "I've been thinking."

"Max…"

"Not about the book tour. Well, yeah, sort of about the book tour. Listen, if you won't go with me, I—I'm going home to Florida for Thanksgiving. Will you come with me?"

"Are you sure your father and stepmother won't mind?"

"They won't."

He rolled on top of me and kissed me. Sitting up, straddling me, he said, "Then, yes, I'll go."

· ·

Tristan walked out of the bedroom, naked. "Why aren't you dressed?" I asked. "I thought we were going to lunch."

"We were, but I have a better idea."

"Oh? And what would that be?"

"Come here and I'll show you."

V called several times, and for forty-five minutes, their calls went unanswered. When I finally answered, they barked a question, like a death toll. "Is Tristan coming on the rest of the book tour with you?"

"No, he's not."

"Good," they said and hung up.

I threw my phone across the room.

I was pouring myself a drink when Tristan spoke, startling me. He glanced from the drink in my hand to the clock on the wall. I looked at the clock. Two fifteen. I shrugged. "It's five o'clock somewhere," I said and winced at the lameness of my defense.

Tristan nodded at my phone lying on the floor. "V?" he asked.

"Yeah. They can be infuriating at times."

"They're in love with you, aren't they?"

"No. Don't be ridiculous. V is in love with my genius."

"You're such an idiot sometimes. I see the way V looks at you. They're in love with you," Tristan insisted.

TRISTAN

WITH HIS FINGER, Max traced the stubble on my face—just now, at twenty-three, making its presence felt—down over my Adam's apple and lower to caress my neck. "And I'm in love with you," he said, effectively shutting me up.

Chapter 61

TRISTAN

V GAVE ME THE blackest of looks when I walked into the lobby. "Hi," I said. "Max will be down in a minute."

They nodded.

I tried again. "V—"

"Tell him I'll be in the car." With that, they turned and walked out the lobby.

"Where's V?" Max asked me when he stepped off the elevator.

"Waiting in the car."

"You two didn't have words, did you?"

"No, but I get the feeling they're still hoping I'll go away."

"They hope in vain. You're not going anywhere."

When I didn't answer, Max turned serious. "Oh God. You're not going away, are you?"

"They're probably going to try to seduce you."

"Don't be ridiculous."

"Why's that ridiculous?"

"They're not my type. I'm an old-fashioned dullard. I stick to the binary. I like to know what I'm getting. Dating someone shouldn't be like opening a box of chocolates."

I laughed, then frowned. "Don't make me laugh when I'm trying to be mad at you."

He stepped close and, putting his hands around my waist, nuzzled my neck. "You know I love you, right?"

"I do, sir. And I love you."

"OK, then. Look, I have to go. I'll call you every day."

"OK."

I wasn't jealous, not really. I was...*irritated*. Suddenly, I understood why Max had found Judy's presence in my life so irksome.

MAX

WHEN I'D FIRST met Tristan, I'd thought he was my Hail Mary. These last few weeks, I'd realized he was and had always been my destiny. Now, as I turned to leave him, I realized he was also my Hallelujah. I walked back to the front desk where he was still standing, watching me.

"V is V," I said, "but you are my Hallelujah."

"And you're mine," he said.

Chapter 62

MAX

OURS WAS LIKE a great friendship founded in childhood where the friends could go months or years without seeing each other and whenever they met, they simply picked up the friendship where it had been left off without even prefacing their meeting with a hello.

TRISTAN

I SUPPOSE SOME people would find it incredible that our love simply resumed. But in all honesty, I'm not sure it ever ended or even paused. We'd continued to love each other as if one dark night, one of us had gone off to war or to prison for a crime he did not commit. And while to all eyes it appeared the love had been effectively interrupted, it had simply gone underground, a lifeline connecting two hearts, waiting, waiting for daylight.

JAVIER

TRISTAN INTRODUCED MAX and me at last. We spent the better part of an hour sizing each other up, listening, reserving judgment. Now, with dessert on the way, Tristan excused himself to go to the men's room.

"This is going to be awkward, isn't it?" Max said, swilling his bourbon around in this glass before downing it.

"I've never seen Tristan so happy. I have to say I believe—no—I *know* it's because of you."

"Thank you for telling me that. I've never been happier either."

"When he was dying, Tristan's father asked me to take care of Tristan because literally there was no one else. I think you'll take care of him now, but I need you to know that I will always be here to back you up. If you can't take care of him, I will."

"You're in love with him."

"No, I'm not."

"But you were in love with him?"

"No. It was never like that between us. When I met him, I was in love with somebody else who, it turned out, wasn't really worth loving. But even if I had been interested in Tristan, his heart was locked and only you had the key."

Max smiled.

"When Tristan told me about the two of you, I worried you chose each other because you had no other options. I worried what would happen when you both got out into the world and saw there were others waiting to be loved by you. Having watched the two of you these past few months, I realize there were *and never will be* any others—for *either* of you. You were meant for each other. And you were both wise enough to realize that."

"I have been his from the day I met him," Max said.

Chapter 63

MAX

Y FATHER'S NEW wife was a sweet dumpling of a woman with a face round as the moon. Her carrot-like legs were thick at the thighs, tapering into surprisingly attractive knees, and further tapering to impossibly delicate ankles. She lurched towards us, elevated and pitching slightly forward on four-inch wedges. She embraced me, exclaiming, "Max!" as if I'd been too long gone and was sorely missed. Then, looking behind me at Tristan, whom she looked up and down, she asked, "So this is the young man you've been pining over since I met you?"

My face grew hot. "Yes. Hana, this is Tristan."

Ignoring my embarrassment, she released me and hugged Tristan, promptly sweeping him up into the family dynamic. "At last," she sighed, falling into his surprised embrace as if she'd been waiting to meet him too long and was on the verge of exhaustion.

Dad came down the steps from the house. When he got to the last step, he stared across the lawn at his wife and Tristan. Blinking in the sunlight and calling up his old nickname, he asked, "Bam Bam? Is that you?"

"Yes, sir. It's me."

"Tristan, my son," he said, stepping forward and hugging him as if Tristan were indeed his own son.

I glanced at Hana, who mouthed, "I didn't tell him who the young man you were bringing was."

TRISTAN

I WALKED INTO the kitchen, a bright cheerful space full of windows covered in red-and-white gingham curtains. Hana was wearing a red-ruffled apron that matched the curtains and standing in front of a Chambers stove, a vintage chrome and enamel behemoth with multiple ovens. Up until that moment, I had hated the color red. Now I saw all its warmth and possibilities.

"Can I help?" I asked.

"No," she said. "You're a guest."

"He's not a guest," Max's father thundered from the dining room. "He's family. Put him to work."

"I don't know the last time I saw him so happy," she remarked stirring a pot. She lifted the lid off a saucepan and dipping a spoon into a bubbling sauce, tasted it. Satisfied, she set the spoon in a spoon rest as red as her apron and added, "And it goes without saying that I've never seen Max so happy."

She hugged me. She smelled like flour. "What was that for?" I asked.

"For being you. And for bringing so much happiness to my boys. Now come, let's join them for a drink before dinner." She took my arm and led me out of the kitchen.

MAX

"DRINK, SON?" DAD asked.

"Just a club soda, thanks."

He looked at me in surprise but also with approval and relief. "Have you stopped drinking?" he asked casually as he handed me a club soda with a wedge of lime.

I wasn't sure how to answer his question. Tristan's return had made me realize my flirtation with alcoholism needed to end if I was serious about a relationship with him. "Yes."

"Good."

TRISTAN

I'm NOT SURE what I expected Thanksgiving dinner to be like, but whatever I could have imagined would have paled in comparison to the reality of what was.

There was a turkey brined in beer and stuffed with apples and sausage, which Max's father made a great show of carving. There was a honey-glazed ham served with a pumpkin-seed crumble; creamy mashed potatoes rich with butter and garlic; string beans with sliced, toasted almonds; homemade Zinfandel cranberry sauce, thick and alcoholic; Chinese dumplings filled with pork and cabbage and redolent of ginger. There was a pecan pie and, finally, a rich chocolate cake with a big red heart that had our names inside.

There was grace and a toast and laughter. I felt, for the first time since Dad died, a part of something larger than myself, larger than my grief. Grief sat down, reminding me that joy and happiness were still possible.

"Glad to see you're eating better," Max said to his father. Then, turning to his stepmother, he said, "You know he raised me on pizza and Chinese takeout, right?"

His father glared at him, but there was no mistaking the affection in his eyes. "You survived, didn't you?"

"Barely. Thank God Tristan used to invite me to his own family feasts regularly."

"How *is* your father?" Max's father asked me.

"He died," I said.

"Oh, I'm so sorry. I didn't know. He was a gentleman."

"Thank you."

"You know, he paid all of Max's hospital bills, after…"

I looked at Max, who looked at his father. "He did?"

"Yes. I take it you didn't know," Max's father said to me.

"No, I didn't."

"Well, he did—through his lawyer."

"His lawyer?"

"Yes. I'm afraid when he came to the house right after the… *accident*, The Aunts wouldn't let him come in. So, he sent his lawyer to see me."

We all fell silent for a moment, lost in our own thoughts. Max squeezed my knee under the table.

"Thank you for dinner," Max and I said in unison.

"You are most welcome, my excellent sons," Hana said.

Lying in bed, Max pulled me close. "Thank you for being here."

"My pleasure. I've always liked your dad, and I like your stepmother just as much."

"Mother. I don't think of her as my stepmother. You know, I never knew my mother and so I never thought I needed one, and then Hana came along."

MAX

"I GET THAT," Tristan said. He was lying on his back looking up at the ceiling fan turning lazily above us.

"You ever think about going to Paris?" I asked.

"I've been to Paris." He turned on his side to look at me.

"I mean with me. Like we used to talk about doing."

"You want to go to Paris and climb to the top of the Eiffel Tower—"

"And see the *Mona Lisa* and see your sweet face reflected in the mirrors at Versailles."

Tristan sat up and folded his hands in his lap. "Yes, but I want to go someplace else first."

"Where?"

"Korea. I want you to go to Korea with me. I want to take you to my mother's grave. I want to stand there, side by side, hand in hand with you."

I burrowed my face under his hands.

"Stop that," he said. "I doubt your parents want us having sex here."

"Oh no? Look in that bowl on the nightstand."

TRISTAN

I LOOKED IN the bowl, which contained condoms and tubes of something called Gun Oil.

· ·

I was drowsing, lazy and satisfied, when Max moved from under the covers and snuggled up to me. "There's something else," he said.

"Mmhmm?"

"I want you to move to New York with me."

Fully awake now, I sat up. "I'm sorry, what?"

"Come to New York with me."

"What would I do in New York?"

He propped himself up on his elbow. "I have this crazy idea. I want to turn *Cazzo* into a musical. On Broadway."

I stuffed a pillow behind my head. "You want to turn *Cazzo* into a musical? On Broadway?"

"Yes. And I want you to work on it with me."

"Max—"

Max grasped my chin between his thumb and forefinger and gently turned my head until we were facing each other. "You don't have to give me an answer now. I have to finish the book tour after this, so maybe when I get back, we can talk about it some more. But think about it at least. OK?"

"OK."

Chapter 64

JAVIER

"MAX WANTS ME to move to New York with him," Tristan said almost as soon as I walked in the door.

"And?"

"And...I don't know what to do," he said, looking around the living room.

"You could sell this house," I suggested gently. "It's become like a mausoleum or maybe a monument to everything you've lost."

"Sell this house? I can't sell—"

"Fine. Don't sell it. But you have to move on. It's time to move on."

"I can't just leave...everything. It would be too hard."

"Tristan, listen to me. You've been an excellent son. But excellent sons have to grow up into men. You're a man now. And being a man means doing hard, uncomfortable things. It means doing things you want more than anything not to have to do."

"You don't understand—"

"I do understand. Listen, you don't have to decide now, but soon. Just do me—do *yourself*—a favor. Go to New York with Max."

"But what about you?"

"What about me? Tristan, you should know by now that for me, home isn't defined by longitude and latitude. It's defined here." I touched my chest, "Since I met you at seventeen, home—

299

the only real home I've known—has been with you and Papa. Now there's just you. Home will never be a city or a state or a country. It will be *you*. And when I return home—and I always will—it will be to you."

TRISTAN

JAVIER KISSED ME on the top of my head and was gone. I knew without asking he had a date. He'd call in the morning and tell me about how woefully wrong it had gone.

After he left, I wandered through the rooms of my parents' house, which seemed more crowded with shadows than usual. I stepped outside into the backyard. The creek which ran behind the house had mostly dried up, and now it was just a slow, sad rivulet of dirty water.

Chapter 65

TRISTAN

"TRISTAN," MAX CALLED, having let himself in the front door. "I'm in the den," I called out and frowned at the echo. The movers were coming the day after tomorrow. Everything had been sold: the Brutalist copper foil table lamps; the Eames desk; the Harry Bertoia sculptures; the Marcel Breuer leather and steel Wassily chairs; the Saarinen pedestal table with its tulip chairs in the dining room; the Noguchi ceiling lights. The only things I was taking with me to New York besides my clothes and classical records were the grand piano, my father's collection of vintage fountain pens—which I was giving to Max—and my mother's Imperial Hotel china and vintage Tiffany sterling silver chopsticks.

I'd written Marta a letter of recommendation, but I hoped that the combination of my leaving, her age and what Dad had left her in his will would persuade her to retire. All that was left now was the leaving.

"Hey," Max said.

"Hey, yourself."

"You look sad."

"I am—a little. Except for the year we lived in Paris, I have lived my whole life in this house. Anyway, what's up with you?"

"I got you a present." Max pulled a flat box out from behind his back. It was festive with Christmas paper and red and green ribbons.

"I thought we weren't opening presents until Christmas at your parents'."

"We're not, but this is special. Go ahead, open it," he said, handing me the box and grinning.

Catching his excitement, I tore off the paper and opened the box. Inside, wrapped in red and green tissue paper, were plane tickets. "Paris?"

"This spring—you and me."

I looked at the tickets again. Puzzled by the departing airport, I looked at Max questioningly. "I don't understand."

"We're going to Paris, but we need to go somewhere else first."

. . . .

Max and I stood side by side, hand in hand on the grass. The sky seemed pink, weighted as it was with cherry blossom trees in full bloom. I thought I smelled kimchi. In my pocket, my phone sounded. Pulling it out with my free hand, I read the text message from my realtor: *You have an offer on the house. $10,000 over asking. It's a solid offer. Settlement in 45 days. Will you accept it?*

With my thumb, I texted back: *Yes.* I slipped my phone in my pocket.

Max tugged at my hand. "You ready? That plane to Paris won't wait."

I glanced at the black granite tombstone, at my mother's name etched on it in delicate but emphatic Hangul script.

"I'm ready."

THE END

About the Author

Bronx-born wordsmith, Larry Benjamin considers himself less a writer than an artist whose chosen medium is the written word rather than clay or paint or bronze. He is the author of three previous novels: *The Sun, The Earth & The Moon*, *In His Eyes*, and *Unbroken*. He is also the author of the allegorical novella *Vampire Rising*.

He lives in Philadelphia with his husband and two rescue dogs named Atticus and Gatsby.

Website: www.larrybenjamin.com

By the Author

Unbroken

Vampire Rising

The Christmas Present

Black & Ugly

In His Eyes

The Sun, the Earth & the Moon

Excellent Sons: A Love Story in Three Acts

www.beatentrackpublishing.com/larrybenjamin

Beaten Track Publishing

For more titles from Beaten Track Publishing,
please visit our website:

https://www.beatentrackpublishing.com

Thanks for reading!